BICYCLE'S OF BRUSSELS

BICYCLE'S OF BRUSSELS

A War Love Story

ALTON A. MASSEY

Larry Massey

IngramSpark

Contents

INTRODUCTION

The clock on the wall, left of them, chimed two o'clock and Allan asked, "Is that clock, right? I didn't think it was this late."

Michelle responded, "It is quite accurate. I think we should consider finish drinking our wine and going to bed" She briefly hesitated and thought for a moment, then; asked, "What do you normally wear to bed."

"He answered, "I usually sleep in my underwear."

"Not in my apartment!" She shook her head and went to her bedroom and a few minutes later emerged with two sets of silk pajamas with military insignias. He looked at and studied them then asked, "Where did you get those German military pajamas? They look like one's Army and the other Gestapo. Is anybody like Bert, Phillipe, or your aunt aware of them?"

"Yes, they are! You're not going to sleep here in your underwear or naked either!"

When he said he couldn't sleep in either she told him, "Then you will have sleep elsewhere!"

He didn't want to argue and asked, "Is it all right if I sleep in one of the bottoms only."

"Fine!" Then, looked away from him and asked; "Would you like to sleep in my bed?"

He thought about the words, in the café, about her being a mistress and stupidly answered, "I didn't come to sleep in your bed."

Mimi caught the insinuation, "My offer was for you and my bed! Not with me in it!"

Allan was shaken up by that firm response and Mimi recognized it. He tried to apologize and stammered, "I di..di..didn't mean what you think," and meekly continued, "I...I...I didn't understand," as he drifted to and sat on the couch. She angrily secured some sheets, pillows, cases and two covering blankets from her bedroom. Still stammering, with a bright red face, he gratefully thanking her for a place to sleep. She didn't answer him and gave him that look with daggers in her eyes as she made up the couch to sleep on. He apologized again saying he was sorry to question anything she offered him and added, "I'm dumb about girls and life; I always was. I think it best if I dress and leave you now. I'm so sorry about all this."

Mimi calmly said, "Now do not get so excited! Forget this until tomorrow. Go to bed!"

He crawled between the sheets she made up on the couch and when she roughly tucked him in, he was overwhelmed.

From Bicycles of Brussels

Italicized words in the story are those spoken in Flemish...

The authors intent of the story is fictional. However, it was created from his knowledge and experiences of missions and encounters by the pilots of the 8th and 9th Air Forces during W.W.II. Any relationship of names of the characters in the story to any persons living or deceased is purely co-incidental. Also, the 8th and 9th Air Force Groups' numbers used, if related, in any way, to any actual WW II or current numbers, is accidental.

One

USA to PARIS

Friday Night 3 November 1944: Boston Harbor

Troopship Royal Queen was docked with the bow facing toward the sea at the Boston Harbor military docking area. The ship was a former Cruise ship, with a maximum carrying capacity of three hundred and fifty passengers. The ship was built to book vacation cruises to various island stops in the Caribbean Sea area. During poor vacationer periods it was one of three ships supplying transport service for goods and passengers to Cuba. It was booked by the United States as a troopship in September of 1942.

Commander, Thomas Fulbright, wearing his rain gear, was leaning on the stern rail of the Troopship on this, slightly fogged and misty, dark night. He was waiting for a couple hundred of Army 101st Airborne enlisted men led by a Captain

David Knight, and three other officers scheduled to arrive at approximately six thirty. The orders he was rereading also included sixty Army Air Corps pilots, escorted by a Lieutenant Colonel Howard Salisbury, a WW1 fighter pilot, scheduled to arrive ten to fifteen minutes after the paratroopers.

Fulbright seemed he was out there waiting on deck longer than he expected to see the arrival of his passengers. He looked at his watch to see what time it read and realized it was six thirty-five; five minutes after his first scheduled passengers were to arrive. As he looked up, he heard the sound of a group of men walking on the dock. The men were walking in a line of two's and as they approached the ship, he noticed an eagle patch on one of the troop's shoulders when he turned to say something to the person behind him. Now he knew they were his first group of Army troops were two hundred and fifty replacement paratroops of the 101st Airborne Division. Fulbright watched as an Army captain leading them with three additional lieutenants with each of three groups that looked like over a hundred troops. A Merchant Marine officer met the Captain at the foot of the gang plant and exchanged salutes. They talked a moment as the merchant marine officer was reading the boarding papers the captain handed him that was apparently a list of the names of the men in this group. After receiving clearance to board, the captain and the merchant officer exchanged salutes again and the paratroopers, with duffel gags slung over their shoulders, followed their officers up the ship's gangplank in single file. They were led down several flights of stairs to the ship's hold where they were given three tiered bunks to sleep on during the trip to Europe.

At five to seven a large group of Army officers, led by the lieutenant colonel, appeared also in a column of two's carrying B-4 Bags. The same Merchant Marine officer waited and greeted them at the ship's gangplank. The merchant officer also checked their boarding orders and again after the officers talked for a moment the colonel led his pilots, up the gangplank to the ship's stateroom area on the ship's second floor.

By 1935hrs all military personnel scheduled to board the ship were settling in their quartered areas. The paratroopers were quartered in three groups of ninety men each in the bow and center half of the ship's hold. They were assigned three-tiered bunks aligned in groups of nine sets across and ten rows long. The pilots all Second Lieutenants except for two. First Lieutenants were to be quartered in staterooms containing two sets of three tiered bunks. The paratroop officers were assigned to two large double bed staterooms. Colonel Salisbury had his own personal stateroom.

Just as most of the paratroopers and pilots were completing their process of settling in their quarters, Fulbright was seeking Salisbury. He found him in his stateroom just before eight o'clock and informed the colonel. "It is required to have an Army officer on deck at all times from 2000hrs to 0800hrs every night. That is approximately from to sunrise to provide deck security each night while we are at sea."

"May I ask what is the purpose of this duty," questioned Salisbury?

Tom explained; "The duty is basically to keep non-navy personnel, the paratroopers, and your pilots, off the deck during the night. And you can schedule it any way you desire, i.e., any combination of hours to cover the required hours of duty. Basically, we don't want anyone wandering around out there and accidentally fall and injure them-selves in the dark. One of my officers or I will be on deck to greet your officers at six each evening and relieve them at eight every morning. There is one additional condition; severe storms are very common during this time of the year in the Atlantic. In the event we run into a storm, one of my men will relieve your officer and handle the duty until the seas calm down."

Salisbury lifted his cap, a bit, and put it back on and asked, "I was going to ask about a storm, but you just adequately covered that. When do you want my first officer to begin the duty?"

"I would like you to have someone," Fulbright hesitated and looked at his watch, "Ah...it's 1750hrs already now, so I'll have one my men take the duty from now to midnight."

"Salisbury answered, "I can have one of my men begin at eight. If your officer will not mind waiting five minutes or so, my man will be there as soon as possible."

"That's very reasonable colonel and it's close to 2000hrs. I'll have one of my officers out there until yours arrives."

They saluted and parted. Salisbury quickly found and looked up the roster of pilot names on the ship. He remembered someone talking about a pilot named Manston, an Ivy League university athlete, when they were assembling at Fort Miles Standish to be transported from their blacked-out barracks to the dock. This pilot was listed on the personnel orders as Alan Manston. Salisbury didn't waste any time and immediately went to the pilots' quartered area. He rushed to the second-floor stateroom area to find the pilot. After opening several doors seeking this pilot, he found him, Manston, who had just found his assigned stateroom. It was five minutes to eight and the colonel assigned him to the security duty from 2000hrs to 2400hrs, before Alan had an opportunity to meet his five roommates.

Manston went out on deck immediately and a Lieutenant Senior Grade Navy officer met him as he stepped out at the bow section of the ship. The Navy officer saw Manston arriving and greeted him and as they saluted, he said, "My name's Daniel; what's yours?"

"I'm Alan Manston, assigned to report here for duty."

"OK Alan; the objective is to keep all of your Army personnel off the deck at night. It's dark out on deck as you notice there are no lights. We don't want anyone falling overboard in the dark. Also, we can run into a violent sudden storm on this trip and it's pretty slippery out here anytime it's wet. Two Army officers will cover the center and stern sections of the ship with their enlisted men. These areas are separated by three sets of stairs beginning with the one you came out; then said excuse me," and left.

Alan was standing on the starboard side of the bow deck and about an hour had passed when he felt the ship beginning to move. He checked the time on his iridescent watch and saw it was 2116hrs as the ship began leaving the dock. He walked around the bow rail, from the starboard to the port side, to watch the ship leave the harbor and maneuver into its convoy position. When the convoy was properly aligned the entire convoy began increasing their speed and created a larger wake at the bow. Peering into the dark seas he could see ships, pitching up and down, and moving along both sides of his as though they all were in cadence. Most ships appeared to have crane booms, barely visible, and were most likely carrying supplies. On both sides and beyond the three lines of ships he could barely see smaller ships, probably destroyers and corvettes, steaming up and down the outer lanes of the convoy. It seemed a lot of time had passed before he shined his dimmed flashlight on his watch and realized three hours of his assigned four-hour duty had passed.

Fulbright had walked from the stern to the bow of the ship where he stopped and talked for a moment to each Army officer on deck duty. An approaching voice called out to Alan, "Are you the officer assigned to keep this section of the deck clear of personnel tonight?"

Manston shined his dim flashlight at the voice, now two arm lengths from him and responded, "Yes sir. I'm here on orders from Colonel Salisbury. Oh, I see you're a Naval officer. Would you please step back so I can get all of you in my flashlight to see all of you?"

Fulbright stepped back two steps and answered, "I am Lieutenant Commander Nathan Fulbright, the officer in overall charge of this ship with the assistance of two other Navy officers and numerous seamen assigned to this ship."

"But...but...this is a Merchant Marine ship. I wasn't aware Navy people were onboard."

Fulbright put his dimmed flashlight on Alan and said, "Haven't you noticed there is a four-inch gun turret gun behind you? And there's one on the stern." And then asked, "Are you one of the Army's fighter pilots onboard?"

"Yes, I am Sir; I have to ask for some identification."

Fulbright got his Navy ID card out and stepped forward to hand him the card. Alan took it and asked him to step back. He saw the ID card was authentic, handed it back, then saluted and said, "I'm sorry sir, I never thought an officer with your authority would be out at this hour. I do apologize if I offended you in any way."

"Ok, Lieutenant; just call me Nate. What's your name?"

"Sir, I mean Nate, my name's Alan Manston."

"Happy to meet you, Alan. I'm not offended by your challenge. You performed the duty was as it should be done. Incidentally, did you ever consider being a Navy pilot?"

"Well sir, I did. I tried to enlist with Navy Air Recruiting group when they were at my university. I was a second semester freshman at the time and failed acceptance due to a minor physical problem.

"Then; how did you gain acceptance in the Air Corps?"

"That's a long story. I don't think I should bore you with it."

"I'm all ears; I'm listening?"

"I was attending a close friend's funeral in Binghamton during Thanksgiving and saw an Air Corps recruiting office in the bus station. On Sunday afternoon, before returning to the university, I tried to enlist in the Army Air Corps at the bus station. The examining Army Flight Surgeon initially rejected me for the same problem the Navy did. After a complete discussion of my problem, he said it was too minor to really worry about if it never bothered me. Then he accepted me!"

"That was not long." Responded Fulbright and then continued, "I have some checking to do, so; take care," and just turned and walked away into the dark toward the ship's stern.

The rest of his watch was uneventful, and he was relieved at 2400hrs (midnight, Saturday morning) by Salisbury escorting another pilot. He then immediately went to his stateroom and found everyone sound asleep. One of the middle bunks with bedding on it was empty and obviously his. As he began to undress, by beginning to take his trousers off, the guy in the top bunk above him fell out of bed on him. Boom: down they went; everybody woke up, the lights went on and someone asked, "What are you guys doing on the floor?" Then they all had a hearty laugh as they watched Manston getting up with his trousers around his ankles and the top bunk guy trying to crawl back up over the three-inch ridge on the edge of his top bunk. Someone told Alan to turn off lights when he was ready to settle in his bunk. He finally undressed in a few minutes, clicked off the light switch and crawled in his bunk and fell sound asleep.

A bugle blew reveille at 0700hrs, over room loudspeakers, waking up all the pilots. They were also informed; breakfast was at 0800hrs in the dining room. It took almost an hour for Alan and his five roommates to maneuver around each other to wash, shave, dress and be ready for breakfast. During that hour he became acquainted with his five roommates as each told who they were and where they were from. He found Pete was from Georgia, Jim from Florida, Ben from Missouri, Andy from Nebraska, and John from California as each introduced himself. Shortly after getting slightly acquainted with all the different accents, they went to breakfast together where Ben suggested they should sit together at one of the tables set for eight.

They each looked around the room to see if they could possibly recognize anyone among the other pilots before sitting down. They sat down at the nearest table when they found no one saw anyone they remembered from anywhere. Shortly Harvey Daniels approached their table and thought he knew Alan from somewhere or someone he knew from Binghamton, New York. He asked if the vacant chairs were being saved for anyone? Ben told him to take one and he selected the chair facing Alan. He introduced himself and as each at the table said their names he then remembered from where he knew Alan. He remembered attending the same funeral and the following week enlisting in the Air Corps at the same times in Binghamton. He didn't see or meet Alan at the funeral, but knew they were from the same Ivy League university. Then asked if he remembered where and when he attended a funeral on one weekend and enlisting on the Air Corps the following weekend.

Before Alan could answer another pilot approached the table, looked at Alan, and asked, "Is that you Manston?"

"Yeah; that I am and who are you?"

"How could you forget me; and I, you? You slept in our upper bunk in Primary flight training."

"You're Harris...Richard, right?"

"That's right. Would you guys' mind if I take this available chair?"

"Go ahead and take it," responded Ben."

Harris sat down and continued, "Do you remember we arrived at Primary Flight School late at night and ended up assigned to the same double bunk and adjacent wooden stand-up lockers. And after showering the next morning do you remember while dressing, you said something like; Jees, my clothes are damp; thought Maxwell was bad." Dick talked to Alan about the bases they went to for their flight training after Primary. They found they were at different bases through RTU. All this time Harvey was waiting to ask Alan about their university and the two weekends.

An opening occurred and Harvey interrupted and talked to Alan for a couple of minutes. Then excitedly told everyone, at the table, they enlisted together and all he knew of Alan's athletic activity at their Ivy League university.

The first thing he told everyone at the table said openly, at the table, Manston played in every football game at the university except the last one in 1942. "I knew who you were, I never heard you were injured and looked for you in that last game wondering what happened to you? Would you tell us why you didn't play in the last one?"

Andy looked at Alan quizzically and asked, "Yeah; how come you didn't play in that last game?"

Alan hesitated, scanning everyone at the table before answering; "I only have this to say, "I attended a funeral in Binghamton during that last game for a person very close to me."

Then Harvey asked, "OK so I was at the same funeral; and on top of that did you know you ended up as a contender for the Ivy League Light Heavyweight Boxing Championship in December '42? And didn't fight in the finals for the Ivy League title at Dartmouth in January!"

"And why didn't you fight for that title," asked Jim?"

"You guys are asking too many questions about different things at the same time. I can only do one thing at a time."

"Ok Alan; why don't you explain about not boxing in the finals," asked Ben?

"Oh Jesus; OK. The guy I defeated in the semifinal was a senior and the former Ivy League Champion. He was about the same weight, four-inches taller and had or two inches with his reach on me. I don't think I threw enough hard right-hand punches; he was so hard to reach and maybe he was better than me. But I out jabbed him and was told I caught him with a couple of right-hand blows that noticeably buckled his legs. He hit me a lot of times, but; I wouldn't show any sign of his damaging blows and just bored in as though he never hurt me. I left there that night with my head spinning, wobbled all the way home, and was still spinning the entire following week when the exams began. I had a hard time just trying to read and understand the questions besides trying to answer them and decided not to box anymore. Then, I received a warning from the university because my marginal grades did not meet the acceptable level, to maintain a scholarship, required by the Civil Engineering School. Now does that tell you that I am or am not a super guy because I wasn't a starter in football; and would you or would you not speculate after I had the crap beat out of my brains that was a 'shoe in' to win the Ivy League Light Heavy Weight championship?"

The entire table was quiet for a few seconds when Pete asked, "Why didn't you go back for the spring semester anyway?"

"I went home after the exams, and I thought about returning or not. Then I remembered being informed, at the Air Corp Office when I enlisted, to expect to be 'called up' in early February. It didn't make much sense to return for the spring semester, pay tuition due, buy books and go to school for a week or two then leave in February." He looked at Harvey he asked, "Did you return for the second semester?"

"Yeah; I did." My tuition was refunded, but I had to keep the books. And another thing; would you believe the guy you defeated for the campus championship substituted for you and won the Ivy League Light Heavy Weight Championship."

John asked another question, "Now what's this about football; were you a starter?"

"No; I wasn't. I was a freshman walk-on in the spring practices and placed on the Junior Varsity Team. Due to the war the restrictions, freshman were permitted to play in all Ivy League varsity sport teams. I was initially placed on the Junior Varsity Team and surprised, after first day of practice, to find eighty percent of the JV guys were on football scholarships. Two days later I had the opportunity to play on offensive and defense plays against the varsity. It just so happened I messed up a lot of plays when put on defense and blocked well on offence. The following first Friday, the JV coach told me to turn in my JV stuff and pick up varsity equipment that I found was newer and better than the JV stuff. The next Monday, I ran out to the JV squad and the line coach told me to go over and practice with the varsity.

"So, what happened then," asked Andy?

"To shorten all this; I ended up being a back up as left guard and was accepted as a buddy by the varsity guys and in the following fall of '42 I reported to and played with the varsity."

"How about games Alan," questioned Pete?

"You see; I played at a guard position. The starting left guard was an All American and the right guard was an Honorable

Mention. No one could replace either as a starter no matter how good they may be. And about playing, the following fall I got to play around fifteen minutes in the first three games. When the All-American left guard sprained an ankle against Brown, I got my chance and played the rest of the second half of that game. I played the entire next two games and then was benched as a backup when the All American was healed and returned. Anyway, I had enough game time to get a letter."

As the conversations progressed it wasn't long before everyone at adjacent tables, knew of Alan's athletic background that Harvey began. He then wondered why he told them so much about himself and asked, "I'm sure at least one or all of you guys were athletes in something. Why doesn't one of you start and let us in on your experiences.

It was quiet for a couple of minutes as each of the others looked for someone to begin with something. Finally, Ben said," I played football too at Missouri University. I was on the JV squad as a freshman and made the varsity as a sophomore. I got to play in one game during the 1942 season. We were ahead by forty-seven to six in that game and the coach put me in for the last five minutes. Hey...that made me feel good. Then Peter chimed in saying, "As a Junior, I was on the golf team at the University of Georgia. Our team won the Southeast Conference in 1942 and I made All American Honorable Mention.

Before he could continue Jim interrupted with, "I remember you now; I was on the University of Florida's golf team the same year Georgia won the Conference and played against a guy named Phillip Maxwell. Man, he was good. He beat me seven up with six holes to play. I'd say his score scratch score could have been around a sixty-eight."

John and Andy said neither of them played in any sport at their colleges, but; John said he played the trombone in the band and Andy said he sang in the chorus.

Harvey then said, "I only was on a scholarship, and I had to work hard to maintain a B+ average."

They finished their breakfast and were the second last to leave the dining room and went up and out on deck. The sky was overcast, and the sea was relatively calm that first day, but; it began to churn up a little with rain that evening. By the second day's afternoon the sea had calmed down to small rolling waves and most pilots were out on deck. That day, Alan met and was reacquainted with Martin Fredericks whom he met on the train when activated. They got into a conversation about the areas of the south where they received flight training before noticing the overcast sky becoming dark and overcast. They changed the subject to the weather and made a weather forecast based on the meteorology learned in flight schools. Via good and thorough courses, they predicted the possibly of rain and rougher seas during the night. Shortly after they made that prediction a voice overload-speakers told everyone to return to quarters.

That one-inch ridge around the edge of the dining room

tables, that so many were complaining about, demonstrated their value the next morning. The ship was pitching fore and aft combined with a starboard to port roll and this edge prevent plates, silverware and serving dishes from sliding into the pilots' laps. The few pilots who became seasick ran out and on deck and 'urped' overboard. That night it was also fortunate that all bunk beds had that three or four-inch ridge boards on their outer edge, except for Andy, to protect one from rolling out of bed. Everyone in Alan's room fell asleep despite the tossing and turning of the ship, and no one fell out of bed that night.

The rough sea tossing the ship around, during breakfast cause a few pilots stomachs were not up to the challenge and ran up and out on deck. Salisbury approached Manston and his group of roommates, before they finished breakfast, and again assigned him to duty in the hold. He was to 'sit' the same paratroops beginning at 1600hrs.

"Do any of you guys know why he always picks on me and no one else in our group?"

Peter gave him an answer; "He likes you!"

They left the dining room and walked up and out on the bow of the deck. They didn't remain out there very long. The bucking of the ship into the waves threw seawater up on to the deck getting everyone a little wet. In less than ten, they were back in their stateroom, drying off...

Andy asked, "Whose idea was it to go up on deck in the first place?"

Jim said, "It was Peter's and Ben's."

"The hell it was it was Alan's," answered Ben.

"It didn't take long for everyone to point the finger at someone for venturing out on the deck," responded Alan and added, "Let's just drop it. No one was dragged out there!" He then waited, in silence, for someone to tell him to keep his thoughts to himself. He heard no challenge and smiled at everyone saying, "We have a good group of guys here; let's keep it this way." After a few silent minutes Ben suggested they play poker or pinnacle.

Peter immediately spoke up, "I don't play poker; besides I don't know how it is played?"

Ben then questioned, "Well, how about Pinnacle; how many of us know how to play that?"

Everyone said they knew how to play Pinnacle and John asked, "Where do we get the cards?"

"I have a couple decks and one is for pinnacle," added Ben.

The room being so small and not having anything to easily play on. Then Andy suggested they try to play in the Dining Room? "I'll go up and find out if it's, OK?"

Ben thought it would be best to just go there and play and proposed, “No we don’t ask; we just and play and if they try to chase us out Alan can always clear it with the ship’s Navy captain.”

“I told you guys; I only know him from deck duty and talking to him ‘once’ for a few minutes doesn’t mean he’ll let me do anything I want to do. And I don’t think it would be good for me to approach him again after what I did for the troopers in the hold.”

“What did you do for the troops in the ship’s hold that involved the Navy guy,” questioned Ben?

“Oh, let’s forget about that for now. I’ll ask him if we need to.”

“I won’t play if it’s for money; I’m not that good.” Added Pete.

“Neither will I! And for the same reason” added Jim.

“Ok. We can play for the Stateroom Championship. The criteria will be which two-man team beats the other two teams first.”

"How does that work,” asked Pete?

“Let’s go up to the dining room and I’ll explain it all there.”

Lt. Commander Fulbright saw them walk in and begin to play cards. He approached their table and said, "I'm sorry fellas', the dining room is Off Limits, except for meals."

When he noticed Alan among the players he added, "Well; I'll see what I can do for a way to play cards in your stateroom."

They went up on deck and returned after fifteen minutes. They found it was too cold out there and returned to their stateroom. Ben started a conversation about girls and started with. "Let's talk about girls until it's time for lunch. The morning went by rapidly and it was soon time for lunch. After lunch, fried boloney sandwiches, dill pickles and ship's tough coffee, they went back to the stateroom and found a small round table and four large pails to sit on in the middle of the room.

On seeing the set-up Ben said, "We gotta start the Pinnacle Tournament before who knows how many interruptions we might get. Alan has one almost before we can start."

It was 1530hrs when they returned to their stateroom from lunch and Alan had to leave and go down to the hold 1545hrs. The match was put on hold and the remaining four; played pinnacle until Alan returns before starting the tournament.

As he approached the hold, on the last set of the stairways, he was engulfed by the odor of seasickness. Sergeant Williams warmly met him on his arrival and Alan asked where the stench was coming from? Williams told him the men had been using the shower room next to their quarters, to relieve themselves. The seasick problem was escalating at 1754hrs when Alan had to take them to dinner. The main dish was fat juicy mutton. Manston wondered, why would anyone serve that ugly smelling mutton, especially, during rough seas. It smells bad enough in fresh air and we still have the vomiting odor all over the place. Most of the troops didn't go into the mess hall. The few men that did go returned holding their nose and dumped their trays into the trashcan. After they returned to bunk area they ate some K-Rations for dinner. There was so much seasickness in the hold by 1830hrs it became unbearable for everyone near the shower rooms. Alan had a strong stomach and barely made it to 2000hrs when his replacement finally arrived ten minutes late and he could leave the area.

A young paratrooper interrupted Alan and he stopped as he was hurriedly passing his bunk to exit the hold. He was just a kid, no more than seventeen. He asked if there was any way they could get some fresh water? Alan told him he would find out if there was a way. As he climbed the stairs, he could not rid his mind of the stench in the hold all the way up two and the third on below their stateroom level. He had to go out on deck for some clean fresh air.

The following afternoon the sea was calm, and the paratroops and pilots were out on deck at the same time. Manston saw Fulbright walking through the bow area checking deck conditions. The paratroopers in the ship's midsection saw

Alan approach a Navy officer, but did not hear him tell Fulbright of the conditions in the hold. Seeing the paratroopers approaching them he turned and walked toward the bow with Tom. As they were walking Alan asked Tom if he could find some fresh water for the paratroopers instead of having them drink stale canteen water every day. Fulbright said there is lot of good water on the ship and said he would see what he could do?

The next couple of days they played pinnacle every chance they had when the sea was not calm enough or too cold for them on deck. During the mini-pinnacle tournament the conversation ended up more on girls than the game. John told tales that were hard to believe, i.e., how he had dates with movie actresses like Jo-Anne Nealson and Cora Miller who were not leading ladies, but; well known for their supporting rolls. He also claimed to have slept with Rita Hayworth who was a leading actress. Ben told how he made out with three of the Cheer Leaders during two football seasons. Then Peter presented his experiences with Georgia Peach girls.

Alan was the only other one to say something about a girl. "I only had one girl and our relationship was strictly platonic and I really broke up when I found out how she died." Looking at Harvey he followed with, "That's when I saw you in Binghamton at her funeral."

"Alan, I didn't know that you knew Mary-Lou. I was there too. Remember how I told everyone at breakfast that first day we were at sea, we were at the same funeral in

Binghamton. She was my sister's best friend in high school before we moved in my junior year to Philadelphia." Unknowingly he brought tears to Alan's eyes by adding, "Remember those beautiful blue eyes and the blond hair. She was such a wonderful person."

"You guys did so much talking during the pinnacle tournament that the weakest pair, Jim and Pete won the tournament," claimed John.

Pete responded to that with," What are you talking about? You were the one who started telling us 'How you made out in Hollywood' almost as soon as we sat down to play."

Alan had another assignment in the hold, on the sixth day at sea with paratroopers. This time they heard four depth charges explode an hour after his arrival. They sounded like they were very close to the ship. A few men began to panic and shout about being sunk while trapped in the hold. Manston asked Williams if he could quiet his men so he could talk to them. It took a few minutes of shouting, to quiet most men. When it was relatively quiet, Manston spoke as loud as possible, "I learned from, college Engineering Physics, that sound travels a hell of a lot faster in water than in air. The depth charges you heard were really exploding very far from us, in the outer lanes, where the patrol ships were escorting the convoy." The four charges were all they heard during the next couple of hours and that more than Manston's explanation about sound in water, quieted them down for the rest of the evening.

Williams thanked Manston, just before he completed his tour, for the buckets of fresh water and ladles brought to them twice a day to fill their canteens, also for getting the shower rooms cleaned up. He informed the sergeant, "Thank Lt. Commander Nathan Fulbright, the Navy's ship commander. He is the one who was responsible for anything you receive."

Williams answered, "Yeah, we will, and we thank you too. We have a good idea how he found out about our personnel problems down here."

The last two days at sea the ship approached northern Scotland, maneuvered around the Outer Hebrides Islands, the English Northern Channel and through the Irish Sea. The ship continued past two prospective ports of entry for England, Blackpool, and Liverpool. Then on to St. Georges Channel where the ship finally steamed around Lands End Island and across the English Channel to the port of LeHarve, France. The Royal Queen docked late the eighth day of the trip at approximately 1815hrs European Standard Time. All personnel debarked between 1900hrs and 2000hrs. The pilots were first, off the ship, and Salisbury had then wait ion formation until their Paris escort arrived.

LeHarve to Paris, France on 11 November 1944

Colonel Salisbury turned the command of the pilots to an administrative officer, who was introduced as Captain

Charles Fields, after leading them off the ship. The captain gave them a brief presentation of what they would be doing for at least the next hour or two. Then after lining them up in a column of fours, he led them, carrying their B-4 bags, into the train station where their footlockers were alphabetically lined up in four rows. He led the pilots in a column of twos into the station and instructed them to locate and stand behind their footlockers.

A roll call was made, to verify all pilots and belongings were accounted for, after everyone identified their footlockers. The captain ordered them to pick up their B-4 bags and follow him out of the station to two passengers' railroad cars. They were instructed to board in groups of eight in each compartment. Several French workers followed the pilots, with wheelbarrows carrying their footlockers, and loaded them on a boxcar behind the compartment cars.

The Paratroopers were led past the pilots' cars, a half hour later, and climbed into boxcars with '40 HOMMES ou 8 CHEVALS' printed in large letters on the sides. Numerous pilots thought, "It was a hell of a way to transport a bunch of young guys who, in a few days, were to be engaged in combat."

The train pulled out of the railroad yards at 1930hrs and arrived at the Paris station at 2330hrs The pilots were then trucked to the Montmarte section of Paris and escorted behind a mansion to large area containing several rows of tents. Four men, in some sort of alphabetical order were assigned to each tent. Manston and his tent-mates Ben Maybury, Andy Starr and Will Mitchell were surprised to find their footlockers placed in front of their assigned tents. There were some goofed up footlocker placements and those misallocated were readily corrected. All were found, in the same rows, a tent or two away from their designated locations.

A good warming fire from a coal stove and a full bucket of soft coal set next to it was centered in each tent. Bare cots with footlockers at the foot ends were placed, one on each side, in the four-sided tent. After having a few minutes to settle, everyone was led to the rear of the mansion to receive two pillows and three GI blankets. They went back to their tents to make up their cots. Then returned and were given high altitude gear consisting of pants, jackets, caps, and boots. They wondered why they got all this stuff until they went to bed. They made up their beds with one blanket doubled over the cot and the other two used for cover then crawled in bed. It was so cold, everyone realized, the cots could use some sort of additional insulation to lie on. That night their only solution was to get up, put on their high-altitude gear. It helped enough to fall asleep normally, but they were still slightly cold. A Bugle Reveille woke them at 0800hrs on Sunday 12 November. They shed their high-altitude gear, except for the boots and put on their three-quarter coats and caps. They were lined up in a column of fours and were led to the Mansion they remembered passing the previous night.

On the way to the mansion, they were shown where the soft coal supply was stored, on the outside of the building in a large bin, on the left of the basement entrance. On the way to the mess hall, they passed a short hallway, on their left and it was pointed out that's where the bathroom and showers were located. The mess hall was a cafeteria style, and breakfast was the typical scrambled powdered eggs, strong coffee with powdered milk, boxed cereal, and thick hard toast, if so desired. They were given an hour after breakfast to clean up, but; not enough time to shower, before being led to a large room in the mansion. There, after filling out more personnel papers they were taken to a classroom and given an introduction lecture on the subjects they would receive before being assigned to fighter groups.

During their initial lecture, it was explained how the mansion had been a former German propaganda radio station and the English named the broadcaster Lord Haw, Haw. They were informed, at the end of the first day of lectures, reveille every morning would be at 0600hrs; beginning Monday; breakfast was at 0700hrs and be ready for classes by 0830hrs.

Most military bases in the United States and now also in Europe do not serve a lunch or dinner on Sundays. So, lunch and dinner were self serve delis. Plates of cold cuts, Parisian bread, pots full of coffee pots, bottles of milk and Coca Cola were made available at noon and 1700hrs. Most pilots went to the Mess Hall for lunch and found four long tables set up with plates of cold cuts, Swiss cheese, bread, several jams, numerous pots of coffee, small pitchers of powdered milk and small sugar bowls placed on tables. It was like an uncontrolled madhouse with everyone trying to be first at everything. Alan and his tent-mates, rather than getting tangled with the maze of pilots quietly sat at a dining table drinking coffee until the rush settled down. Most of the thinly sliced Spam and thicker sliced bologna was gone when they went to the food tables. The hard Parisian bread, butter and several jam bottles were still plentiful. Will went to the kitchen and in a matter of minutes came out came out with two plates; one with a few thick slices of Spam, the other with bologna and Swiss cheese. When he arrived at our table several pilots confronted him looking for seconds. Will told them, "Back off. We haven't had our firsts yet; these few slices are for my tent mates and me!

Some smart guy said, "Who made you the boss?"

Will retaliated with, "I did! You guys emptied the plates, and I got a few slices of cold cuts for us! And if you want some more; you know where the kitchen is," and that statement settled that problem!

Dinner was not available, except for another deli, therefore; all personnel were permitted to leave the base at 1600hrs, for dinner if they wanted it off base, and were to return by 2330hrs.

Alan and his roommates rushed to the bathroom, showered, shaved, and dressed to leave the base as soon as possible by 1600hrs. It was 1635hrs before all were finally ready to leave the base and look for a good restaurant.

Sunday Night, 13 November – The Parisian Restaurant

All four rejected the first three restaurants for not appearing clean. Will had dined in the very acceptable fourth one they approached during the 1936 Olympics. They entered this restaurant and were in a relatively wide long lobby. It was well furnished with three large sofas, two love seats and several high back, upholstered, armchairs. A few large, wonderful country scene and landscape paintings were appropriately placed on embossed walls. The pilots had walked past the restrooms on their way to an open section passage at the far end of the lobby that appeared to be the entrance to the dining room. Ben stopped and thought it would be a good idea to wash their hands before going to the dining room. They went in and a couple relieved themselves. When they came, they saw a group consisting of three formal dressed couples entering the lobby. They came out and went to the dining room entrance. They waited for the matre d' and as he approached them, he noticed three couples standing behind the pilots. He smiled at them then greeted them. He turned to the pilots and asked them for the name on their reservations. When they told the matre'd they did not have a reservation he apologized to have to informed them, as reservations were required for dinner on Sundays, he could not seat them that evening.

Now completely ignoring the pilots he addressed the three waiting couples behind them. His wide smile to the mid-aged couple in the group indicated recognition. He bowed and addressed them as monsieur Minister Hubere and Madam Marie. A tall, beautiful, blond girl, in her late teens or early twenties, standing next to the couple overheard, the 'no reservation rejection' and asked the Minister, in French, "*Uncle Hubere; we do not have a reservation; or do we?*"

Her uncle answered, "We do no; and it is not a concern of ours."

Will, the son of a wealthy family, understood what his answer was to her question and became upset with the matre d' for ignoring his group. He angrily, interrupted the matre'd and addressed him in fluent French, "*What about us? My parents, sister and I were here in 1936; we didn't have any reservations or any problems receiving dinner. Is this now a restaurant reserved only for European politicians and wealthy Parisian families?*"

The mid-aged man's niece, overhearing this glared at Will and Alan standing next to him. It made Alan blush and put his arms and hands up in a surrendering position. Then noticed the young lady was smiling at him; so; he moved his hands to a prayer position.

She continued to smile pleasantly, apparently attracted by this humble gesture, and asked her uncle to intervene for the pilots and asked, "*Why did the matre d' not seat those pilots?*"

"Michelle; never mind what he is doing, he knows the restaurant's policies."

"I suppose that includes not permitting American pilots to dine here."

"It is none of our business. Do not make a spectacle of this!"

Then the young girl pleading asked, "Uncle Hubere have you forgotten it was American aircraft that assisted the soldiers who liberated Belgium in September. You know the matre d' very well. Won't you please; ask him, if not for me, for Belgium, permit the pilots to have dinner here? Her escort was visibly disturbed by her request of her uncle's intervention. The other, short, young man, escorting a very pretty young brunette said nothing.

He hesitated before telling is niece, to leave well enough alone, his wife interrupted and said, "For heaven's sake; have the matre d' permit those pilots have something to eat!"

Hubere was quiet for a moment then whispered quietly to the matre d', "Would you please seat those pilots in a suitable area a good distance from where you intend to seat us."

The matre'd nodded without questioning and reluctantly seated the pilots at a table, on the floor level area far from the front side of the room. Upon returning to the Minister he asked, *"Sir, does the seating of the pilots meet your satisfaction?"*

"Mais oui; merci beaucoup," Hubere said, nodding to show his satisfaction.

The pilots were watching to see where he would seat them as then the matre'd courteously escorted his group to the section two steps above and centered in the rear section, of the room. The blond girl ended up facing Ben he wondered why she took Alan's breath away as his face turned bright red when they she was smiling at them. When Ben began returning her smiles and glances, he became aware they had truly attracted her attention.

This led Ben to ask, "Did you notice those deep blue eyes?"

"You bet and did you notice those shapely legs on her," Alan replied?

Will returned, "Yeah, but did you notice her boobs were not very big."

This led Andy to return, "They're not small, but look like a good handful."

"Oh yeah, "She's a hand full if you have small hands," returned Will.

"Remember when we, Ben, Andy, and I were on the ship and Turner, from Los Angeles said most movie girls didn't have big boobs. They used fillers to make them more attractive," returned Alan.

Will then said, "Well, I'm a 'Boob Man' anyway you want to look at it."

"So am I" agreed Ben.

"To me, she is beautiful enough to be a movie star. How

do you know she's not one here or better, arriving with a 'Big Wheel' government minister," Alan had to add?

While this girl talk was going on Andy said, "Didn't any of you noticed how the girl's escort noticing our activity and her returning smiles bothered him?"

Andy was right. He was objecting to her interest in the pilots' table, and they could tell by the way he looked at them and kept saying something to the girl and the way she looked responding to him. At that time, Michelle was telling him, "You are not my keeper!"

Claude being upset at her attitude brought al this to her uncle's attention and he noticed the continued glancing activity. The activity began irritating Uncle Hubere's observations and made him glare at Ben and he temporarily stopped glancing at the young lady. That did not affect the young lady's interest and she continued to glance and smile at the pilots' table. Her aunt, Marie, noticed when her niece's glances were at Alan, he looked down at the table, and began blushing, as their eyes met. She then leaned close to her niece, whispered something, and both turned to smiled at him.

The escort also observing this continuous glancing became noticeably frustrated. He turned toward Hubere and said, "*Do you see what Michelle is doing? Notice how they are looking at her and she is exchanging smiles with all the pilots!*"

Hubere turned and starred at Ben smiling toward his table.

Then looked at Michelle and asked, "What do you think you are doing? You are cooperating with the pilots' insolence!"

"Oh uncle, please; they are only responding to what I began."

"Well; stop it now! You are embarrassing us. Here now, change chairs with Claude."

"Why?"

"Never mind why; just do it!" She frowned and pouted as she exchanged chairs. This seating arrangement now faced the young lady more at Alan than Ben. Will noticed all of that activity, leaned close to Alan, while laughing nudged him, then pointed at the girl's escort, who was upset and was squirming in his chair.

The matre'd had a waitress take menus to the pilots and in broken English she asked if they wanted something to drink after taking care of his special guests. They all ordered a dry red wine and in a few minutes the waitress returned with their wine and asked if they were ready to order. They said they were, and everyone ordered steak from the menu. Ben Will and Alan's intermittent glances to and from the young lady continued during dinner. After about fifteen minutes the young lady's glances appeared to be directed more often toward Alan and he could not keep from blushing every time their eyes met.

The pilots finished dinner and ordered coffee. While

consuming a few cups of coffee they began a conversation about the young lady at the other table. Will and Ben looked over at her and said how much they would like to take the young lady to bed. Andy's comment was about her beautiful features and how she could be a gorgeous model and how much he wished he could have a girlfriend like her and then go to bed. Ben and then Will told Andy they wouldn't wait if they had an opportunity to date the young lady and how they would go about exciting her. Alan was just sitting quietly as the three of them continued fantasizing about the girl. Alan's absence of adding any comments or giving an opinion about this subject, they were currently discussing led Will to ask, "Why have you not added anything to our evaluation of that girl?" Alan just shrugged his shoulders and nodded a no to Will. "No what! Are you insinuating you have no interest, or she doesn't arouse you? Don't just sit there; say something!"

The conversation stopped when the waitress returned with the bill and a pot of coffee. She asked' "Who would like more coffee before I leave the pot with you?" They all wanted more, she refilled their cups, set the pot on the table, and left.

"How about an answer to my question about your interest in the girl?"

"If I am or am not, is the question. The question is, under what circumstances and conditions would you have the opportunity to take her to bed. I don't think I would ever have one with her."

"You mean she hasn't excited you with all her glancing and smiling at us looking for our response?"

"Look; you guys have only one thing on your mind. Andy said most of it right. He talked only about her beauty and being a model and no sex. I don't have any inclination about taking a girl to bed unless I love her, and she loves me enough to want to get married."

"Are you trying to tell us after all your athletic activity you still are a virgin, questioned Ben?

"Jees; being an athlete has nothing to do about all this!"

"So, we have some kind of a star athlete among us who's never been in bed...not even with a cheerleader? I never met one who hasn't claimed to have been in bed with less than ten girls."

"I never said I was a great athlete; maybe that's why I have not even taken one girl to bed!"

Andy interrupted them and injected, "Look you guys; we're getting nowhere on this subject except for a lot of pushing and shoving. Let's pay our bill and get out of here into the real world."

Will figured out what each should contribute, including a reasonable tip and motioned to the waitress when she was in their area. She came to their table and when Will handed her the money, she knew from the cost of the dinners the size of the tip she received was exceptional. She curtsied gave them each of them a big smile, and added, "Merci beaucoup, beaucoup!"

Upon leaving they had to pass the glancing girl at the three couple's table. Prior to reaching them, Will suggested they should all ignore the uncle and his niece's escort, then; give his niece a big smile as they walked by her. Ben, with his cap off, bowed and two of the others did the same except Alan who smiled and blushed as he walked past her. The young lady watched the pilots walk all the way to the exit and smiled every time her and Alan turned, and their eyes met on his way out. Her uncle and escort's eyes were on Ben and Alan who the young girl winked at each time they turned their heads. Her aunt just sat back in her chair and held back her laughter. Alan was still blushing as he walked out of the restaurant.

Will continued the discussion about the young lady on the way to the base, by saying, "I had a girl just like her; she was good looking, hot and fit to travel. That girl we saw was a pretty good 'looker' and you could tell the way she smiled she had the 'hots' for one of us."

"Jees; Will; I don't understand why sex is so big and the first thing of," Alan questioned?

"Come on; don't tell us that you are the perfect innocent gentleman and never think of it," questioned Ben?

"You guys are something! Can't you appreciate a girl for being beautiful," Alan commented?

"She certainly had more of your attention than any of ours. You did a lot of the smiling. The rest of us were mostly observers," responded Ben.

"Come on you guys, ease up. That girl was looking at you, Will and Ben, as much or more than me. I know she wouldn't ever look at me again outside of that restaurant," Alan angrily responded.

"Take it easy Manston," stepped in Andy, "They were only needling you. Don't get mad."

"I'm not mad! I'm upset because that girl was looking at all of us. Did you forget it was she who asked her uncle to have the matre d' seat all of us; not only me!"

Ben then looked at Alan, "Why you snake, you understood everything she said to her uncle. You never told us you understood French."

"I never told any of you about my French because I only know so little. I studied French for three years in high school. I just filled in what she and you said when all that French was being said."

"You didn't look surprised when I responded to her uncle?

How come you just stood there looking innocent during the entire French conversation and not showing any emotion what-so-ever?"

Steve changed the subject to keep it from getting into an unwanted discussion and suggested, "Lets drop this and go see a movie."

One of them said, "That's a good idea," and they went up directly to the Movie floor and room on their arrival.

Monday 13 through Friday 17 November 1944: Paris

Their initial class was survival in the freezing waters of the English Channel, how to inflate a dingy, get out of the water and into it in an acceptable survival time. This was the major subject among the lectures and demonstrations they received. Also, several continental languages were taught, and they had to respond, useful phrases, in an acceptable manner. Survival kits and its contents, including the useful language phases in phonetics among other items, and the purpose of each item was explained in detail. In addition, they were shown and informed of eatable earthly things such as snails, worms, and plants to survive on.

The major topic was 'how to surrender if down German territory'. They were instructed; if they were down, they should attempt to find a Luftwaffe or an Army unit or base before surrendering to anyone. And it was strongly emphasized to avoid civilians and especially the Gestapo if at all possible! Other subjects were the identification of German cities, and memorizing how they appeared, in clear skies and through broken clouds. In addition, they had to know the relative compass headings from several German cities to Paris. Strangely it seemed that VD presentations dominated lectures at various times between the presentations and they so strongly impressed Alan, he believed it would be best to evade sex with any European women.

Friday morning, the 16th of November, pilot assignment orders were posted on the board outside of the Personnel Office. Forty-four of the fifty-five P-40 replacement trained pilots received assignments in Eighth Air Force Groups. One P-40 trained pilot was among fifteen P-47 receiving assignments to Ninth Air Force Groups in France. Martin Fredericks seeing Manston on the Ninth Air Force orders with Jim Keene assigned to the same group looked for Alan to introduce him to Jim Keane who was assigned to the same, 378th Fighter Group.

In the meantime, Manston was wondering why he, the only P-40 trained pilot, was the one assigned to a Ninth Air Force Group that most likely were flying P-47's.

Two

NINTH AIR FORCE

Friday 17 November to Friday 15 December 1944: France

Fourteen P-47 trained pilots were scheduled to leave Paris in two six by six trucks, at 0850hrs, Friday, 17 November 1944. Six were to travel in one six by six and the other eight in a second six by six to three different bases near the French-Belgian border. Alan was watching them load up and climb into the back of the truck. Fredricks, before he climbed into his six by six, turned and said to Alan, "Now you watch out for yourself. The Jug can be tough on a pull out at a high air-speed; even from five thousand feet. I'm sure you'll transition before you'll be permitted to fly combat, so make sure you practice dives between sixty and seventy-five degrees 'with the throttle cut back just above idle, then; from ten thousand feet. Practice these adding a little air speed on each dive until you feel confident at any controlled airspeed from any altitude. That's all I have to say; I want to see you in Paris, on leave, some day."

"OK, I'll remember that. Thanks for your consideration; you be careful too," answered Alan.

Fredricks climbed into his truck and sat on the last bench seat on the left side of the six by six and waved to Alan as the truck disappeared from their view. Alan returned into the HQ building and talked to Jim about this diving stuff in a Jug. He told Alan the same thing because they did a lot of that in RTU. "Looks like we'll be doing it a lot too!"

Twenty minutes later a Weapons Carrier arrived and parked in front of the Base Mansion. An Air Police sergeant stationed at the Headquarters entrance went to and arrived at the truck as the driving sergeant was getting out. He approached the truck driver and said, "Sergeant, you can't park here, in front of the Base Headquarters. You have to park in the parking lot you went through to get here."

The sergeant informed the Air Policeman, "I was told to park here, by the Gate Sergeant when I told him I was here to pick up two pilots and their baggage for the 378th Fighter Group."

"You must be the guy to pick up two Second Lieutenants this morning. Those two footlockers to your right are theirs and they are waiting inside. I'll get them for you." He turned and hurriedly walked into the building.

The 378th sergeant, waiting for the pilots looked at the footlockers to check the names on them. A minute or so later two pilots carrying B-4 Bags came out of the building, escorted by the policeman. The waiting sergeant saluted the pilots and asked as they approached him, "Are you Keane and Manston?"

As Jim and Alan returned his salute Jim said, "Yes; we are. We are waiting for a 378th Group sergeant to pick us up. If you're here 378th I believe you've found them; that'd be us I believe."

"Would you mind telling me which of you is which?"

"I'm Jim Keane and this other officer is Alan Manston."

The sergeant introduced himself as Staff Sergeant Whiting and asked, 'Sirs, if you hand me your bags, I'll load them and your footlockers on the truck while you get in the cab to ride up front with me."

The pilots climbed into the front seat of the truck while the sergeant was taking care of their footlockers and B-4 bags. They were surprised to find the truck had plenty of cab-room after the sergeant got in and asked. "Are you all set and ready to go; sure, you haven't left anything behind? It's a more than a three-hour drive to the base."

Jim looked at Alan who nodded yes and responded, "We're all set if you are?"

They left the Replacement Depot a short time later and drove for about three and a half-hour before they arrived at the of the outskirts in the town of St. Dizier. He then drove them to the 378th Fighter Group Headquarters at 1425hrs where a sergeant met them as they entered and led them to the group administration offices. A Master Sergeant Wendel, group administrator who asked for and took the sealed personal files. Then he had them fill out a few different personal papers that took them fifteen minutes to complete and handed them to Wendel. He scanned their papers, finding them in order, escorted them to the Group Commander's office where they had introduced them to the Co. They entered the office stopped at the CO's desk and saluted while at attention. "I'm John Bennett and you are," he said as he held out his hand for a shake.

"I'm Jim Keane Sir" and this guy is Alan Manston, he said as they each shook hands. Bennett pointed to two armchairs against the wall to his left saying, "Bring those chairs up her in front of my desk and let's get to know each other." He initiated the conversation, "I understand you, Keene, flew Jugs in the states," and you Alan had P-40s in RTU. Do I have that right?"

"Both replied, "That's right sir."

Looking at Manston he asked, “You have a lot of work to do to catch up to our P-47 guys. Think you’re up to it?”

“Sir, I believe I am. It’s just another fighter that you have to learn to care for like...like a girl.”

“You’ve got that right; then asked where they were from? He was surprised when he found Jim’s home was in an adjacent small Texas town and Alan was from Buffalo. He continued by telling them where his home was. Then questioned them about where their pilot training bases were and who were their instructor pilots. He did not recognize the names of their instructors and asked did either of you hear of a Colonel Bill Wentworth? He was a double Ace and I’ve heard he is now an RTU Base Commander.”

Jim answered, “I know him; he was our Base CO at Dover, Delaware. He is a great guy!”

He was always so friendly to all the pilots. When he saw a student pilot, in the club he hadn’t met; he’d stop, sit with him, buy a drink, and have a short conversation. Every time he did this, He approached the students table, stop, and look at the student, the other instructors, knew what he was up to and had to laugh when the student jumped to attention and saluted when he began talking to him. He’d sit down, buy a couple of drinks, and spent at least a half hour talking.”

‘That’s my Wentworth! He always was friendly with everyone. I remember when any pilot, new or experienced goofed up on him during a mission, he never raised his voice. He would take the pilot in his office, get out two glasses and fill them from a bottle of good whiskey. While having two or three drinks he was friendly, almost like a mother, not your father. He would explain, what you did wrong or caused a problem, like he was your buddy. When a pilot came out of his office, he followed him and invited everyone in the Ready Room to have a drink on him when they went to the club." He hesitated and then said, "I can tell you both are wondering how I knew him so well. I flew combat with him. When he completed his second tour as a Major, and elected to return to the states, he told me he still wished to fly, but wanted a desk job wherever he was assigned. I guess he got what he wanted."

While enjoying their conversation he had them toast with a shot of his bourbon with him. Then he informed them, "You are assigned to different squadrons. Keene you're with the 375th and you, Manston are with the 376th then dismissed them with, "When you leave this office, go out there and see sergeant Wendel again. He will tell you about your squadrons, where they're located, where your tent quarters are and where to get your supplies. I'll check with you from time to time."

Wendel informed them Sergeant Whiting was waiting to take them to the various places on the base they had to go to become established with their squadrons. As they walked out the door, they saw Whiting sitting in the truck, waiting for them. They climbed in and he and drove Jim to the 375th and Alan to the 376th. Captain William Clancy, the Operations Officer was waiting for Alan in the doorway of their squadron's Ready Room. Clancy introduced himself, while sergeant Whiting was unloading Alan's baggage, then; took him to meet Major Thomas H. Cassidy, 376th Squadron Commander, in his office. Usually not both are available because one of them led the squadron on each mission. On this day both were in the building as the Group Commander was leading 376th as the lead flight on that day's mission.

After a short introduction and discussion about his flying P-40s, and not Jugs, Cassidy informed him," "You'll have to transition in P-47s. Does that bother you?"

"No sir. If these Jugs have the same controls as a P-40 I don't think there would be any trouble flying it as well as anyone else. And one thing do I know; the P-47's landing gear separation would make it much easier to land than a P-40."

"You're pretty confident, aren't you?"

"Sir, I don't mean to infer I can do anything better than anyone else, I just feel if you're a fighter pilot you should be able to learn how to fly any fighter aircraft, Army, Navy or Marine to the 'edge' of its flight capabilities or hang up you wings; cause you won't live long!"

He smiled at Clancy and said, "I think we can use him. Ok then; Clancy, you can leave now; and take him to the Ready Room. On the way stop in our clerk's office and assign him to a flight that is short, a pilot. I think its Butler's; anyway, check it out with Tony?"

The clerk's room separated the CO's and Clancy's office and had doors on opposite sides and one out to the hallway. Leaving the CO's office Clancy stopped and introduced him to Sergeant Tony Pellegrino, the Operations Clerk. Tony confirmed Butler was short a pilot, and had Tony assign him to his, 'B' Flight. After a brief conversation with Tony, he led Alan to his office where he reviewed his flight records with him. Completing that, the Ready Room was the next and final stop.

Upon entering the Ready Room Clancy looked for Butler and didn't see him anywhere and asked, "Anyone seen Butler or know where he is?" Someone said, "I believe Butler is in his tent with Cooper." Well, OK; we'll catch him at dinner between 5:30 and 6:00 o'clock." Then proceeded to introduce Alan to the six pilots that were there. Most pilots were very receptive and freely talked about some of their close calls. A few didn't hesitate to boast about their air victories. When Clancy interrupted one of the boasting pilots boldly said "And some of our guys get a little shaky and begin to drink a little more than they should. I watch those guys carefully when they stay up late and get loaded. I don't want them on a mission the next day and unnecessarily get himself or someone else killed. I'm not insinuating it's bad if it isn't done an only on a night before a mission. We have a couple in our squadron now. I watch them carefully and as long as I'm operations officer it won't happen here. Let's drop the subject for now. Just remember what I said," added Clancy!

A half hour later a sergeant Henning arrived in a jeep to drive Alan to the base supply building. There, he was issued bedding and flight gear that included flight suits, a helmet and an A-2 leather flight jacket and then returned to his tent where he found a bare cot with three others made up. He found an empty scotch bottle and a large note on that cot with, "for Manston" on it in large letters. He tore up the note, took the bottle off his cot, set it down of the wooden floor and put the clothing from supply on the empty cot. His footlocker was there, placed at the foot of his bed. He turned to Henning and asked, "Would you take me back to the Ready Room? I didn't get something there I could use."

Alan came out with a lot of newspapers he picked up laying around the room and took them to his tent. He hung his suits, uniforms and coats in a freestanding empty wooden clothes closet and layered his cot with newspapers before making up his bed. Henning was kind enough to wait for him and take him to the Mess Hall. Alan didn't finish setting himself up in the tent until 1739hrs.

Cliff Butler, his Flight Leader was waiting for him at the mess tent entrance and was the first pilot he met. Butler led him through the serving line to a table were some of their squadron pilots were eating introduced him to one of his tent-mates, Captain Howard Cooper and his other two tent-mates John Benson and Fred Bauer. During dinner Cliff informed him he was scheduled for Ground School, on the P-47, Monday morning after reporting to the base hospital.

Saturday 18 through Friday 24 November 1944: Ground School Saturday

-

Saturday morning Manston reported to the base hospital for a physical examination where he met Captain Donald R. Burton, the squadron Flight Surgeon. After the examination he spent the rest of the day in the Ready Room meeting pilots. Sunday was an off day for Alan, and he ended up first in a poker game, in the club tent with pilots not on the mission and a few ground duty officers.

Everyone ran out of the tent to count the number P-51s when they heard them returning. Manston left and went to the Ready Room for the mission debriefing. All the mission pilots sat in front of the Intelligence Officer, sipping their two ounces of whiskey, for the mission debriefing. Apparently, they all felt good about their few ground victories on a field with several scattered Me-109s. All indicated there was just machine gun fire and no 20's or 40's. When that was concluded Alan sat, in on different conversations, listening to various mission stories. Shortly most pilots went to their tent, before dinner, to take a nap, since they were woken around four o'clock in the morning.

Alan ate dinner with most of his squadron pilots and later watched a high-stake poker game in the large tent club for an hour. He walked around the club a little then went to the taproom area where beer was available. The hard stuff was mission issue stuff, and some had their bottles and drank 'boiler makers'. He had only one glass of beer and sat around watching some going back to the bar for more. A few pilots were getting a little tipsy and Alan decided to leave and return to his tent.

None of his tent-mates were there, so he relaxed and looked and read a few articles in a couple of Life magazines. Just before eleven o'clock, as his tent mates had not yet returned, he checked the placement of his paper insulation under his bed blanket. Then put on his flight gear and crawled under the top blankets.

Monday morning, he met master sergeant Less Madden, P-47 line chief and aircraft instructor, in a base hanger. He first, thoroughly discussed the Curtiss Electric controlled propeller and in the afternoon the Jug's hydraulic system. Tuesday, he taught everything from the airframe to the flight controls and electrical system. Wednesday, the 22nd, 1st. Lt. Edgar Patterson taught P-47 flight characteristics. In the afternoon he introduced the K-14 gunsight and theory for air-to-air combat. The next day, Thursday, he demonstrated the use the gunsight for strafing, bombing and rocket firing. That afternoon Alan reviewed the P-47 flight characteristics and cockpit contents while Lt. Chuck Matthew's was giving the tests to those ready for a check out flight. Jim Keane and two other, P-47, trained pilots made their initial Jug flights on Friday. Alan passed his blindfold cockpit test on Saturday and was scheduled to check out in a Jug, 'B model', on Monday.

Saturday 25 November through Friday 15 December 1944: Flight Transition

-

That Saturday Staff Sgt. Chet Matuzak met him at 0900hrs in the morning to assist him with the pre-flight aircraft walk around check. Pilots could only fly aircraft, not on combat missions. This limited Alan to an average of a flight to every third day. He flew his first flight check on Monday and Wednesday, the 29th, he was instructed to practice power on and off stalls. Thursday, 30 November, was Thanksgiving Day and the group was assigned to fly several missions. His squadron had twelve pilots on the first mission and lost three. Two of them went straight in at the target. They said one pilot screamed about one of his legs took a 20 mm and couldn't feel if it was still there. It was quoted that his last words were, "I'm going to make a forced landing. They surmised he must have lost a lot of blood quickly from his wounds, shortly lost unconscious, and control of his aircraft as his radio went silent within a minute. He crashed behind enemy lines but did not burn.

Thanksgiving dinner consisted of turkey, mashed potatoes, corn, local bread, and coffee. Alan while eating with Cliff and his flight pilots seemed extremely quiet during dinner. He hadn't said two sentences during the entire dinner. The silence was apparent to Cliff who asked, "Are you engulfed by the men we lost today?"

"It's not them Cliff; it's just a death on this day still haunts me."

"Still haunts you? Is there's something in your past that bothers you? What's so bad about this day or is it just not being home for Thanksgiving?"

"Alan pointed an unoccupied corner of the tent and said, "Let's go over to that corner. "I don't want anyone to hear this."

Cliff, following Alan, said they needed a drink and got himself and Alan a coke. They sat in a corner table and Cliff asked, "Now; what is all about this day?"

"Alan looked down and said, "I'd rather not get into that now, OK?"

"If something is disturbing you; better let it out before it affects you on a mission and do it now."

He very sadly said, OK. I had a girlfriend in college. We were great for each other; she made my life complete. Her father picked her up, at the university, for a Thanksgiving weekend at home. She brought her father to my fraternity house to meet me before they left the campus at seven o'clock. A thunderstorm hit the university area just after they left for home where two brothers, a Navy officer, an Army officer, and her mother were waiting for them. The next morning one of her sorority sisters was at our door looking for me. She told me, my girlfriend and her father died in the city hospital a few miles from their home from a head on collision in that same thunderstorm."

"You can't let things like that, as hard as it may be, stay with you now. You're in a war!"

Cliff then took him to the club and had only a couple beers, over thee and a half hour period while he tried to get Alan to let this thing pass. At ten o'clock, Cliff said he had to go to bed, as he was on a mission the next day. The next morning Cliff was up early, and Alan wet him at the mission briefing. He returned from the mission unscathed, but unfortunately the squadron lost three pilots who parachuted and were seen safely landing.

The next day Cliff scheduled himself and Alan for on an eight o'clock local flight. He demonstrated and had Alan practice simulated evasive maneuvering off a dive bomb target. On one flight Cliff had him fly formation one plane length, slightly right and behind him and went through some acrobatic maneuvers to see if Alan would stay with him?

Alan flew six; approximate two-hour solo flights, within a radius of thirty miles of the base from Friday the 1st through Friday 15 December 1944. He made simulated strafing, dive-bombing and skip- bomb runs on various typical selected landscape targets in the area.

Combat: 16 Saturday through 23 Saturday, December 1944: France

-

Alan flew his first mission on 16 December first day of the Battle of the Bulge. He was scheduled to fly as Cliff's wingman in 'C' flight. The large briefing tent had on a large a map mounted on a large of plywood board of the France sector we were in, the Netherlands and western Germany. On this morning the map was marked to show the Germans had penetrated of our front through Luxembourg and into Belgium to show the approximate location of German forces. A fog was reported covering the entire attacking area and air support for the ground troops appeared to be impossible. Alan's squadron put up four flights of four P-47s to be directed to targets by a forward controller. The squadron approached the Bastogne area and found that the area was fogged in as predicted. Their Forward Controller was notified it was impossible to attack in that area; and the squadron separated into two groups of eight P-47s for further ground control direction. Cliff, leading flights, C and D, was directed by ground control to bomb and strafe a convoy of supply trucks a few miles east of Luxembourg City.

They found the Germans had more 20 mm. antiaircraft guns located throughout the entire area east of the fog, to protect their supply forces, than reported at the briefing. The flights' attacked and destroyed two antiaircraft positions before wiping out several supply trucks. One truck was carrying bombs and a tremendous explosion resulted when it was hit. A price was paid by two "D Flight" pilots getting hit bad. One, went in on sort of a glide path, crashed and began burning. The other was hit on a dive-strafing run and must have been seriously injured because the plane was seen to never waver on went in on his dive angle. He crashed in a bolt of fire.

Several planes in 'A' and 'B' flights were hit hard hit by small arms fire. Two were also hit by 20 mm anti-aircraft guns and severely damaged. One crashed and burned, with the pilot, and another pilot had to bail out and was covered, by circling P-47s, until he disappeared into a wooded area.

During the debriefing almost everyone was eager to say something about the mission. A few were real jokers, but; Alan only sat quietly until he was asked something. This was his initiation, attacking ground forces. He was shaken up flying into flashes of anti-aircraft fire and tried to conceal it at the debriefing, but; it did show. Cliff noticing his discomfort and after the debriefing, told him, "It is only normal 'after' flying into anti-aircraft positions firing at you. All of us feel that way, but; when you begin making your passes if you concentrate on the target and use some evasive action your concentration should take over your mind. It is always after and on the way home when it all really hits you."

Hearing this Alan was mentally much relieved knowing he wasn't the only one who was shaken by all that anti-aircraft gunfire at the target.

The next day, Sunday, Alan was Capt. Don Peters, B

flight, wingman. They were directed to dive bomb and strafe armored vehicles escorting troop trucks northeast of St. Vith. On his second attack, after dropping his bombs, he strafed trucks with troops and saw men fly into the air when his eight 50 caliber bullets hit them in their trucks. Flying into ant-aircraft fire still bothered him, but not as much as his first encounter. They were on their way back to the base when he began to think about the anti-aircraft guns and explosions around him. He wondered if he was going to last on this kind of stuff.

On their return Manston taxied to the pierced planking ramps and parked his plane in B Flight ramp. Sergeant Pete Mueller got up his right wing helped him out the cockpit. The plane took a 20 mm. in the left wing and several 9 mm. holes in the fuselage. Meuller noticing the 20 mm damage to the aircraft asked Alan if they lost anyone.

He hesitated and after a few seconds he sadly said, "We lost, Cooper's close friend, Capt. Caldwell of the 375th Squadron." Jack Dwyer and Adam Cory who also flew with 'B' flight, left the parking ramp with Parker before Alan, who just sat quietly, in his P-47, watching Captain Henry Sanders, of 'C' flight, being helped into an ambulance. Mueller saw Manston who had been so quiet as he left the flight line, looking so sad with his head down, walking alone toward the Ready Room.

Only Cliff was aware Alan didn't say a word during debriefing and also didn't notice he left immediately at its conclusion. He went directly to his tent and was glad his mates were not there because he just didn't want to talk to anyone. Lying on his cot looking straight up at its peak he could see Germans literally flying out of their trucks he hit on the mission. That vision gave him a strong queasy gut feeling. He dozed off in full flight gear and woke up at quarter after five and he was still alone in his tent; then walked out to the watershed, washed his face and hands before going to the mess tent. He found an unoccupied table and ate dinner alone. Cooper noticed his strange behavior and saw him quietly leave alone and thought it strange he had not talked to anyone for several hours. He had the feeling Alan went to their tent and went there, quietly entered the tent, and found him alone knelling by his cot with tears in his eyes. Coop sat on his cot facing Alan's, waited a few moments, and asked, "What's the matter now?"

"I can't help feeling bad about the German troops I killed today."

Cooper stated, "Alan; why the hell do you feel bad about killing Krauts; that's your job!"

"It was the killing; not who. I never believed I'd kill anyone and am praying to be forgiven."

"Oh, that's nice. Those guys were going to the front lines to kill our guys tomorrow with no regrets. Look at it this way; you saved a lot of our troops from dying tomorrow by disposing of some Krauts today! Understand? You gotta know there's a lot of our guys out there needing our help and dying faster than we are!"

"Yeah, you're right; I guess?"

"You guess? You got to know!"

"I guess a lot of guys need to be forgiven on both sides."

"No! You don't understand. You gotta know these are troops extra loyal to the Hitler's dream who slaughtered a lot of good people. You have to visit some village graves near here and see the women and kids they killed." The tent became very quiet for the rest of that evening after Copper stopped talking.

On 22 December, the weather permitted attacking targets in some areas around Bastogne. Ground control directed all squadrons to attack several targets east of the fogged in area. 'A' Flight hit a train under full steam loaded with supplies heading for the Bastogne fogged area a few miles away and caught it before it got there. They were surprised on their second pass by flat bed cars dropping its roof and sides revealing 88mm guns. They climbed to four thousand feet and made four more strafing passes at about 400 miles per hour. They knocked out the two 88's and shot up the train's engine and about ten cars. One exploded and burned as if it was loaded with fuel.

'B' Flight found a convoy of trucks carrying supplies and

personnel. They went in low, used up most of their ammo, destroying enough up-front trucks to stall the entire convoy. Then called ground control to get another unit in there to clean up the area.

C' Flight Leader, with Alan on his wing received general ground control directions to find some tanks and found a line of Tiger tanks rushing down a road toward Bastogne. With eight 500-pound bombs they took out six tanks, then; Butler called 'D' Flight and four Jugs with eight more 500-pound bombs to came into their quadrant area. They did a job on the destroying or damaging four of the remaining tanks and scattered the supporting personnel.

The Germans placed numerous anti-aircraft guns in a ten-by-ten-mile area. The squadron lost four Jugs and their pilots. Two from 'A' flight, one was definitely a KIA and the other was listed as MIA when last seen baling out. Someone saw his chute open but lost him before he landed. These two pilots made two more strafing runs after they were seen taking cockpit 20mm hits at the target. One 'C' flight pilot was hit and bailed out at low altitude. No one saw his chute. It was a wonder that two 'C' flight P-47s returned. One was smoking on the last few miles, after taking severe a lot of flak that damaged his engine and landed without incident the other landed 'wheels up' at the base. All other returning P-47s had numerous 9mm holes and two had 20mm damage.

On this occasion Manston sat quietly in his cockpit after most pilots had left the flight line. He was close to one of the

KIA, Jack Schlee, another football guy. He was from another Ivy League school, and they opposed each other in a game between their universities. Cliff who was waiting for him noticed he was on a quiet binge again and told Cooper about him who landed later. The mission debriefing was already in process when Alan reached the debriefing. The two 'A' flight pilots, Irv Schlee and John Peterson were recommended for the Silver Star for continuing to strafe and destroying their targets after obviously being seriously injured by shrapnel.

After the debriefing Cooper approached Alan and asked, "How do you feel now about killing Krauts today?" Before he could answer Cooper continued, "Besides the two we saw at the target did you know 'D Flight, ran into a hornet's nest and had a rough time? Their flight leader, Capt. John Hamilton, made it back and landed wheels up here on the base long after we landed. His wingman, Lt. Elmer Campbell, was hit bad and crash-landed near Metz. Lt. Joe Parker, his element leader, took a lot of flak and crash landed at Metz."

"OK. I understand what you're telling me. I didn't think of this a couple of days ago."

"One other thing; did you know that some of our pilots are not very aggressive, but; those we lost today 'went all out' for our guys down there in the snow."

On 23 December they were directed to railroad yards just east of Clervoux. 'A' and B' flights, (Cliff) dive-bombed and a strafed railroad yards loaded with mobile equipment on flat bed cars. They destroyed the engine, armored vehicles, trucks, munitions on flat bed cars and sections of the tracks and yard buildings. It was a good day for them. No one was lost, a few had some flak damage, and everyone safely returned to the base.

Tuesday, 26 December 1944 north of Trier/St. Vith area

-

Capt. Clancy led two flights of four P-47s on 26 December mission with Alan as his wingman. This mission was to have an effect the remainder of Manston's life in Europe. The two flights destroyed six and severely damaged several other "Mk. IV" Tiger tanks. Alan flew Major Cassidy's (Squadron CO), P-47 on the mission and returned with severe flak damage. When he parked the P-47, the crew chief, tech sergeant, Calvin Knudson saw the damage and was bent out of shape asking, "What the hell did you do to Cassidy's and my Jug?"

During the debriefing Cassidy laughed hilariously when Alan told him about Knudson's comment about the damage to his Clancy's airplane. Cliff, who led "B", flight verified Manston's destruction of two tanks when he dropped both bombs on his skip bomb pass, and a 20 mm or maybe 40 mm hit in his right wing that nearly turned him over. Cliff acknowledged his survival must have been due to a super reflex to recover at that attitude of approximately one hundred feet.

Wednesday 27 through Saturday 30, December 1944:
France

-

The Group lost six, (6), aircraft, two, (2), MIA and one, (1), KIA pilots on 8 missions during this period. The group dive-bombed artillery placements, bridges, and railroad-yards, then, strafed troops. Other targets were dive-bombing and strafing, trucks; and some with troops and others carrying supplies. A hit on a munitions truck was quite impressive when it went up in a tremendous explosion. Another pilot, 1st Lt. Henry Harding who recently was made "E" Flight Leader, another good friend of Alan's, was the KIA.

The Malmady area, where some of the US troops were murdered was everyone's prime target for strafing any German troops found in or near the area on the 27th and 28th of January. On the 30th, eight to ten, Me-109's appeared in the area and engaged them in a low altitude 'dog fight' shortly after Cliff's 'B' Flight dive bombed and strafed, artillery placements. 'C' flight leader, Capt. Fred Hauser, shot down a second one after Alan, on his wing, damaged it. Cliff's flight downed two in the same area and the remaining 109's fled. None of the squadron's planes had many hits.

Monday 1st. through Thursday 11 January 1945: France

-

The group lost 2 aircraft, 1 pilot MIA and 1 pilot KIA on the next eight missions. Directed targets were bombing and strafing of bridges, retreating Tiger tanks, trucks, and troops in the area. On the 6th of January, on the way back to the base at 10,000 feet, Cliff sighted what looked like six Me-109s at twelve o'clock and about five thousand below them. He circled his arm to his flight and pointed down and the flight peeled off in twos and thinking they were not seen came up behind them and three each broke in opposite directions. After a couple of luftberry circles the 109s had not shot at anyone and were presumed to be out of ammo. Cliff shot down two, one of which Alan had severely damaged before Cliff finished it off.

After parking it was found that Manston's camera and film were tangled up from a 20mm piece of shrapnel. They couldn't understand that because the 109s didn't fire on them. Cliff gave the most plausible answer. "He took flak at the bridge because the film did not show any of those dive strafing passes." Later on, in the debriefing Cliff said, "Manston got what may look like my second one it was his. He had severally damaged it and all I did was to fire a few rounds to get it on my camera to verify what Alan did.

Manston did know why Cliff said that and when he looked at Cliff he just winked. "What a guy" Alan thought. He found Cliff at dinner and asked, "Why did you do that?"

"Do what?"

"At the debriefing."

"Manston, for 'Christ's sake' you hit the guy good enough. Didn't you notice he was in a slight left banking dive and was smoking. Now just let that be! OK!" The mounting number of losses on ground missions got to Manston as he now joined most other pilots by hitting his bottle of Scotch every so often.

On 8 January his P-47 was severely damaged after dive-bombing a very dense artillery position. Alan's 'Jug' took a 40mm. hit on the top cylinder(s) of the engine and it began smoking severally. Cliff said to him, "Don't push your lick. I'll lead you to Metz and you land, understood!"

"Yes Sir," Alan returned. Cliff made an emergency call and led him in right to the point of landing and buzzed off waving his wings.

Alan's plane stalled just after he was led to a parking ramp. Two crew chiefs were immediately with him, got him out of his plane and drove him to the base Operations Shack. Alan asked them what they were going to do with his P-47 and was told they would check it over and decide whether it was worth fixing. If it were, it would go to a major repair and overhaul depot.

Alan walked into the Operations Shack and encountered Martin Fredericks, now a Captain and Group Operations officer, waiting for him. They exchanged a few stories them Martin immediately made arrangements for Alan to remain overnight and be picked up the next day for a return his base. The following morning Fredricks took him to breakfast then to a waiting jeep to drive him back to his base. On the way he had to wonder how he became a Captain in less than two months on the continent. He dismissed that saying to himself, "He sure looked and acted the part getting me settled and arranging for this ride back. No regrets, he obviously earned it!"

Two days later he was as Cliff's element leader and took a 40mm in his right wheel well on his second dive bomb at some artillery placed along a road and behind of a line of trees before strafing the truck convoy. He knew he was hit and nothing in the cockpit indicated anything serious was wrong nothing. On his second strafing pass Butler saw the damaged wheel well and instructed Manston to get the hell out of there and head for the base with his wingman. He honored the order and left the area.

He tried to put his wheels down over his base and only the right wheel came down. The tower notified him and had his wingman land while Alan burned some more fuel off in wide circles around the field so he would not interrupt any incoming planes. Cliff arrived with the rest of the group, landed, and was told, the P-47 circling the field was Alan burning fuel off. Fifteen minutes later he called to make a one-wheel landing on the left side of the pierced planking runway. The emergency crews were in position as he turned on his final approach bearing left as much as was reasonable. He definitely did not want to land anywhere near the right side of the planking strip (runway). He had his right wing up as he touched down on his left wheel kept the right wing up until the 47 slowed to around sixty mph. The wing came down hit the planking then swung him into the mud on the right side of the strip. This spun the plane around to the right violently, almost taking the right wing off.

Alan was thrown around and both arms and hands were hitting both sides of the cockpit before the Jug stopped. He was dazed from also hitting his head on the left side of the cockpit when the plane began to spin. The emergency crew got to him in a hurry and pulled him out of the P-47 now laying at a forty-degree angle on its right-side Alan was conscious and on the way in he told the ambulance to take him to the ready room, he was OK now.

There, the flight surgeon, Burton, immediately asked. "Manston what the hell are you doing here. You should be on the way to the hospital!"

Alan said, no one told him, so he came to the debriefing. Burton not too happy, looked Alan over sort of thoroughly down to his flight suit, and directed him to report to the hospital as soon as the briefing was over. Later in the hospital Burton thoroughly examined him for any injuries and for the state of his mind. Burton could smell the alcohol on his breath and asked, "Where were you drinking," as he had him stripping down to his GI boxer shorts and asked, "Where did you get the alcohol? And asked do you hurt bad anywhere?"

"I got the whiskey at the debriefing and no I don't hurt except." pointing to, "This little lump on this left side of my head. It is tender when I press it and these damn bruises on my left shoulder and elbow have an annoying slight burning sensation."

Burton had him stand with his arms, hands palm down and fingers extended. He placed his fingertips gently under Alan's and felt his hands slightly trembling. Then put his hands on his shoulders and lightly squeezed. Next, he put slight pressure and squeezed here and there on his limbs and body and asked, "Does anything hurt when I pressed anywhere?" Alan nodded no and he added, "Well, I think you are all right physically. These bumps and bruises are sort of the same things kids' experience and then snickered, and said, "I can't give you a Purple Heart, you're not bleeding. How do you feel otherwise?"

"I'm OK Doc. I feel good right now. And I don't want a Purple Heart for these scratches. How would I feel, if I met a guy with one leg and asked how I got my Purple Heart?"

He finished the examination with a discussion about the amount of scotch he was drinking and told him he really didn't need that stuff for his nerves. "I've noticed you joining a lot of others after missions, a little is OK. Your background tells me you can easily slow down. Manston agreed and said he could easily cut out most of his scotch drinking. Other than his minor bruises found from the landing he was believed to be physically and mentally, shaken up despite his denial. Then after his examination of Alan Burton approached the Cassidy and told him, "Manston is experiencing a little shock and shaken up pretty good. I was able to recognize it though he tried not to let it show, but his slight trembling told me otherwise. He had two very psychological challenges being shot up the past few days. Three days ago, Monday, his engine was badly shot up, was smoking, and severely vibrating all the way to Metz where he had to make an emergency landing. Now today, only two days later, he was severely shot up again had to make a one-wheel landing and had to be helped getting out of his aircraft. I recommend that you should consider giving him some leave time.

A half-hour later Cassidy called Group Headquarters and arranged a leave for Alan. At dinner Cassidy informed him he had a seven-day leave for Paris beginning tomorrow, Friday. And added, "When you're ready to go contact me and a jeep will pick you up, take you to headquarters where you'll receive your leave orders. The same driver will then drive you to the Red Cross Club in Paris where you can get a room."

Joe Hopkins, a 347th pilot sitting at a table behind Alan, heard Cassidy telling him of the leave. A couple of hours later Joe went to his tent, where he was packing his B-4 bag, and gave him a detailed map of Paris having with all the good café locations and places of interest circled in red. He stayed a while to point, out the locations and tell him about the other marked locations. Alan thanked him as he left, then continued packing. At ten o'clock Cooper, Benson and Baker came in the tent, having heard of Alan's leave, and gave him all kinds of advice about the places and girls in Paris until they turned their light off at eleven.

Three

SEVEN-DAY LEAVE

Night Friday 12th: Paris and Saturday 13 January 1945:
Brussels, Belgium

The next morning, Friday, a sergeant arrived at Alan's tent at nine-thirty to picked up Alan and honked his horn. Alan came out of his tent with his B-4 Bag and saw a sergeant was standing next to an armament truck who saluted him as he appeared. Alan returned the salute, the sergeant introduced himself, "Sir my name's Alec Jordan," then took his B-4 Bag and placed it in the back.

When Alan was about to tell him who he was the sergeant interrupted him and said he knew he was. Alan thanked him and climbed into the front seat, and they went to Base Headquarters for his leave orders. On the way Jordan told Alan he was driving him all the way to the Paris Red Cross club where he can get quarters. Alan got out the truck and entered the

HQ building for his orders and returned in a few minutes. Alan smiled as he climbed into the truck and asked, "Does it take about four hours to drive to Paris."

Jordan said, "That's about right Sir," on the way to the base gate. They left headquarters at eleven o'clock and went through the gate after another enlisted man saluted. The road was rough as soon as they got on the road to Paris.

Alan asked, "Is the road as bad or worse than a couple of months ago," and Jordan told him it he thought it was worse? Alan followed with, "Well it seems this truck rides a little better than a jeep."

Alec nodded his head and away they went. Alan dozed on and off all the way to Paris and was wide-awake on when the road became smooth upon entering the city. They arrived at the Red Cross Club at four-thirty. The sergeant grabbed out, picked up the B-4 bag and followed Alan into the club and waited for him to register. Alan looked around the lobby before he walked toward the desk. About halfway there he thought he recognized a captain talking to a lieutenant. He approached the captain and asked, "By any chance, are you Martin Fredericks?"

The captain turned around and said, "Alan Manston! When did you get here?"

"I just got here and am on my way to check in when I saw you."

"We were just about to go to dinner, want to join us?" He jovially said he would be happy to go with them if they waited. "Ok, we'll wait while you check in. Take your time we're not in a hurry and this is a friend from my group, Lieutenant John Hayden...meet Alan Manston."

After checking in he took his B-4 from Alec and relieved him to leaved and do whatever he had to do. Then talked to Fred and John for a few minutes before going to his room. He returned to the lobby and the three left for dinner. They had a pleasant walk for seven blocks to a nice little restaurant. As they arrived Martin said, "This is one of the best restaurants in Paris. It's not a big fancy place, but you can't beat the quality of food here. This is Henri Richard's restaurant. Henri and I became close friends through my uncle who discovered the place."

On entering Henri saw Martin enter and met halfway to the Matre'd. Alan met and was introduced to Henri, a short stout man with a giant charisma. He escorted them to a table and on the way asked how his uncle was? Fred told him he hadn't seen since they were there in early December. Henri, seeing he was now a Captain, told him he has done well since then and excused himself to greet more diner guests. He sent a waiter to their table, and they ordered steaks with one glass of red wine before eating and a second during dinner. John had suggested they ought to try the Follies Bergers after dinner and Fred said that was a good idea.

When they finished eating Alan said, “Martin, you’re sure right that was a good piece of tender meat I had and what kind of wine was that? It really went good with the steak!”

They had agreed and, left the restaurant at six-fifteen for the follies and arrived a little before ten to eight for the nine o’clock performance. It was packed when they arrived, and they weren’t permitted to enter because there wasn’t any seating and standing room available. They hesitated on the sidewalk in front of the Follies when Martin said he knew a good café and suggested they go there because the booze was good at reasonable prices. John and Alan said they were ‘game’ and they walked several blocks from the follies to the café.

Upon entering the café’ and walking toward the bar a bar tender came around from behind it, hurried to them and happily greeted Martin.

Alan asked, “Martin, is there anyone in Paris you don’t know?”

Martin and John laughed as they introduced him to Leon Gallant, the owner of the café. Leon then he said,” Martin, I have not seen you in a month and it is pleasing to have you here.” And pointing said. “Sit at that table,” and then asked Alan, “What would you like to drink? I know what Martin and John want.”

“I’d like a glass of good red wine more on the dry side if you have something like that.”

"Leon, make that three glasses of your good red dry wine," responded Martin.

While walking them to the bar he waved to the bartender while finding a good place at the bar with seating. When he finally reached them, he said to him, "Give these gentlemen three glasses of Cabernet Sauvignon wine," He remained with them until he returned with the wine. He talked to Martin in French until the waiter returned with the wine, then said in English, "I'm very busy. I'll have to leave now. I will come to your table if I find some time?"

Martin asked Alan, "What group are you with and what fighter do you fly?

"I'm with the 378th stationed in the vicinity of Nancy flying P-47s." From there they began talking about their missions and targets. They were only in the beginning of the missions when three sergeants walked in, looked around, spotted the officers with wings, and walked toward them. Martin noticed them looking, walking, and mumbling as they approached him.

He turned toward John and Alan and said, "There's three 101st paratroopers heading in our direction. They look like they have something on their minds."

"Yeah," said John and added, "Somebody on our side probably shot at them."

The Tech Sergeant leading them was Bert Williams with two buddies, Casey Koslowski and Danny Benner. As Bert approached Martin, he directed all his attention on him he asked, "By any chance, do you guys fly P-47's?"

Martin answered, "As a matter of fact we all do!"

"Would you mind if we asked some questions," asked Bert?

"No if you don't get too personal," responded Martin.

"OK, were any of you in any area near Bastogne on 26 December?"

"Why," Martin asked?

"We have been looking for some P-47 pilots who destroyed Tiger Tanks in that area."

Martin said, "I'm pretty sure we didn't, why?

The staff sergeants were asking John and Alan a similar thing at the same time. John said, "Martin and I didn't," then, looked at Alan and continued, "I don't know about this guy, he's from another group?" Then asked Alan, "Did you happen to be in that area on that day?"

He responded, "Our squadron had two flights of four P-47s dive bombing Tiger tanks and strafing troops in that

Bastogne area on the morning of 26 December 1944. Our flight destroyed some tanks in that area. I remember it well because I was a little nervous coming in real low, about fifty feet, and dropped both of my bombs a little too close to the tanks than I should have and got lucky. I hit two of the Tiger tanks on that skip bomb pass and 'took out' both of them. As I pulled off the target area in a sharp, tight, left climbing bank a 20 mm. hit my right wing. The impact of that 20mm almost turned me upside down. I got lucky again and reacted in time to stabilize the bank and got out of there. We then made strafing passes and shot up a lot of other equipment and ground troops. Our two flights, skip bombed, destroyed six tanks, a couple of trucks and scared the crap out of those Krauts."

That led to Casey to ask, "Do you remember where you were when you got those tanks?"

"We were just northeast of Bastogne. I'll never forget that mission! I was flying my CO's P-47 and knew I took a lot of 9 and a 20 mm hit. When I landed and parked the sergeant crew chief saw the 20 mm hole in the right wing and a bunch of shrapnel from an 88's in the fuselage. He jumped up on my left wing and as I opened the canopy. He didn't ask me if I was all right, he was only concerned about the holes in the damn plane. When I got out, he asked me why did I get his plane all shot up, like I did it on purpose and the CO would be mad? I couldn't believe he said that and told him I couldn't dodge all the anti-aircraft and machine gun firing at me." and I added, "I will apologize to your pilot," the squadron CO, "For the damage at the debriefing." After the debriefing I told my CO how his crew chief reacted when he saw his Jug with a lot of holes. He and everybody that heard me laughed so hard I thought someone was going to have a hemorrhage."

Hearing all that the sergeants turned and called to Bert, "We found one of the P-47 guys we've been looking for!"

Bert turned and while approaching Alan said to Martin, "I think I saw him somewhere" and asked if he knew anything about him? Martin told him of his playing football and boxing at an Ivy League university.

Bert said, "That's great" and continued, "But, what about his flying?"

"He landed at our base around the eighth or ninth smoking and shot up that day. I knew him from a previous occasion and had dinner with us. He stayed overnight slept in my room, which had two beds. During dinner he told me about his mission on the day after Christmas. When I asked him about the mission, he told me about skip bombing those MK-IV Tiger Tanks, you've been asking about, and the damage he had. And told me the dumb crew chief was so concerned about the damage to his CO's P-47 and he never me if he was all right."

Bert then took a good long look at Alan and recognizing him from the Royal Queen asked, "Are you Lieutenant Alan Manston who came overseas with us."

"Yeah, I think so, Captain Martin was on that ship too and if you're the sergeant Bert Williams I met in the hold of the Royal Queen?

"Yes Sir, that's me! Did you know, a circle made by a combination of Tiger tanks and Kraut troops had seventeen of us trapped? Then you guys showed up and hit those tanks and made the Jerry troops scrambled all over the place for cover. When you came back and started strafing all the ground troops went into holes or whatever they could find. The only things still firing at you were a couple of machines and a few 20mm guns. You opened up one side of their circle we were trapped by and kept them occupied long enough for us to scramble out and run back to division in Bastogne. You did so much for us at your risk we don't even know how to thank you enough?"

Further conversation ultimately led to the enlisted guys asking Alan about the amount of leave time had and he told them, "I have five days left as of tomorrow. Today is my second day."

Bert began a discussion about good places in France to visit and ultimately asked, "Lieutenant Manston have you ever been in Belgium at all?"

"No not yet. I've never had an opportunity and besides no one really talks about visiting any place there. All everyone I've talked to recommended places in France if you have the time to see them. For example, a pilot from my base, whose been here a while gave me a detailed map of Paris with circles around the good places to eat and go."

Bert asked Alan, "Have you ever been in or considered visiting Belgium. Brussels, is really British territory and we have a few outfits stationed there." It took Bert a while describing some of the good things about Brussels to acquire Alan's interest. He then questioned Martin and John's of their leave time and asked if they would like to go with Alan and them.

Martin responded, "We've been there a few times, but our leave time runs out on Sunday. There 'is' a lot to see in and around Brussels and suggested he go with Bert and his buddies for at least a day or two since you have the time.

Aftcr a lot of coaxing, Alan finally agreed to go and said he'd go for one day, tomorrow. And then we must come back to Paris on Sunday the 14th. Bert agreed and said, "Yeah, that sounds good, but you ought to think about another day to really see the place?"

" Bert, do you have wheels?"

"Yes, we have a six by six with us,"

"OK. Let's go whenever you're ready."

Friday Night 12 January 1945: Paris to Brussels

-

Alan thanked Martin and John for a good evening and asked, "Are you sure it's OK to leave you guys. I've only been with you for a few hours.

"Gees, Alan go!" We don't mind, just go, and enjoy yourself. You may not have another chance!"

Alan shook their hands and said, "God willing, I'll have another time, and will I contact you and maybe we can spend more time together. OK? Bye now."

They left Paris at 1825hrs. Alan sat up front with Casey and Bert while Danny rode in back. On their way Bert asked, "Did you play football and box at that university you went to?"

"Yes, I sort of did that. Why do you ask?"

"Captain Fredericks said you did, and I've wondered if everything he said was true?"

"Would it make a difference in your asking me to come to Brussels, if I wasn't true?"

"No, not at all. It proved to us you were the kind of guy who would go what you did to get us out of that Jerry trap, come hell or high water."

"I don't think I alone can take that compliment. There were four of us in my flight. So, thanks from all of us. I'll give them your 'Thank You' when I return to my base."

They arrived at the Grand Palace in Brussels just after 1310hrs and a short drive through the city led them to the Cafe de Amite Gai. They couldn't park on the narrow street, so, Bert, Casey and Alan entered the cafe and Danny left with the truck to find quarters. Mostly British and Canadian pilots occupied the café. A few Americans pilots were also scattered around the café. The café bartender saw Bert, as we entered, and waved to him from the far end of the bar. Bert led Alan to that end of the bar and said, "This is Alan Manston, one of the pilots I told you about, meet Phillipe Severin, bartender, café and building owner."

"Are you one of the pilots Bert has told me so much about?"

"It seems I fit his puzzle."

"He fits perfectly, he had a thorough interrogation before we were sure he was one of those pilots."

"Bert and his friends think you were a hero!"

"I was one of eight other guys, if they want to pin any medals, they better find the other seven too!"

Shortly Danny returned and said he found the three of them quarters, but no officer's quarters were available at any of the Red Cross Clubs. Bert then approached Phillipe and asked if he knew where my friend might stay overnight and was told there were several hotels in the area, but not many open. Bert felt bad about the entire situation and said he would pay for a hotel room in a Grand Place hotel if they couldn't find him a room. Alan attempted not to be upset and said, "Look Bert, I should have asked about quarters in Brussels when we were talking about coming here. It's not your fault, it's just one of those things."

A Canadian pilot standing at the bar next to Alan overheard their quarter's conversation. Half facing him he said, "Hey Yank, you won't find any quarters anywhere at this hour. This is Friday night! Every club and available hotel rooms were reserved two days ago. I know! I just found one on the other side of town."

"Oh hi! My name's Alan what's yours?"

"I'm Lionel, glad to meet you." During further conversation they found Alan lived in a USA town not far from where the Canadian pilot was born and lived. They were familiar with the same Canadian fishing lakes and towns in Canada and the USA.

Three girls entered the café about 2345hrs and caught everyone's attention, including the Canadian's. Alan turned to look at the girls everyone seemed to be mumbling about and then, thought he had seen one of them someplace. He was told they were volunteers from a British Red Cross club in the Grand Place area.

The Canadian told him, pointing to Mimi, "She had been

a Parisian trained Belgian mistress for the Resistance, the Belgian underground. She was a mistress for A German Army General and a Gestapo Colonel to supposedly secured strategic and sabotage information from them. One really great piece of information she secured was that the areas Germany was expecting our invasion north of Normandy somewhere between the Somme River and Calais. She passed this on to the Resistance who informed our Allied planning group. It seems no one I'm aware of wants to confirm that."

Phillipe, called Mimi to join him and Bert at the far end of the bar. As she passed Alan, half facing the Canadian, she thought she recognized him. Before reaching Phillipe, she hesitated, thinking she wondered if he was one of the pilots she saw in a Parisian restaurant. When she approached Phillipe, she looked back at him and asked Bert, "Do you know who that American pilot is? I think I may have seen him somewhere?"

"Yeah, I know who he is, we brought him here from Paris and just got here at 11:30. We've tried to find him a room in the Red Cross here, but they and all the hotels seem all to be full."

Before she could answer Phillipe said, "*Mimi, you could call your uncle. He should be able to arrange for someone to take the American in overnight.*"

"*It is too late to call anyone tonight. We had officers come into the Red Gross Club after 11:00 o'clock who told us almost all the available hotels are full.*" Then she looked at Bert and asked, "How did you meet him?"

"We, Casey, Danny, and I met him in Paris, he's one of the pilots we've been looking for. Remember, we told you about the pilots who dive bombed some German tanks and strafed troops around us when we were separated from our Division in Bastogne. We're almost positive he was in one of the pilots who destroyed several Tiger tanks and strafed troops that helped us escape from being the circle we were trapped in during the Battle of the Bulge. We know he was the pilot who flew so low, we thought for sure the tanks' 88 mm guns would get him before he destroyed two Tiger tanks. Some 20 mm anti-aircraft batteries hit him as he was climbing and doing evading maneuvers over the tanks. He almost flipped upside down when they hit him. We think he's our hero, cause he was one of the pilots who liberated us."

She put her left hand her on his shoulder and looked him straight into his eyes as she said, "You brought him here to meet me, like you did with that tank Captain friend of yours, did you not?"

"No! I didn't this is different, then looked down towards the floor and answered, "Honestly, we brought him here to see Brussels for a day. I felt we owed him something for being there when we needed someone during the Bulge."

"Now, as usual, you desire I should meet him to settle your debt?"

"Don't you want to meet him?" Before she could answer he turned and asked, "Lieutenant can come here?"

Mimi looked and recognizing him thought, "He is one of the pilots from that Parisian restaurant!"

As he approached them, Bert asked again, "Are you sure you can't find a place for him?"

She hesitated while looking at him, and he turned bright red. She smiled remembering his blushing in Paris and asked Phillipe to introduce them. He said, "Mimi van Bortonne this is Alan Manston," and they stood silently looking as each other for a moment. She looked at Phillipe, hesitated, and asked for four glasses of red wine. She picked up two asked to Alan, "Will you pick up those two glasses and follow me to our table?"

At the table, she introduced him to her friends Jeannette and Claudine and returned to the bar and asked, "Bert, tell me, what is so wonderful about him. Is he not just another pilot?"

Bert said, "I heard he was an excellent college football player and a champion boxer."

"Where did he do all of this and what else is he," questioned Mimi?"

"Have you ever heard of the Ivy League universities in the United States?"

She did not answer, turned, and started for her table. On the way she thought, "He acted so shy in Paris. I should find out if he is really shy or a great actor?"

At the table the girls asked him when he came to Brussels, and he told them he arrived about eleven thirty from Paris with his GI friends. Shortly they started a conversation about girls. He began to blush, and they discovered he was sort of shy at the thought of talking about girls. When Mimi asked, "Do you have a girl friend in the United States?"

His face turned red, and the girls began giggling and he sort of looked down at the table while asking, "Why do you do you ask"?

Mimi answered that with, "Most Americans we have talked to have told us, their wives or girlfriends left them for someone else back home and now they became lonesome."

"Do you really want to know," he questioned?" Convincing him they were serious and, had no intention to tease him, he then answered, "OK I'll tell you one thing. I had a girl friend and lost her when she and her father had an auto accident over two years ago. I met her in April and lost her in November 1942. I felt so bad for more than a year. Fighting tears from entering his eyes he said, "It hurt so much when it happened..........and it still does."

They responded, "You look so sad. Are you not comfortable with us? Would you or do you not care tell us a little about her," asked Jeannette?

"Losing her was tragic and I get depressed just thinking about her. I'd rather not talk about that." His shyness leaked when he asked, "Is that OK with you?"

Mimi recognized this was something very serious with him and interrupted, "Girls it would be better if we did not to probe too much." They dropped that subject and asked where he lived, what he did before becoming a plot etc.? Mimi had a strange feeling about him. Then after she thought about him for a moment of weakness, feeling sorry for him, she unconsciously said, "I'll put you up for the night."

Alan asked if she was serious? She hesitated then, realizing what she just said, took his right arm with her left hand and led him to Bert and Phillipe at the bar. Everyone looked at her when she loudly said, "Phillipe, you and Bert won, I am going to put him up for the night in my apartment."

Everyone was more amazed, especially, Lionel, the Canadian pilot, when Mimi began walking him to the door with her arm curled around his and without looking back walked him out of the café. She led him to the right end of the café, opened a door leading to a stairway. While climbing the stairs he asked, "Why did you attract all that attention when we walked out of the café together?"

"Many of those officers have frequently attempted to date me. I have refused to date any of them to preserve what dignity I have had nothing to do with them because most of their rumors. I only talked to them when I am a waitress in the café.

"Rumors? What kinds of rumors are so bad they steal your dignity?"

"Most of them think I am easy to take to bed as a result of my activities during my occupation responsibilities and think of me as anything but a lady. Well, they are wrong, and you were my message tonight to tell them that there are still some gentlemen in the military ranks."

"How do you figure that will be a result of selecting me?"

"The Canadian we were talking to figured you out and he will tell everyone about you, The Gentleman."

When they arrived at the first door on the right of the hall Michelle said, "We are home."

Friday Night 12 and Saturday 13 January 1945: Michelle's Apartment - Brussels, Belgium

-

She unlocked the door and as they entered the kitchen Mimi took his coat, cap and hung them up with her jacket, scarf, and ski cap on a wall hook between the sink counter and the bathroom door. Then took his hand and led him though a wide arch at the other end of the kitchen around a corner to a couch in the sitting room near the end of arch. She told him to sit down while she gets a couple glasses and a bottle wine for a nightcap.

While sitting on the couch he thought, "This is unreal. It's too good to be true. Here I am in a beautiful girl's apartment and now I wonder what's next?"

Mimi took two steps away from him then, stopped and turned facing him. She wanted to be sure and asked, "Was it really you I saw blushing in a Parisian restaurant last November?"

He confirmed, "Yeah, I guess so. I can't help it if I was blushing. Will embarrassed me in your presence." His face turned red again as he continued, "It looked like I created a problem for you with your uncle and your escort. Did I?"

"You did not. They were upset with me not you. Uncle Hubere wants to save me for his nephew whose father is a close friend of another Minister somehow related to the King of Belgium's family. He feels very strongly about me marrying his Claude. I shall never accept him!"

Then she went into the kitchen and returned with two wine glasses and a half-filled decanter of red wine. She sat down next to and close to him, filled their glasses half full, picked up her glass and had him do the same. As she clicked their glasses the clock, on the wall left of them, chimed two o'clock.

Alan asked, "Is that clock, right? I didn't think it was this late."

"It is quite accurate. I think we should consider finish drinking our wine and go to bed soon." She briefly hesitated and thought for a moment, then, asked, "What do you normally wear to bed."

"He answered, "I usually sleep in my underwear.""Oh, not in my apartment!" She shook her head and went to her bedroom and a few minutes later emerged with two sets of silk pajamas having military insignias on the shirts. He looked at and studied them, then asked, "Where did you get those German military pajamas? They look like they're Army and Gestapo. Is anybody like Bert, Phillipe, or your aunt aware of them?"

"They are, you wear one of them or sleep naked, but, not in your underwear!"

When he said he didn't want to sleep in either one of them, "She answered, "Then you will have to leave and sleep elsewhere!"

He didn't want to argue and asked, "Is it all right if I sleep in one of the bottoms only."

"Fine!" Then, looked away from him and asked, "Would you like to sleep in my bed?"

He thought of the Canadian's words, in the café, about her being a mistress and stupidly answered, "I didn't accept your invitation to your apartment to sleep in your bed."

Mimi caught the insinuation, "My offer was for you and my bed and not with me in it!"

He was shaken up by that firm response. Mimi recognizing it slightly smiled. He tried to apologize and stammered, "I di..di..didn't mean what you think," and meekly continued, "I...I...I didn't understand," as he drifted to and sat on the couch. She angrily secured some sheets, pillows, cases, two covering blankets from her bedroom and made up the couch. Still stammering, with a bright red face, he gratefully thanking her for a place to sleep. She didn't answer him and gave him that look with daggers in her eyes. He apologized again saying he was sorry to question anything she offered him.

Still blushing profusely, he risked a conversation about his friends' comments about her in Paris and said, "My friends in Paris referred to you as a lady with a body for a bed. I strongly objected to their comment. I knew you were more than pretty and polite; you were a lady I told them! And also told them you were too beautiful to care if you ever saw us again. I don't mean to patronize you. I say dumb things and am showing you how dumb I am about girls and life, I always was. I think it best if I dress and leave you now. I'm so sorry about all of this."

Mimi calmly said, "Now do not get so excited! Forget this until tomorrow. Go to bed!"

He crawled between the sheets she made up on the couch and when she roughly tucked him in, he was overwhelmed. He was afraid to say anything and when he looked up at her she was smiling. He lay still and thought, "She isn't mad at me and knows she has me in her grasp. I don't know how to deal with her after all this." Then, he innocently daydreamed, she may like him and fell asleep.

Later Mimi returned saw he was asleep and took his shirt, socks, and underwear from the chair next to the couch. She washed, hung them to dry over the kitchen coal stove on a line across room and walked to the couch, looked at Alan sleeping on his right side. She lightly brushed his bare shoulder with the fingers of her right hand, then lightly touched his hair and thought, "Are you really naive, shy and innocent? I have encountered so many American pilots in the café who have told me unbelievable tales in an effort to bed with me. It is very difficult to imagine this American pilot and especially an athlete like you being anything other than aggressive? I shall attempt to bring, whatever you are, out in the open tomorrow! I do not know why, but something in you stirs up something in me.

I believe he should be rather easily to control compared

to my experiences with Eric, the German General, and Hans, the Gestapo Colonel, I had to deal with during the occupation. Then, just maybe, my subconscious mind tells me there is something in him I have to find. A visit with Aunt Marie and her opinion shall help me resolve what kind of man you really are?"

Four

BELGIUM

Saturday 13 January 1945: Brussels to Leuven, Belgium

Mimi woke up early, washed, dressed hurriedly went downstairs into the cafe to call Aunt Marie in Leuven. Uncle Hubere was home and answered the phone and she talked to him briefly before asking to talk with Aunt Marie. He called to Marie to take the phone and she heard saying, "*It is Michelle, she sounds as if she is up to something,*" then, handed her the phone. She took it in her outstretched hand saying, "*Hello my dear: I am so happy you called. We have not heard from you for three weeks. Remember we discussed the possibly of having a birthday party for you with us. Have you decided what you would like to do? Remember I suggested we have some family friends and those of yours you desire?*"

"I decided we should have a simple family birthday party with a small cake and maybe a friend."

"A friend, do you mean one friend? Are up to something? What friend do you have in mind?"

"Do you remember the American pilots we saw in a Paris restaurant last November?"

Marie then questioned, *"In which of the several restaurants we dined in do you mean?"*

"The restaurant where the matre d' would not seat some American pilots."

"Oh yes." Marie answered, *"I remember by the way you appeared to be attracted one of them."*

"Well, 'that one of them' is here in Brussels and we have become friends."

"When did this begin and how long has this been going on?"

"Since last night. He is the one who was blushing a lot when I looked at him. He seemed to take a liking to me and had me glancing at him. Remember you also became interested in him? He arrived innocently with Bert Williams last night. Remember the sergeant who helped me, in September last year, when several citizens attempted to block me from entering the University of Brussels.

He brought this pilot with him to see Brussels and they arrived so late he had nowhere to sleep. So, I decided..."

Marie interrupted, "*You took him in your apartment overnight! How could you? You took an oath to never be with another man unless he means something to you. Hubere will be furious as you have been avoiding Claude since the liberation and now you have a total stranger in your apartment. Do I have to say more?"*

"Aunt Marie you do not understand. He is a gentleman and before I could say anything.

last night about where he should sleep in the apartment, he insisted he sleep on the couch alone."

"You did not entice him?"

"Aunt Marie, do you not trust or believe in me anymore?"

"I am truly sorry. I did not mean that, it just came out and why I do not know."

"He is with me now. May I bring him with me and stay with you for a few days?"

Startled, Marie hesitated and asked, "*Why do you want to bring him here?"*

"He seems to be a very nice person and I would appreciate your opinion of him."

Marie finally said, *"All right. You may bring him with you, but, for one night only!"*

Phillipe came in as she hung up and asked her, "*What are your plans for today?*"

"I am taking Alan to go to Leuven to visit my aunt with me."

"Mimi, do I have a feeling I know of your intentions? You want him to remain there more than a day with you? If you do, what about Bert," asked Phillipe?

"Do not worry about Bert. I have a feeling he had a motive for bringing him here. Wait, you will see how easily he understands everything, and it shall be fine with him."

"What about your uncle, what will he say if he knew of your intentions?"

"Phillipe, I do not care. Now about my intentions I have none except to befriend an American who happens to conduct himself like a true gentleman." As she was walking out the door she added, "tell Bert I am keeping him for another day and took him to my Aunt Marie's house, in Leuven, for the weekend. Tell him that if you see him before I do."

She went through the café kitchen to go back up the rear stairway and return to her kitchen. As soon as she was back in her apartment, she also got out her ironing board. Then she got a frying pan out placed it on a warm area of the stove and placed her iron to put on a hotter place on the stove. She placed four strips of slab bacon in a pan and began preparing breakfast for Alan and herself. Then simultaneously began ironing Alan's clean shirt.

He woke up at 8:35 AM and heard something frying. 'Bacon,' his nose told him. He stood up, looked around the corner into the kitchen and saw her ironing his shirt.

She saw him peeking around the corner and asked, "How do you like your eggs cooked."

"Are you cooking eggs for me?"

"No, am cooking eggs for us! How do you like your eggs? And no more questions?"

"If you don't mind, I'd like mine over lightly if it's not too much to ask?"

"You shall have your eggs as you requested." She stopped ironing and prepared his two eggs as he wished and scrambled two for herself. When ready she put them on two plates with the bacon and added to two half slices of toast on each plate, then, called to him, "Our breakfast is ready!" She sat directly across the table from him after he sat down on the sitting room side. He couldn't understand why she stood until he was seated. He was dumb struck and couldn't think of how to begin a conversation. After a silent moment said, "Why are you doing all this for me?"

"I want to sit where I could look into your eyes as we did in the Parisian restaurant," she responded, and he began blushing. She smiled as she responded and continued, "That may be one reason and another is, it is much easier for me to clean up the table and get to the sink from here. Now no more questions"

"Oh, I see, do you want me to help with the dishes?"

"Did I not say no more questions or did I not!"

"Well, I saw you were ironing my shirt. wh...."

"Don't you dare ask me why. 'Because' you are here and are my guest. How else do you expect one to treat a guest' in their home? Do you understand?"

He pinched his lips together, as he was sealing them before finishing his first bacon and egg breakfast and said nothing until she finished eating hers, then, he graciously thanked her for everything and began to apologize for being a burden.

Mimi, smiled and shook her head thinking, "I never met anyone so shy as you and one who is apparently very confused by some female giving him a bit of attention."

As she picked up the breakfast dishes and silverware Alan again asked if he could help. She looked at him for a moment then took his left hand and led him to the bathroom, told him to take a bath. The tub was, half full and he found it was at the right temperature.

Meanwhile, she cleaned the dishes and silverware and ironed his shirt while he was bathing. It seemed this was also a good time to go down the rear stairs and talk to Phillipe about him. She found him arranging all the cleaned glasses in the bar area. She startled him when she said, "*Bon Jour mon ami.*" Then brought Alan into her conversation beginning with, "*I think my guest is something special. He was so well-mannered last night I must take him to meet my aunt in Leuven.*"

Phillipe answered, "Yes, I know, you told me." Are you excited about your plans and have you told him about this yet. What if he refuses to go? And what if Bert does not accept your plans with him? Remember he brought Alan and may feel responsible for his whereabouts?"

"I'll take care of that one way or another," and went back up to her apartment a minute or two before Bert walked in. Phillipe told him about Mimi's plans. Bert said he had an idea of what she was up to and said he'd wait till they came returned and have a talk with Alan about his and her plans for the day.

Mimi returned to the bathroom carrying his washed and ironed underwear and shirt. Alan was relaxing in the warm water. She placed his clothes on a chair, then, approached the tub and asked if he needed his back washed?

His face turned red again as he quickly covered his privates with his hands and said to her, "My back is fine and doesn't need washing and if it does, I'll do it."

"Really, now! How do you do that," she said, then, walked out laughing.

As she closed the door behind her, he quickly got out of the tub and dried himself to put on the clothes from the chair. He found his trousers on a kitchen hook and his shined shoes below them. As he was putting on his trousers, she shocked him from behind saying, "I talked to my aunt and she is expecting us, hopefully, before noon." Before he could answer she continued, "You would not mind visiting my aunt, in Leuven, with me today, would you?"

"I don't think...."

She interrupted, "On the way we shall have some good morning air while we exercise by riding our bicycles to Leuven."

She talked incisively about Leuven down the rear stairs before Alan could finally get in a word and curiously asked, "Why would you want me to meet your aunt in, in, wherever it is? And "What about Bert who brought me here? He is supposed to take me back tomorrow. I can't stay anyway! My leave orders do not include Brussels, they are for Paris only!"

"If you are concerned about all that, I could have Bert

return for you in a few days? I would not take you to meet Aunt Marie before receiving Bert's approval."

He stated, "A few days! I can't stay that long! Give me a good reason for going there?"

"My aunt remembered you from Paris and would like to meet and get to know you," she said, as they walked through the kitchen.

As they entered the café, from the kitchen, Bert was sitting at a small table with Phillipe drinking coffee. Seeing them enter, he asked, "Are you ready to see Brussels today?"

Mimi interrupted, "Did not Phillipe mention to you Alan and I intend to visit my aunt in Leuven?"

"Yeah, he did," and asked, "How do you feel about this, Alan? Do you want to stay?"

"I don't know. I'm not even supposed to be here. It's her idea. My orders are for Paris, and I could be charged with AWOL or even desertion if found here or at her aunt's house?"

"Bert, I am sure you know, I can show him much more of Brussels and the area than you can here and in Leuven. Also, you always said you know all the MP's and they were your friends. If that is true, why could you not have them take care of him?"

"Yeah, I know them, but this is a big request, and I can't guarantee anything? Alan, I need your serial number, full name, and rank before I can talk to them and find if they will cover for you if anyone comes looking for you." One other thing, you will have to let Phillipe know where you are each day i.e., in Brussels or Louvain and where you are because if they want you, they will call here looking for me."

Mimi made Bert swear he would take care of arrangements with the MPs in Brussels within the next hour. Bert shook his head and said, "Mimi, you are something! If it were anyone else, I would tell him to go blow it...! OK I'll do it for Alan, and for you! I did bring him to meet you. He's a great guy and he deserves someone like you."

"Thank you, Bert. If you told me that last night, we would not be talking now."

After all that dickering Alan finally agreed to go to her aunt's house 'over the weekend'.

Saturday 13 January: Leuven, Belgium - Mimi and Alan visit Aunt Marie.

-

Bert informed them, "They, the MPs, understand and will try to take care of anything that arises involving Alan and you, for me, if need be. They left shortly after Bert called the MP's office and before noon. Mimi rode her bike and Alan used (the real) Mimi's bicycle, which was still in the Phillipe's café's utility shed.

They took the side road north to the main road to Leuven. Most of the local traffic consisted of bicycles, a few military jeeps, and small trucks. When they reached the city limits both British and American mobile equipment occupied most rural roads. They bicycled for a little more than a half hour when Michelle had them stop at a small intersecting stream.

They walked thirty feet off the right side of the road and parked their bicycles next to a tree that appeared peculiar. The tree grew as a triplet out of a solid two-foot stump. The center branch must have been the largest. It was cut level and covered with a concrete slab to protect it from the weather. That probably saved the rest of tree from rotting. Mimi insinuated the tree was cut this way intentionally to provide a place to sit and admire the terrain to the west and possibly the sunset. This center space, of the tree, was a little shy of seating for two. Mimi sat Alan first, then, squeezed her butt tight up against his.

The pajamas were still on his mind and asked, "Mimi, please don't get angry with me for asking about those German pajamas again. I can't rid my mind of how you got them?"

In a slightly disturbed tone she responded, "It would be best to include Aunt Marie when you receive an answer to that question."

Confused he asked, "How is your aunt Marie involved with the pajamas?"

"She knows the why, the circumstances and was involved more than you can imagine."

Mimi, testing Alan's reaction to her, squeezed as close as she could to him until their butts could be glued together. She turned her head for her face to be very close to his blushing face. The blushing Alan was lost for words, looked at her and scrambled for something to say. Then came up with, "Is...is your name really Mimi? Who, who was the girl that looked like you named Michelle in Paris?"

"That is a complicated question. You would need the knowledge of several incidents to understand. I do not wish to involve you in that now. You shall also hear it all in Leuven."

"Involve me? I don't know anyone here other than you and only since last night. How am I involved?" That question made him blush profusely.

Mimi held back a snicker and smiled instead. She told him his blushing was cute and changed the subject, asking him if he would tell her something about the girlfriend he lost.

He responded in a muffled voice, "Even though it all happened two years and two months ago it's difficult for me to talk about her. How about you telling me about your fiancés?

My boyfriends? Oh, I had some, you may call crushes on

some boys when I was young. I never had a fiancé, but I did have someone more like a friend when I was eighteen. My relationship with him was purely platonic. He was a nice gentleman like you are, but I never could become serious about him. We should discuss this and any of my other experiences at Aunt Marie's. We have plenty of time for you to tell me about yours here."

"Why do you think I have enough time, but you feel you don't? I don't understand."

"Alan, there is so much that relates to the name Mimi, men, and the pajamas. There are too many events to which the name Mimi and the pajamas relate to me to explain now."

"I hate to keep questioning. But I have to ask one more, why is your aunt, involved?"

"I feel you will be more comfortable, relaxed, and understanding when Aunt Marie and I, together, tell you of these things. Would you not be more inclined to believe why I am referred to as Mimi and how I received those pajamas if you heard it from her. Yes...no?"

"You're making me think something is so serious it may be too difficult to understand."

"You are right it shall be difficult to understand. That is why it shall take more than an hour. I will tell you this. Uncle Hubere has pushed his nephew Claude on me since we were children. Claude's father and my uncle are brothers in the Belgian Ministry. Uncle Hubere wants me to ultimately marry Claude to be a part of their social life. I have never felt I could want Claude for a lifetime. He is overbearing at times, and I have to occasionally put him in his place. In addition, I believe I would be happy living with a man I truly loved. That is part of my story. Believe me it is best if you hear the rest with Aunt Marie.

Alan gave in and said, "Look, my relationship with the one I spoke of, and one other was purely of a platonic nature, but, with the last one, we did develop some serious provisions."

She responded, "I believe you could be like that; won't you briefly tell me about them?"

January 1938: Town in western New York State – USA

-

"OK. There were actually two girls with whom I had a platonic relationship. The first one, Katherine Krauss, and I became really close friends. She was a neighbor who lived two doors from my house. She and I were in the same 8th grade class. I never was really very interested in her, even though she was fairly pretty until one day, in early January 1937. I saved her from a couple of kids trying to molest her. I escorted her to and from school the rest of that semester. The following fall we attended the same high school and developed a close relationship after she asked me to walk her to and from high school that semester. I told her I would and did. I really enjoyed her companionship until March of 1938 when she caught Scarlet Fever. I remember it was, a Sunday when she died and left me devastated. Katherine remained in my mind's eye for years. I dated girls for football parties for four full years and I could not get serious with any of them."

He stopped and asked himself, "Why am I telling her all of this personal stuff? She asked him why he suddenly stopped, and he answered, "I asked myself the same thing."

"Are you telling me because you must like me and believe I might like you?"

He thought a moment and asked, "Do you really like me?" When she with her head down a little nodded yes, he concluded, "I came this far, might as well finish it. I graduated in June 1941, applied for an Ivy League University, and was rejected for not having taken a chemistry course. I returned to high school for one semester to pick up my necessary chemistry credits. I completed a year required that fall and was now academically qualified for the university. I was accepted in January 1942 with a partial football scholarship, which covered most of my tuition costs.

Spring football practice began in March. Almost every day, after practice, several players, who had girlfriends, went to the student union for a cup of coffee and to visit with them. I met Mary Lou Bailey there and a platonic relationship became a promise to wait for each other until we graduated. We wrote to each other through that summer of 1942.

Our relationship was really wonderful up to Thanksgiving weekend of that year. I met her mother, unfortunately, under other than happy circumstances. Her father picked her up in the early evening before Thanksgiving Day during a thundering rainstorm. She and her father, later that night, died from a head on collision, during that same rainstorm, on their way home.

I attended their funeral on Saturday in a town just outside of New York City and remained overnight in her home until I had to leave and return to the university on Sunday afternoon. One of Mary Lou's brothers, a Navy officer, took me to the bus station in the afternoon where I noticed an Air Corps Recruiting office there while waiting for my bus. A week later, with parental consent, I enlisted in the Army Air corps. The recruiting station Captain told me I would be activated in late January or most likely in early February of 1943. Therefore, I completed all of the semester courses' examinations in January and decided it best not to return.

January 1943 to November 1944: USA

I was inducted on 26 February 1943 and completed pilot training in May 1944 after being detained for three months. One month was due to an administrative error and the other two months due to bouts with the flu. Thus, I was commissioned and received my wings three months behind the class with which I entered the service.

After graduating I went to a Florida RTU (Replacement

Training Unit) and flew P-40's for three and a half months, that was up to mid-October 1944. They gave him a seven-day leave for home and he was processed for combat in five days at Fort Dix when I returned. Three days later I boarded a ship for Europe from camp Fort Miles Standish, Boston, Mass. It took seven and a half days to cross the Atlantic and dock at Le Harve, France.

We arrived on Saturday, the 11th, and were taken to the Officer and Pilot Replacement depot in Paris. They gave us the next day's afternoon off. The day being a Sunday, breakfast, as you probably know, is the only meal served on American military bases. So, we, the four you saw, had to find a place to eat." He began blushing as he told her.

"That's when you caught me with those precious smiles in Paris and now here, we are on the way to your aunt's house.

They got on the bicycles, started out and shortly Mimi asked, "Were my smiles in Paris really precious?" Her questioning made him blush and her smile as she added, "I believe you really thought my smiles were precious."

They arrived at her aunt Marie's just before four o'clock. Her aunt and butler greeted them at the door. The first thing Alan noticed was the large crystal chandelier in the entrance hall. Then he noticed the woodwork was a medium-colored black walnut that was beautifully sculptured. His observations did not go unnoticed by Aunt Marie who took his coat and cap along with Mimi's hat and jacket. She handed them to the butler and asked if they could use a cup of hot tea. Mimi looked at him and nodded yes for them and Marie informed the butler to have the maid prepare a pot of tea. Michelle then introduced, him as, "Alan Manston, American fighter pilot this is my Aunt Marie Louise Petremont."

Marie suggested they go into the sitting room and sit near the fireplace where she sat in a love seat, Michelle on the floor next to her and Alan in one of the two armchairs that faced them. He appeared to be hypnotized with his eyes surveying the matching black walnut hand sculptured mantel while waiting for tea. Marie suddenly said, "Happy Birthday Michelle."

This startled him, "Yeah Happy Birthday, who is Michelle and how old is she?"

"Thank you both. Alan I am Michelle not Mimi. She was my cousin who you shall learn all about her later. I am 22 years old, today. How old are you," she asked?

"Maybe this is some kind of coincidence, I'll be 22 this next July 13th."

"That makes you exactly six months younger than Michelle and her your elder," said Aunt Marie.

"So, you're Michelle? And now I also have to listen to and answer your demands?"

Marie laughed, "It does appear strange how something has brought you two together?"

"Aunt Marie, you have concluded exactly what has seemed so strange and bothering me about him."

The tea arrived in a porcelain pot in fine porcelain cups with a birthday cake on a platter. They sang Happy Birthday, she blew out the candles, made a wish, cut the cake, and served it with tea. Their conversation led Alan to ask about Germany the occupation and the pajamas.

"How did he discover you had those pajamas," asked Marie?

"He wanted to sleep in his underwear, and I insisted he use pajamas or sleep nude. He became upset when he saw the German pajamas. I told him he would discover why I had them later and later is here."

Marie addressed him with, "Why did you become upset over the pajamas?"

"There is still a war on, and those pajamas represent the enemy."

Aunt Marie asked her if she really wants him to know everything about the pajamas?

She answered, "Yes, I promised he would learn of them here at your house from you and me."

Michelle *whispered, "I seem to have, more than just friendly feelings for him. When we came face to face in Phillipe's café last night and I was sure it was he from Paris. Something made me feel like I wanted to throw my arms around him. It was as if he has a spell over me. Now I want his respect and feel he should know as much about me and the Occupation to believe I am a lady as he thinks I am."*

"Michelle my dear, it is not a spell. You have experienced an infatuation at first sight. Has he shown any affection toward you?"

"Not really! He seems shy and occasionally blushes. On the way here he told me I captured him with my smiles in Paris. He calls them precious smiles."

"Michelle that was your notice he could care for you if you were willing? Why else would he be here and said things like that, if he did not have some feelings for you?"

"I had a difficult life during the occupation and now, I find it difficult to relive and tell him of the intimacies. Would you explain how the pajamas came into my possession?"

Aunt Marie addressed Alan with, "Michelle has a great deal of respect for you and feels it is difficult for her to explain about the names and the pajamas that you are so curious about. Young man, we want you to understand what we are to tell you is very personal. Do not interpret it in any other way than as it is told to you, and you must never tell anyone of what you have heard this evening. Everything is really personal."

Marie told Michelle, "*It is 5 o'clock and we want to be in church by 5:30.*" Then looked at Alan and asked, "Is it asking too much of you to wait until we return from church for me to explain?"

He answered, "Why don't we just forget this. I have no right to be probing into hers and your lives. I don't want to know all this stuff. She's too beautiful for me and herself to talk about her that way."

Again, she whispered to her aunt, "*I want him to respect me. He must know about how the pajamas entered my life and to understand the real reason for my involvement with German officers. I feel I want him to know everything if there is any possibly, I find he is the man I've waited for all my life.*"

A few minutes later, 1711hrs, Michelle and her aunt Marie left for the university chapel. As they walked Michelle asked her aunt if she believed she was infatuated or could it have been love at first sight.

"*Love at first sight does occur and occurs to many couples. Do you feel you want him for a close friend or someone you would like to become serious about?*"

"*I have this feeling that I want to be with him since he arrived. I do not know if it is love I feel,*

I only know he has been constantly on my mind, and I want him to love me."

"So, the more of those glances in the Parisian café were for him and not all for the entire group of pilots there. That was why Hubere and Claude sensed you have been becoming too interested in them. Now I also fully understand why Hubere had you and Claude change chairs. Do you think Uncle Hubere will remember him and being with Alan now may upset him. Hubere knows Claude loves you and he wants you to love him. He has wanted you for Claude since you were children."

"I do not care. When I first saw Alan, something stirred inside me. Now that he is here in my life, I have made up my mind I must know if he could possibly be that one person I have been waiting for. I will not marry, for a position and social status as Uncle Hubere desires. I shall marry for love only and love alone!"

Marie answered, "If you are serious and find you are meant for each other, and a problem looms with Hubere, I shall do my very best to find a way to help you with what you want."

"You would attempt to make uncle Hubere accept him in place of Claude?"

"I did not say that. I think I can make him accept Alan, at least, as a friend first. Then we can go further after we have established that."

"Aunt Marie, do nothing before I spend some time with him to find if I can love him."

Five

UNCLE HUBER'S - INVOLVEMENT

Saturday Night 13 January 1945: Leuven, Belgium

Alan, relaxing near the fireplace heard one door close and another open as Michelle and Marie left for the chapel. A few moments later a voice behind him said, "Hello. Are you enjoying the warmth of the fire?"

Alan stood up, turned around and smiling said, "Hello. Oh yes, I am. I'm a friend of Michelle's. She and her aunt left for church a few minutes ago. I didn't know anyone else was home?"

He smiled, momentarily, then with a seemingly lengthy dissertation, he introduced himself with, "I am Marie's husband,

Michelle's uncle, and guardian Hubere Albere Petremont. And I heard you are Alan Manston an American fighter pilot. I answered the phone when Michelle called this morning and knew you were coming." How did you meet Michelle?" And, before Alan could say anything he asked, "Why did you came to Brussels?"

Alan thought his questioning attitude was a strange way to introduce oneself and answered, "I came to Brussels with some GI friends to visit Brussels. We arrived late last night, from Paris, went to a café and later met Michelle and two girlfriends who came there after their Red Cross Club volunteer work."

He stroked his chin while asking, "Was one of your GI friends Bert Williams? You said friends, who else was with you?"

"Yes, one of them was Williams and two others were Casey and Denney."

He then turned his head toward the fireplace and asked, "How did you, ahem, manipulate to stay in Michelle's apartment over night."

"Alan was now becoming frustrated and responded, "I didn't manipulate anything! There were no quarters available or hotel rooms available any were in Brussels. Bert Williams, you mentioned and café owner Phillipe, with Michelle and her two girl friends solved my problem. I didn't do anything!

I believe she felt sorry for me and gave me a place to stay! And, before you ask, no I didn't sleep with her last night! I slept on her couch!

"Is that the only explanation your have after being in her apartment overnight?"

"I have to ask, why are you interrogating me?"

"I am not interrogating. I am concerned about anyone taking advantage of my Michelle."

"For an uncle, you don't know her very well! She doesn't need any bodyguards, I'm sure you know how she sheds all the men in that café! And I still don't know what else you want to know. Except maybe she remembered me from the restaurant in Paris and felt sorry for me being in that predicament. We talked about that yesterday, Saturday. Don't you remember when all of us were in Paris in November? You were there."

Uncle Hubere now admitted he remembered seeing him there with three other pilots, then looked directly into his eyes and stated, "Being Michelle's guardian, I want to know how you talked her into coming to Leuven with her?"

"You don't know? When you walked in here you told me you answered the phone this morning and knew Michelle asked me this morning! She also mentioned her aunt wanted......"

Interrupting again he changed the subject and asked, “To what unit are you assigned?”

"I cannot say," responded Alan!

Then, Hubere became visibly disturbed. “Young man I can find everything about you through U.S.A.F.E. if I so desire.” Then, suddenly he changed his attitude and subject again calmly asking, “Would you care for some wine? Do you like red or white?"

A confused Alan responded, “Look I have no idea what you want from me and.... I prefer red, but white is also fine with me!”

The butler brought decanters of red and white wine and he gave Alan a glass of red wine. Now Hubere became personal and asked of his pre-war lifestyle.... and again, before he could answer, he added, “Michelle is from a fine class of social people and needs someone of that class. She has a friend I expect, no I am sure they will be engaged after she graduates in 1946. You would not want to interfere with that, would you?” Alan felt he was coming on to either reject him by status or dump him just for existing when he continued with, “I understand you were a student at some Ivy League university. And again, before he could answer, Hubere bluntly asked, “Did they accept you based on your academics or did your father purchase your admittance.”

A very disturbed Alan asked, “Am I on trial? What’s with all these detailed questions?”

Hubere insinuated that his questions were in Michelle's best interests and added, "Did you know she possesses a fine estate?"

With a surprised facial expression, he interrupted him, "No! I came here as her friend."

With that opening Hubere injected, "She has a fine Belgian 'friend' of her own social status. He graduated two years ago in political science and is now with the Belgian Government. It just so happens, he, Claude, is the person who will soon be Michelle's fiancé," he happily gloated.

"You already told me that. I have no idea what you are purging me for? Michelle has indicated to me; she doesn't want a serious relationship with anyone at the present time."

"How dare you lie to me!" said Hubere!" Then demanded, "Retract that vicious lie!" He repeatedly fired questions at Alan beginning with him and his life, then his family's status, etc. When he repeated, she and he were only friends, Hubere demanded, "What are you after?" He tried to diplomatically allude to Alan being from an unacceptable social heritage. It became obvious Hubere's only interest was in 'status' and nothing else when he emphasized, "Michelle should befriend only men who are one of us."

To that he responded, "Whom do you mean? Someone like this friend, Claude, you mentioned?"

Hubere did not give up on attempting to insinuate Alan was from an unacceptable social class by asking, “Do you have any kind of estate for Michelle similar to what she now has? And are you aware of the income needs to satisfy her in the social class she belongs?”

Alan fumed, “I don’t have any idea about any estate and the social surroundings she now lives in. All I now hear and know is that she is your niece. She has some sort of a worthy estate, and you insist she must be with someone of your social status!” That was it! Alan excused himself and asked the butler to bring him his and cap. Smiling over his victory, Hubere pleasantly led him to and opened the door. When he noticed Marie and Michelle at the bottom of the stairs, he quickly closed the door behind Alan and hurried to his library/office.

Saturday Night 13 January 1945: Aunt Marie’s House - Leuven, Belgium

-

Alan tipped his cap as he was about to pass Michelle and her aunt on the porch. And before he was beyond reach, Aunt Marie grabbed his hand and asked, “Where are you going?”

“I gather from the last half hour none in Belgium knows anything about me, my life or my parents who happen to be very fine people and they don’t care too. I’ve concluded I, or rather we, my family, are not really good enough to associate with your kind of people.”

"Why did you say that," asked Michelle?

Aunt Marie surmised Hubere created a problem and assumed, "You have met Hubere, did you not?"

"Yes, I have met 'the' Uncle Hubere and associating with him wasn't very pleasant."

Michelle stood speechless for a moment and asked, "Why... how did this all happen?"

He answered, "Uncle Hubere told me you had a friend who was about to become your fiancé."

Michelle responded emphatically, "If he said it was Claude, his nephew, it is not true. He tells everyone that. Claude will never have me! I do not care for him to be a fiancé now and he never will!"Aunt Marie told her, *"Not to worry uncle Hubere was just being overly protective,"* Marie apologized to Alan if he was demeaned in anyway and asked him to stay.

Flustered, he responded, "No, I...thin...think it would be best if I just leave and disappear."

Michelle grabbed his arm then boldly added, "If he disappears, I will disappear with him."

Then, Michelle pleaded, "Please remain here with us, at least, for this one night?"

Marie also promised, everything would be all right and asked, "Can you stay just for us?"

He nodded and said, "OK, I don't want to shun you. You've both been so kind but, I don't think I can feel comfortable here anymore and I don't know if I can handle much more without exploding."

Aunt Marie told him, "I assure you there will not further problems with Hubere." Then she stopped there as she turned and hurriedly walked to the office and library. There were only a few quiet moments when some low voices were heard. Then shortly a very audible confrontation began between Aunt Marie and Hubere.

Meanwhile, Michelle was helping Alan with his coat and cap and, her hearing Claude's name frequently, she stood frozen in the hall and then heard, "*That decision is not yours, it is Michelle's and hers alone.*"

Hearing this Michelle suggested they returned to the sitting room. They sat next to each other in the love seat she and Marie sat in earlier. The used wine glasses were still on the coffee table. Michelle rang and had the maid take those and bring three clean glasses. When the maid returned, she took the old and set the clean glasses on the coffee table. Michelle half filled two glasses with red wine. She picked up her glass, took a sip and said, "Alan, when Aunt Marie returns, she and I shall attempt to explain why people called me Mimi. And why and how I have of those German pajamas!"

Alan half listening to her was wondering, "How does Aunt Marie have control of Hubere." Then said, "OK I can wait for the name Mimi and pajamas, but how does she have all that power over Hubere?"

"It's all the money. A fabric manufacturing facility owned by my aunt and my mother, provides them the money. When my mother died her half of the facility became mine. Well, Hubere, currently is my guardian, by a state decree, and controls my entire estate. I can tell by your expression; you are wondering how this occurred?"

Alan then injected, "Michelle I don't need to know unless you feel I should?"

She then continued, "I feel you should know that the fabric manufacturing facility has been in my mother's family for three generations. Uncle Hubere's family was well known through his father's activity in Liege politics. He married Aunt Marie when we lived there and became part our family. Aunt Marie helped him gain social recognition in Brussels when he became involved in national politics there. Hubere, being a politician, was introduced to the right influential people who placed him where he is. When my parents were killed, during the war was when he and Aunt Marie became my guardians and my foster parents, that is how he was given control of my entire estate. Now, when I graduate with my Biology degree in January, I shall assume complete control of everything in my estate."

They finished their wine before Marie came out of the office with a vicious, but victorious look and proceeded to lead them into the dining room. Uncle Hubere arrived shortly after they were seated. During dinner she continued to correct Hubere's side comments and attitudes. Hubere did not confront her, he just looked straight ahead as if he was not hearing her.

After Hubere finished his dessert, she told him she would like to talk, privately, in his office. They were in the office no more than a few minutes and returned to the dining room, smiling, to finish her dessert. She was pleased that Michelle and Alan waited for her. Marie invited them back into the sitting room by the warm fire. She saw the red and white wine decanters on the coffee table, then, had the maid remove those that were used and bring clean ones. She began to fill the glasses and stopped when Michelle began to ask something, then, stopped, hesitated, and said nothing. Aunt Marie looking at her asked, "Is something bothering you?" Michelle said nothing while giving her several positive nods. Marie then continued to fill the glasses and calmly questioned her. *"As you asked, did you want me to begin telling him how you received the German pajamas now?"*

Michelle answered, *"Yes I prefer you should begin telling him, I shall listen."*

The German Military Pajamas

-

Marie began by asking him if he felt anything for Michelle and was aware Michelle may be fond of him? He answered, "I don't think fond is the right word, maybe like is more appropriate? Besides she's too beautiful and wonderful to be stuck with someone the likes of me. There are a million great guys out there who have the looks, personality, and wealth she deserves. There's no way I can compete with those credentials."

"Many boys and now many men have unsuccessfully attempted to court Michelle!"

"Didn't Michelle have any boyfriends before the war? Didn't she..........."

Michelle interrupted, "Boyfriends I had, they were just that, friends as I've told you before!"

"How could a beautiful girl like you not be approached and not have found someone?"

"You do not understand women. I am rather conservative. When I meet the man, I would want to marry it must be 'true love' for both of us. That is, a love that is sincere and full of the devotion to each other, I have been waiting for. I know those wonderful 'guys' and their conduct after marriage. I don't know how it is in the US, but here devotion to each other is in the majority of marriages!"

Aunt Marie interrupted, "To my knowledge, all the boys and men she knew and occasionally dated were only friends.

Michelle's parents were good religious people who taught her well the rules of living a good sincere life. She is looking forward to a life she was taught 'out there' as you say." The mention of her parents was depressing to Michelle and a few tears appeared in her eyes. "Michelle my dear, you must live with the memory of your parents. You know they are with God, so, miss them, but relieve yourself of your misery and live the happy life out there for you." Aunt Marie went to her and hugged her, then, told him she may like him to do the same. He carefully did and wondered how he could possibly fit into all of this? "I do not know why, but you are the only comforting person who has really entered her life since her parents passed on," stated Marie.

Michelle added, "You were the first man, in my life that had an attractive effect on me."

"May I get on with what began this, the German pajamas asked Aunt Marie. Michelle said if she desires to, she should continue. Aunt Marie nodded affirmatively and proceeded with, "Michelle's parents were the entire, and only, reason for her having those pajamas. I will be sincere as possible of what I know." She looked at Michelle and asked, "If I err, please interrupt and correct me." Michelle just nodded yes, and Marie proceeded, "Hitler dragged Belgium into the war after a 1939 pledge of neutrality. He invaded Belgium suddenly and deadly, in May of 1940 who only desired peace,"

September 1939 to May 1940: Belgium

"I remember when Germany attacked you. It was in all our newspapers in the States on 'Special Editions' that came out the afternoon of 10 May 1940 and a big spread about Hitler breaking his vow to maintain neutrality with you and Holland. Did you, really believe he would not overrun you? He broke every previous agreement he made with the rest of Europe."

"We should inform him of everything of how our families became involved," added Michelle."

"I don't want to probe into your lives. If you feel I should know something just keep it brief, don't talk about any details that aren't necessary and are none of my business."

Marie then said to Michelle, *"I think you and I should talk about this first and decide how much it is appropriate to tell him now."*

"Why do you want to discuss this first? He heard rumors about me in the café last night. Sooner or later, I am sure he shall ask, if not me someone, if there is anything to the rumors. And if he is serious about me, he will ask why and how I became involved. Is telling him the truth of everything not the wise thing to do now?"

"Yes, I understand, and I agree. I believe there is much of our background he should know about our families, and what our lives have in common, especially through your mother."

Their discussion in Flemish was making Alan uneasy and

he thought, "Their discussion in their language makes me feel as if I am intruding in their lives about things, I have no right to know."

Marie and Michelle noticed his uneasiness. He couldn't conceal it, he was blushing, as they talked. Then Marie said, *"I think we can tell him everything that is involved in your Resistance activities and explain how our family relates to most everything."*

Before she began Alan again asked, "Are you both sure you want to tell me all this?"

Aunt Marie Michelle smiled, looked at Alan "Yes, I we, then began." "Please excuse us for speaking in Dutch. Michelle is concerned you may not understand if certain events are not explained. For example, we decide you should be aware of how our families became involved."

"OK, but you don't have to tell me anything that only your families should know."

"You see Aunt Marie, he just illustrated that he is indeed a gentleman."

"He is unusual. Most people want to know all they can of someone's family's secrets."

"He is annoyed again, he is blushing," commented Aunt Marie. "Alan, you have to excuse us again. Michelle had to praise and call you a gentleman."

"Yeah, I heard you say something about a gentleman, I didn't think it was me?"

"As I said, both of our families are involved and responsible for everything that occurred. You should first know Hubere is a member of the Belgian Government Ministries. Everything initially occurred in 1940. Hubere was in his government office. Michelle and her cousin Mimi, our daughter, were together in Phillipe's apartment when the...."

He interrupted forgive me but, "I know you are Aunt Marie, but I don't understand about this Mimi or Michelle stuff?"

Michelle now interrupted, "Mimi was my cousin, I am Michelle Ode van Bortonne and she, Mimi, was Aunt Marie and Uncle Hubere's daughter. Aunt Marie will explain it all to you."

Aunt Marie hesitated a bit at the mention of her daughter's name, wiped a few tears from her eyes, and said, "Hubere's best friend in the government was Claude's father who is a distant relative to the King's family. Thus, after he graduated from The University of Brussels he was employed in the French/Belgian embassy offices."

Michelle interrupted again and said, "My father, Jacques Karl van Bortonne, a professor at the Roman Catholic University of Leuven (RCLU) and my mother, Annette Helena,

Aunt Marie's identical twin sister, was at home. My older brother, Charles Joost, died in combat on the 17th of May 1940."

Marie interrupted "Michelle, don't you feel it is better I believe it is best I continue from here. Michelle's grandmother, Annette Louise Hartmann, my mother, lived in Liege. Our father, Joseph, born in Germany died in the winter of 1936 from pneumonia. Franz, our brother, became manager of our, 'Liege Fabriquer de Fabric', a fabric producing mill. Shortly after Franz, a loyal German, became a member of the Gestapo and died in Italy during the allied invasion. Then, Michelle's mother and I became the sole owners of the mill." She hesitated, seeing Michelle in tears, and asked, "Are you all, right?" Michelle while wiping her eyes again nodded affirmatively.

Marie turned to and asked Alan, "Have you understood what I've said to this point?"

He was looking at Michelle, then turned to Marie, and answered, "Yes, I have."

She then continued, "Before the war began, Mimi and Michelle were seventeen and enrolled in a Brussels Prep School. They lived above Phillipe's café in a one-bedroom apartment their fathers had investigated, reviewed, and then selected. Phillipe Severin and his family also lived in an apartment, across the hall from them, above the café. Their Pre-Medical entrance program began in September 1939 and scheduled to be completed in May 1940. Advanced in biology and chemistry, among and others, were required, were at the University Pre-Medical program level."

The girls, in their apartment above Phillipe's café, woke up early in the morning by the exploding of German bombs in Brussels on Friday 10 May 1940. Cities in Belgium and Holland i.e., including Antwerp and Amsterdam, among others, were simultaneously bombed. The bombing quieted at 1600hrs and the girls were going to bicycle home to Leuven, but Phillipe discouraged them, from bicycling for fear the bombing may begin again. Fortunately, Michelle's father arrived before sunset and drove them home in his car. When they arrived home a radio announcement said all schools were closed until further notice. The girls received a notice, on Friday, 17th of May, they received completion credit for their courses in the Prep. School."

Aunt Marie let me continue from here because this may be difficult for you. "Mimi and I went to Leuven University on Saturday morning, the 18th. Mimi wanted to get books on psychology and philosophy. She wanted books similar to those used at Brussels University. Mimi had made up her mind that she wanted to enter the vacated library to find these books. She asked me to go with her and we went to my father's office at the university. We were there approximately ten minutes when she asked my father if he would assist her in gaining entry to the closed library. He told her to go home because the library was closed to everyone, and no one was there. Mimi left my father's office fifteen or twenty minutes before I left for home, and had gone to the library, contrary to his suggestion. I only walked a very short distance toward home when a bomb exploded behind me. I turned, saw the bomb explode in the adjacent street beyond the library. Mimi appeared running from the far side of the library toward an adjacent wooded area across the street when another bomb exploded in the middle of the street and near her.

I was approximately 300 meters away from the explosions when I saw Mimi fall and I ran to her. She had shrapnel wounds and needed immediate assistance and then ran back to my father and told him Mimi was injured from bomb. He called the university hospital, and we hurried back to Mimi. An ambulance arrived in a few minutes, which seemed like hours. My father and I went to the hospital in the ambulance with her. My father immediately phoned my mother as soon as we arrived, and she notified Mimi's mother. Aunt Marie and my mother arrived at the hospital five minutes after Mimi died."

Aunt Marie was visibly depressed, Michelle momentarily stopped and asked, "Do you wish me to stop, continue later, or wait until tomorrow?" After a few minutes of silence, Aunt Marie wiped her eyes with a laced handkerchief, apologized to Alan and who told her there was no reason to apologize. He knew and tried to imagine how tragic that had to be for her.

Marie shortly regained her attitude for the task in hand then asked, "Michelle may I continue from here to your return to the University in September?" Michelle said nothing, only nodding yes. She continued again, "I was too upset to call Hubere and had Jacques notify him of Mimi's death. Hubere was in an important Ministers' meeting and was not to be disturbed. I left a message with his secretary to have him call home immediately. Hubere returned our call, hours later and Michelle's father answered the call. I had Jacques tell him how Mimi' died. I could not tell him.

Michelle seeing her tears interrupted, "Aunt Marie was in shock and never come out of it from the moment she knew Mimi died through the two-day wake and then some. Mimi was buried the following Tuesday, 21 May, in Leuven cemetery. The funeral so depressed Uncle Hubere and Aunt Marie, they barely contained themselves at the cemetery.

Six

MICHELLE AND THE RESISTANCE

May 25th, 1940, to January 1943: also, the: King, Ministers, and Brussels

After Aunt Marie settled down and brought herself back together, she asked Michelle if she would mind if she continued again. Michelle asked are you sure you don't want to just relax a few moments?"

"Not really...I am all right now. And I really want to present the events that follow those terrible days after the initial attack on Belgium.

Michelle hesitated a moment and then agreed and she began, "King Leopold and his ministers met on his necessity to leave Belgium. All of his Ministers, especially Hubere, strongly urged him to flee Belgium with them. The King was determined to remain with his Army and stop the German's advance. Most if not all of the ministers strongly disagreed with his decision and fled to England. The King surrendered Belgium 18 days (May 28th '40) after the initial attack. The Germans subsequently interred King Leopold in the castle of Laeken and his ministers who fled to England, formed a government five months later.

The schools, colleges and universities all wondered when they would be permitted to return to their studies. The Germans permitted Belgian Universities', secondary and primary schools to open for fall 1940 semesters after installing and posting all their rules, Michelle began her first semester at the University in September. The Germans promised everything would be normal after the surrender of Belgium. They made numerous promises, and it was not long before they controlled everything, especially our food. They put everyone on food rations. And not much was available." Marie hesitated, then, and asked Alan, "Have you been able to follow and understand this?"

"Yes, I have. One thing I do remember Hitler was publicizing all of the people of Belgium and Holland happily accepting him."

"We did not. Within a year Belgium formed an underground organization."

The Resistance, added Michelle."

01 May through 31 July 1941: Brussels, Belgium

-

Marie smiled at Michelle and continued, "Michelle completed her first Pre-Med year at the University of Brussels in of May 1941. Then the Germans forced Jacques, Michelle's father, to teach German at the University of Brussels. The Nazis' demanded all schools teach German and accept it as the new common language. The Walloons, who were geographically south of Brussels, spoke French. French and mostly Flemish, were the common languages used in and around Brussels. North of Brussels, to the Netherlands the Flemish, similar to Dutch was commonly used.

Under Germany's rule German was supposed to be the preferred language. Michelle's father, Jacques, rented an apartment near the University and commuted to his home in Leuven on weekends. His apartment was a kilometer from his daughter, Michelle, who still lived above the cafe. Phillipe had catered to the Germans and practically rolled out the "Red Carpet" for their officers and served them the best food available. His efforts won him German confidence and the café became their meeting place.

As a Resistance Cell leader, Phillipe met his objective to win the German's confidence. His and Michelle's ability to speak perfect conversational German assisted this effort. Michelle did not know then of what I'm to tell you now!" Michelle looked surprised.

"Jacques mistrusted Phillipe after he noticed his close

association with the Germans and having Michelle being a part time café waitress particularly disturbed him. He discovered Phillipe was a Resistance cell leader in July and not a Rexist as he came to believe in July. He then realized Phillipe had duped the Germans and because he was previously a Resistance member. Shortly after becoming a member, he convinced the Leaders France had successfully formed an underground and sabotage plan against the Germans. In late August he went to Paris and met with the French Resistance to merge their efforts if they were willing. No one knew a Rexist had followed Jacques to Paris and saw him with suspected persons. He followed Jacques to places where suspected French Resistance members gathered. On his return, the Rexist nodded to the Gestapo, waiting at the station, and pointed to him debarking at the Brussels train station.

Two Gestapo men grabbed him as he entered the train station and took him to their office. They held, questioned, and beat him daily for four days. On Thursday, 28 August, they put Jacques in the rear of a truck and drove in the direction of Koln. At a dense wooded area in the Ardennes, they walked him into the woods executed then, buried his body in a shallow grave. The Resistance followed them, observed the murder and burial of Jacques. They retrieved his body, returned to Belgium that night and buried him in the Leuven Cemetery." Aunt Marie noticed Michelle began sobbing as a few tears appeared in her eyes. Alan had been silent, leaning on Marie's every word before she took Michelle into her arms. He handed her his GI handkerchief and she dried Michelle's eyes who then attempted to smile at him.

Alan slightly disturbed said, "Michelle I don't want to hear any more. Do you understand? I don't want to hear anymore. I realize you did what you had to do! I don't....."

Michelle interrupted Alan saying, "Aunt Marie, please continue. So more occurred from here on, to explain everything I was involved in, during the German occupation, as I said before."

"Are you sure? Alan feels he does not want to know anymore."

Alan shrugged his shoulders, in a questioning manner, after she said that and he added, "Look now, I really don't need to know any more. I'll say that again, I understand you did whatever the situation required you did? I understand, I face death every time I go on a mission. That's what I choose to do!"

"Aunt Marie, please don't stop here. There is so much more I feel he should know," as she was looking at Alan," then nodded her head in a yes motion to Aunt Marie.

Marie looked at Michele and proceeded saying, "On, 29 August the Gestapo began taking our men to work camps."

29 August through 13 January 1941: Belgium

Aunt Marie stopped and asked us if we were thirsty.

Michelle said, "I could use some nice fresh cool water now. I like the dry red wine, but it makes me thirsty."

Marie summoned the maid and had her bring a decanter of cool water and three glasses. When she returned Aunt Marie filled the three glasses with water, drank half of her glass of water and refilled it. She looked at Alan, then asked Michelle who would she desired to proceed from here. "You are aware that this presentation for Alan and me are at the point where the tale of my mother's death will occur." Michelle then added, "You are doing fine. It would please me if you would continue from here."

"All right," Marie said, then continued, "They publicized that Jacques van Bortonne decided to go to Koln (Cologne) with men drafted, supposedly, to work there for them. They also publicly praised him for volunteering to assist in the language translations of the industry's immigrants. On Saturday morning, 30 August, the Leuven Resistance received word of Jacques' death. Everyone now feared his wife, Annette, would be the Gestapo's next victim. The Resistance in Leuven received the word and became concerned for her safety. Three men of the Resistance began looking for Annette, to hide, until they knew if she was or was not wanted. On their arrival on her street, they saw Gestapo officers parked in an auto at her curb. The Resistance arrived five minutes later and parked in a friend's driveway down the street. Fifteen minutes later, just before noon, Annette arrived and innocently walked past the Gestapo's auto. She walked to the house, rang the doorbell. No one answered so she used her key to unlock the door and entered.

She called for Beatrix and received no response; thus, she looked around the house for her. Beatrix had seen the Gestapo parked in front of the house and was hiding in the kitchen closet. As Annette went to the foyer closet to place her hat there, someone knocked on the front door. Annette opened the door and two Gestapo men, one an officer and the other an enlisted man stood facing her. After a short conversation they shot her just inside the doorway. As she fell her head lay in the door opening. The Gestapo looked to make sure she was dead, then turned and returned to their auto, entered it, and drove away.

The Resistance men heard the gunfire. As soon as the Gestapo left the area they backed out onto the street and hurried to Annette's home. They found her front door slightly open and crept in. They found Beatrix crying hysterically kneeling in the doorway, next to Annette's body, and told her they were from the Resistance to help.

One of the men put his fingers on Annette's neck to check her for pulse. She had none. They believed she was dead. Another had Beatrix telephone her local doctor who said he would hurry to them. They carefully moved Annette's body away from doorway into the entrance and closed the door. He arrived in five minutes and confirmed she was dead.

Beatrix cried out, 'Michelle, Michelle,' as though she could warn her of the Gestapo. The Resistance knew Michelle was in Brussels and realized they had to quickly do something.

As Aunt Marie finished that sentence Michelle couldn't hold back her tears and began to quietly cry. Aunt Marie and Alan, both, could feel the hurt she had. Marie put her arm around Michelle and hugged her close and asked Alan to do the same with her for at least a few minutes. Shortly Michelle calmed enough to sit down next to her aunt and found a meek smile for Alan. Aunt Marie asked Michelle if she felt well enough for her to continue, or did she want to continue later.

Michelle then moved and sat close to Alan, who had his knees bent up with feet on the floor. She put an arm around his left calf and said, "I am all right and would you please continue for us.

"All right," then went on with, "The Resistance called Phillipe, in Brussels and informed him of the events in Leuven and said they felt she may be the Gestapo's third victim." And asked him if he knew where Michelle was and find her as soon as possible to hide her until they find out what the Gestapo might do with her if anything. The man on the phone asked, if somehow, they could change her identity. Phillipe told them, that it was an excellent suggestion because Michelle and Mimi looked so much alike, they were often mistaken as twins. They, in Leuven then contacted a funeral home in the area to begin arrangements for Annette's burial. When they hung up Phillipe knew Michelle was in the University library and rushed there for her where he found her researching something. He raced her back to the café and took her down into the basement.

On that Saturday, just after lunch, the entire Brussels Resistance knew of both murders and feared for Michelle's life. One of them heard of the plan to change Michelle's identity and knew a Resistance man who worked in the city administrative office. He phoned him and Phillipe to tell them to meet at Phillipe's café as soon as possible. The city employed Resistance man caught up on his work there and left for Phillipe's café.

Michelle was not aware of her parent's murders and when Phillipe attempted to quietly explain of her father's and her mother's death Michelle became so upset, she demanded a pistol to kill all the Gestapo agents in Brussels. Phillipe had to quickly settle and quiet her screams not wanting to arouse any German military personal in the area. Then with 'blood in her eyes' she demanded they permit her to be in the Resistance.

The administrative office man arrived at Phillipe's, was led to basement, and suggested they prepare a sequence of plans to exchange Michelle's identity with that of Mimi. This man asked how this would be possible and before he could question more, Phillipe described their similar physical characteristics as, "They had excellent figures, almost the same height and weight in addition to blue eyes and blonde hair."

Marie stopped and explained, "They truly were very much alike except for the heart shaped birthmark on Michelle's shoulder. Phillipe finished his description with, "Both girls being as beautiful and shapely enough to be models, inherited that from their grandmother Hartmann." Then she continued, "Phillipe informed the Resistance man that Grandmother Hartmann was one of Germany's premier models when she was young. We, Michelle's mother, and I were also said to be beautiful enough to be models, but Grandmother Hartmann discouraged us from pursuing that profession."

She continued the story of Michelle with, "The city administrative man was convinced and agreed exchanging the girls' credentials seemed to be a favorable option and he could exchange their identity in the official city records and knew someone, in a similar position who could change the records in Leuven." The Resistance developed a day and a night plan when it was required to reach public records unnoticed that had to be completely recreated, i.e., records with photographs. All records for both girls through primary and secondary schools were in Leuven. Some of these records, for finishing school and Prep School were in Brussels.

The Brussels Resistance carefully exchanged the records beginning with all certificates, of birth, the public and the church's, containing any distinguishing marks on their bodies. They exchanged all their medical records and went to all the hospitals and doctors' offices' they may have visited. Then proceeded to primary, secondary, and finally the one-year of Prep. School records. Some were assessable, and easily exchanged during the day. Many others required the cautious entrance of public buildings, at night, to exchange all publicly personal records in stored files and the utmost care was required to avoid suspicious Gestapo personnel."

She stopped for a moment and said she needed some water. They all sat quietly looking at one another drinking water waiting for someone to say something while Aunt Marie was resting. "That water tasted very good, hesitated then continued, "Two days later Michelle, still undercover disguised as an elderly widow, attended her mother's funeral. Phillipe also attended the funeral believing he had to be there to control Michelle. Shortly after the burial, Phillipe convinced me Michelle should remain in hiding for several days. I agreed and she stayed in his apartment with his family for the seven days. Whenever Michelle was alone with Phillipe, she told him she had to do something in the Resistance. Phillipe explained she could create more havoc and be more effective when she was 20 years old. After much conversation on that subject, he convinced Michelle to work in the café as a part time waitress where her German, with a true Berlin accent, would distract any suspicions the Germans may have had.

Meanwhile the Resistance busily exchanged her personal records, at night, in Brussels. Michelle conversed with most officers in the café when she delivered drinks to them and ultimately her Berlin German accent served her well when she had to use it. She was such a good actress; the German officer customers began to flood the café. Phillipe had a piano in the cafe, and she had a voice with which she swooned the officers many requests for her to sing Lilly Marlaine.

01 September 1941 to 13 January 1943: Brussels, Belgium

Alan was so quiet Michelle asked, "Is anything wrong? Want Aunt Marie to stop here?"

"Nothing is wrong. I'm just in awe of what happened here in the beginning of the war. It's difficult to understand how all of you withstood the pain and discomfort and especially controlled your anger."

"It really was not uncomfortable after we settled down and put Resistance plans to work," and then looking Aunt Marie she asked, "Do we still have enough time before we should go to bed?"

Aunt Marie looked at Michelle then Alan, nodded yes and continued, "Michelle began her first university year in September of '41 and completed her second year in May of '42. In January of 1943 Michelle became 20 years old and completed her first semester of her third year, then dropped out of Brussels University for the duration of the occupation. Phillipe offered her a position to secure German military information by associating and mingling with ranking German officers."

Seven

MICHELLE AND GERMAN OFFICERS

January 1943 to July 1944

Aunt Marie stopped, said her throat was getting dry and she needed something to drink. She had the maid bring her three glasses and a decanter of fresh water as the other water had been sitting there too long. When the maid arrived, she took the decanter and filled their empty glasses. Aunt Marie drank half of her glass of water and said, "It is amazing how good water can taste at times, is it not?" Michelle and Alan also drank some water as Aunt Marie was asking, "Michelle, do you really want me to continue now?"

She looked at Alan, hesitated, and answered, "Aunt Marie

you know I am not proud of what I had to do and I will relive it if I continued from here."

Aunt Marie agreed, "Yes I can understand your dilemma." Michelle confirmed her statement with a couple of little positive nods, and she went to the heart of the job Michelle had committed herself to perform. "Michelle was shocked when Phillipe told her the objective was to secure military confidential material by availing herself as a permanent mistress for high-ranking officers. They told her she was to be specifically trained by successful Parisian women how to be an effective mistress to accomplish this task. They also told her, as an example, one method found to be successful was to persuade the officer to discuss some sort of information, as applied to him, that required his action, which may possibly reveal strategic military information. Ranking officers like a Colonel or General, one at a time, would provide a protective shield from other aggressive and challenging café officers when alone for a few days."

Michelle initially told them that seemed too immoral for her, but was satisfied they stated, one officer at a time because she was about to tell them she would do almost anything if several officers were to be taken care of simultaneously at a time. Understanding the one-on-one condition, she felt she had to talk to me for my opinions of the action required and what I thought she should do. I initially agreed it was more immoral than I cared to believe and then we had to thoroughly discuss the matter.

Michelle's grave desire to avenge the murders of her parents was the primary reason for the discussion. She was so deeply injured by the events she felt she would really do anything even if the number of officers would be limited to three. Since the requirement was one at a time she was convinced and, I agreed with her decision, when I realized how she was. She had been holding her parent's tragedy in her heart too long to have decided otherwise."

Alan interrupted and said, "I know, you had to do that!"

"I want you to know everything.," answered Michelle.

He responded, "You talked me into this. Now I can't decide what I'd do if I didn't know how everything turned out. But I'm willing to and guess I should hear it all as that seems to be Michele's objective?"

"Do you do agree to listen to everything with an understanding of what I had to do?"

Alan nodded with one little quick yes nod and Michelle asked Aunt Marie, "Please tell him all of this because I need someone I trust, to share all this with."

Aunt Marie smiled and questioned, "How would she be medically protected against diseases? The Germans are not cautious of whom they went to bed with and what would she do if she became diseased or pregnant?" She hesitated, turned, and looked at Alan then Michelle, then, continued, "Phillipe informed us he recruited the best gynecologist in Brussels for her. He would examine her weekly and make sure she would be healthy and not pregnant under his care. Then after much thought we agreed she could be a mistress, but with only one officer in any period of time." She asked Alan again if all this bothered him and he told her no he was still willing to listen.

She filled her glass with water and topped off theirs and drank, almost the entire glass, before proceeding with, "Michelle began two months of her mistress training by Parisian underground girls, a few years older than her, on January 27th, 1943. Most all the girls she met were in their twenties. They taught her how to entice the interest of the higher-ranking German officers by, how to dress, develop a desiring posture, walk like a model, words to use to entice with a charming charisma and social behavior, etc. Of course, you understand she already possessed most of these characteristics. Near completion of her training in Paris she attracted, a blond, blue eyed German General, Eric von Stassen, who was in his mid 40's."

Aunt Marie stopped, sipped wine, then, asked Michelle, "Am I relating this properly?"

Alan interrupted and looking at Michelle said, "How does Aunt Marie know all this?"

"Yes, you are telling it as it was." She looked at Alan who interrupted her, was quiet for a few moments before a smiled and a no, no nod. Then continued with, "We communicated throughout my entire association with the Resistance."

Aunt Marie then took over, "Michelle returned to Brussels during the second week of March. Phillipe greeted her at the train station and her apartment above the café was still available for her, except it was now rent-free. Phillipe also spent time with her and asked her if she was still sure she wanted to accept the mistress responsibility. He gave her a few days to be sure she still wanted to be a Resistance mistress. She returned to me in Leuven, and we again thoroughly evaluated the position. Our family name was well known throughout the area. Ultimately it was Michelle's decision to make it appear she separated from the family. I had to appear disgusted with her and we publicly disassociated with each other. Hubere was not unaware of anything, in England, and if he was, he would have severed his relationship with her.

She hesitated again while drinking the rest of her glass of water and went on with, "The first week of April Michelle began as a full-time waitress in Phillipe's café. Most of the customers initially were Luftwaffe pilots. A few of them were majors and lieutenant colonels. As word spread about the beautiful waitress, working for Phillipe, more officers began to appear. Von Stassen was assigned to the strategic bomber command in the vicinity of Brussels and in the first week of May he appeared in Brussels and went to Phillipe's café to see Michelle. The following week he invited Michelle to be his escort to a Military Ball in Brussels. She accepted the invitation and being in need of a suitable gown Phillipe helped her acquire a very lovely one. The ball was attended by mostly married couples of the rank of Lieutenant Colonel. Michelle, wearing it looked stunning and she received much favorable attention of both men and women at the ball by her beauty. Her German with an excellent Berlin accent seemed to convince everyone and many German women desired to talk to her. There were numerous comments, such as, "Her diction was so precise she was probably one of the privileged few who attended one of Berlin's finest finishing schools."

After her initial public success, she was seen with Von Stassen at numerous social affairs, stage plays and operas during June. During the first week of July after attending an opera one evening, on the way to the café he asked her if she would be his woman. She finally gave in to Erik's desire to spend the night with her and agreed to be his mistress only, on the condition, if she was to be his only women, he also had to agreed she would be his only one. On the first arrival in the apartment, she surprised him by insisting he bathe before getting in bed with her. The first few weeks the General's military responsibilities restricted his visiting to three days, mostly on weekends. She convinced him she needed his continuous presence and insisted he spend many evenings and nights with her to discourage the advances of the many aggressive officers.

Michelle had always conducted herself as a lady in public with the General. She was admired by von Stassen's associated General officers, but now was resented by many of Brussels citizens who knew she attended numerous social activities with this German general. By August she had won his complete confidence, and that of his associates and told them to proudly discuss how the Germans were going to win the war. She got Eric to talk in bed and in discussions, Michelle frequently played the Devil's Advocate. She used this and developed a technique that tricked Eric occasionally to reveal important strategic information and plans. She passed this on to Phillipe who passed it on to the Resistance and ultimately to U.S.A.F.E headquarters. It was accomplished in such a secretive manner no one ever suspected her of anything. Much of the sabotage was in France or Holland and at a distance from Brussels which supported her in discussions by the German officers."

Aunt Marie stopped refilled her water glass and took a good long drink of water. She put the glass down and said, "If anyone wants more wine help yourself." She rested a moment after her long dissertation. Michelle and Alan had their wine earlier and now also preferred water. Marie refilled the wine glasses and Michelle toasted Aunt Marie for helping tell her story of the occupation. Aunt Marie smiled and said, "There is more. Remember the Gestapo officer?"

"Oh, yes! He was such an aggressive, self-praising egotist and terrible in bed. He had such a filthy mind I had to kick him out on several occasions. I do not believe I shall ever forget that evil man." She had to stop and had a second glass of water before continuing. *"I hate that man so much I do not care to talk of any time I had to spend with him."*

"All right, I shall speak of his time in your life as little as possible."

Aunt Marie sipped more water and said, "Gestapo Colonel, Hans Eichenberg, appeared in Brussels. He came to the café and saw Michelle sitting very close to the General. This was not the normal behavior of Belgian women toward the Germans, and he became suspicious.

He had Michelle investigated and they found she was from a line of German heritage through me and her mother. Further investigation revealed my brother, an uncle, was a Gestapo captain in Italy with an outstanding record. Her uncle's status as a Gestapo officer was more than sufficient to convince him and the Gestapo, she was an acceptable German allied Belgian female. Remember, she was not known as my one and only daughter Mimi and her cousin Michelle was the one killed in Leuven by a bomb.

The Colonel now became interested in Michelle for himself. General von Stassen was transferred to Paris in early December of 1943 with a little assistance from Eichenberg. Michelle now became aware of his intentions lured him to become her new mate. She won him over. He was all hers, but it was more difficult to secure valuable information from him. She did secure the information that the northern French coastal area was the last place the Germans suspected of an invasion. That was passed on to the allies in March or April of 1944."

She frequently called me and asked how to treat the filthy man. When she knew what to do Michelle was quite an actress. She had a talent with men. None were a match for her. The Belgian people became ruthlessly disgusted with her for frequent public appearances and now with a Gestapo Colonel. Eventually she was accused of being a Rexist and found it extremely difficult to shed after the liberation of Brussels. Her association with German officers; especially a Gestapo colonel was very convincing."

Tuesday 6 June 1944: D-Day:
The Invasion of the Continent - France

Aunt Marie took a break in the presentation and asked what plans they had for tomorrow. Michelle responded, "I don't know at the present time, but think we should visit the university first because it is not far from here. Then ride our bicycles or walk around Leven where he can meet some people who believed I was a Resistance member, and I did what any truly loyal Belgian would do for Belgium.

"The Allies successfully landed where the Germans least expected an invasion in Europe. Tuesday, 6 June 1944. Colonel Eichenberg heard of the successful invasion and early in July 1944 fled Brussels for Aachen, Germany. That was the end of him. Michelle called me and never sounded happier than that moment. The Americans advanced toward Paris and the British toward Belgium. During the first week of September the Americans advanced, rapidly, through Belgium from

France and the British from Holland and liberated Brussels on September fourth and all of Belgium a few days later."

She stopped again and sipped some more water. She looked at Michelle and grimaced before saying, "Michelle, I feel it would be best if you continue from here."

She sadly answered, "No I should not Aunt Marie. You can, explain better than I can, how difficult it was to convince people that I was no longer 'that girl from the occupation' which haunted me for so many months and to some degree still remains."

Eight

POST WAR BELGIUM

Sunday 23 July 1944 to Saturday 13 January 1945

Leuven, Belgium

Aunt Marie noticed Michelle's and her own water and wine glasses were empty. Without asking she refilled both of their glasses with the red wine. Michelle responded, "Thank you Aunt Marie. How did you know I was becoming thirsty?" Then, added, "Well we, you more than I, have talked our way through the war and now the post war public life loomed its ugly head."

"Let me think a moment," Aunt Marie commented. "Oh yes! Michelle had a few relationships with men, Belgians, Allied Military, and others, on a purely platonic basis after July 1944. Numerous Belgian men and women snubbed her and avoided any of a relationship with her. So many were convinced Michelle was a Rexist and not a Resistance member, but I recall many conversations with people who knew her parents were victims of the Nazi Gestapo and refused to accept the logic that she associated with the Nazis purely revengeful purposes.

She then looked, with a very serious expression, at Michelle and added, "I would appreciate if you would interrupt me anytime you may have any clarifying comments.

"I am carefully listening to your every word. Not because you may say something derogatory, but for omissions or mistakes."

"I see. I will try to be as thorough and accurate as I can. But interrupt anytime you want." And she continued, "Michelle's reputation was severely tarnished by her relationships with German officers during the Occupation such that Belgian men and women publicly, other than the Resistance, dishonored her after the liberation. Initially men who were completely aware the Resistance had changed her identity still despised her. They accused her of being a prostitute and made horrible sexual advances toward her. This bothered Michelle and me so much I had Phillipe, a known Resistance Cell Leader, prepare a public statement for the newspapers and radio stations acknowledging her loyalty and German relationships as a contribution to the defeat of the Nazis and also Belgium's liberation through her personal physical sacrifices.

Then, Phillipe approached Hubere who returned to Belgium immediately after our liberation, to clear her name. He initially despised Michelle refusing to believe any of her or my explanations of her included the contribution for the success of the allied invasion. She drew out of the Colonel she was seeing, a month before the invasion, that the Germans were arming in an area north of the Normandy beaches more toward the Calais area. This was passed on to the underground who in turn sent the information to the British. Then to still create hazards for her Brussels University shocked Michelle in September by denying her application to resume studies for the second semester of her third year. I had to meet with the Deans of the Science and Medical schools, to draw out of them if anything they may have heard about her was their reason for the denials.

By some miracle, the last week of September King Leopold became aware of Michelle's physical sacrifice during the occupation and had a Social Ball in her name. He bestowed on her 'The Belgium Cross' for her heroic personal sacrifice. The next day, both Deans phoned me separately after hearing and reading of this, to apologize, for not initially recognizing I had initially and clearly pointed out to them she made a personal sacrifice for Belgium. I had to laugh to myself as each verbally stumbled as they were informing me that Michelle was now permitted to enroll in their school. Public acceptance by the Belgian Government remained moderate as most knew of her relationship to a Government Minister and believed he was involved in arrangements to have the King bestow honor honors on her."

She stopped and for a moment was silent, then said, "My mouth is very dry, I need some more water. While drinking her water she addresses Michelle, "How am I doing? Have I been sufficiently accurate as to the events?"

"You are telling it as it happened with more accuracy than I expected; do continue."

"Thank you, Michelle, and went on from where she stopped, "The next day the Brussels USO Club asked if she was willing to return as a part time volunteer. Believing she had to do something, such as, serving the people, she accepted their request and there she attracted and was approached by numerous British and Canadian military personnel for dates. USO rules forbid making dates on their premises that gave her reasons to refuse any and all requests. Phillipe's café now the place favored by British, Canadian, and American officers. She would be there this evening if you were not here."

Michelle interrupted, "Last Friday, I was at the USO working with my previous girlfriends, Jennette, and Claudine. We stopped in Phillipe's café, that night as usual, and he motioned to me, as we entered, to come to his end of the bar. Remember Bert, the American paratrooper?" Marie nodded yes and Michelle continued, "He was at the bar with Phillipe and had an overnight room problem and that is why he is here."

"I love what happened next. Please asked Aunt Marie, "Let me continue from when you returned to the university and living at the apartment above the café. Dating rules did not apply at the café and she was always flooded with dating requests. I remember, that fall she initially accepted dates and mentioned to me none of the men she dated or knew meant anything to her. Also, after she began working in the USO, several of the initial dates made at other places and times were very trying. All her dates were all hands all over her and wanted only her body. I am sure you know quite attractive, without adding her beautiful face, eyes, and hair, which was always well kept. By the end of November, she refused all date requests due to most men's immoral minds. She never knew who was trustworthy of being a gentleman. It appears she now may have found one."

Being so naive he was going to ask who she found when Michelle interrupted, "Alan you have no idea how trying my life was after the liberation. Uncle Hubere rescued me from escaping the clutches of my pursuers. He came to the café and provided a barrier against predators, without my consent, by and announcing I was his Claude's fiancée. Then he arranged for this Claude, to pose as my fiancé, to meet me in the café for dates. His objective was to include him as one of our family by having me eventually fall in love and marry him. I fooled both of them by always making him bring me here to Aunt Marie's for evening visits."

Aunt Marie told Michelle. "I believe Hubere did this fiancé thing between you and Claude for two reasons. One, yes, he wanted you and Claude to come together, but; he also wanted to do the most he could to protect you from the ravage by sex seeking men.

"I have a difficult time accepting that theory. If you remember, he always arranged for Claude to escort me to all kind of events for my entire life when I had other offers. Claude is a nice person, and a friend, but I do not feel I could ever love him as a fiancé. Then, looking at Alan she added, "I believe he, whom I seek, is still out there somewhere."

He, innocently, thought it best not to ask whom? Then, he shrugged his shoulders in an, 'I don't know' manner that made Michelle and Marie laugh.

Marie said after the laughing ceased, "Alan, you are such an innocent person, hold up your wine glass so I can give it one last fill." She poured a medium amount for him, Michelle, and herself, then, she and Michelle held up her glass saying, "Here's to a long and happy life for the three of us and 'anyone else' who may become a part of our lives."

Michelle then said, "Last Wednesday, I completed the second semester of my third year. This following week of 12 January 1945 an American pilot, you, entered my life. Uncle Hubere seeing I have given you so much attention may think his plans for Claude to become part of my life may not develop. I am not sure if he had intentions of maintaining control of my estate through me or, knowing Claude liked me very much and wanted us to get together."

Marie defending Hubere explained, "He believes his responsibility is to assure your security. Alan please understand, he believes you will not be able to provide for the life Michelle now lives and maintains she should continue living in the social class in which she was raised."

This statement bothered Michelle and being outspoken, interrupted, *"Aunt Marie; uncle Hubere has overlooked the strong possibility Alan may vary likely become an Engineer after the war. Engineers have always been accepted as well educated and respectable people. Most have reasonable incomes and enroll their children in the same expensive schools Mimi, and I attended."*

"Maybe? Uncle Hubere will understand your reason for associating with him."

Aunt Marie addressed Alan, "We apologize for using Flemish in your presence. Michelle became upset for anyone to believe she must live in a given financial and social class."

"Don't worry about it. My conversation with Uncle Hubere tells me pretty much about your social and financial class of people. I don't know what kind of a problem you are concerned. As I have no idea how to project what social and income Engineers appropriately fit financially and socially back home?"You must not worry about it because Michelle and I both respect you very much. It also is her problem to determine at what she desires socially and economically in a man. Don't you agree Michelle?"

She answered, "Alan, I think you are a wonderful person. I believe it would not matter what your income was if you were the person with whom I want to spend the rest of my life. I know you would always be a gentleman and an adequate provider. Everyone keeps forgetting I want to be a medical doctor and I shall be capable of determining at what financial and or social level will be acceptable for me.

"I never have considered that, nor do I believe that Hubere has? Forget that for tonight, it is getting late, eleven thirty, and time to go to bed. Are you two ready," asked Marie?"

Michelle answered, "Yes; and I do have so much more of Leuven to introduce him too tomorrow."

Alan wrinkled his brow as he thought, "I was supposed to go back to Brussels?"

Later, in the upstairs hall Michelle said, "I could tell you were wondering about tomorrow? Did you not remember Bert said he if you are not in Phillipe's at noon tomorrow, he would return Monday to pick you up at noon?"

"How did you know I was thinking about when I will be returning to Brussels and Paris?"

"Tomorrow being Sunday gives you one more day more to be with us."

Michelle moved close to him. She put her hands on each side of his face and kissed his right cheek, then, simply said, 'Goodnight', before each entered their own bedroom.

Sunday 14 January 1945: Sunday Aunt Marie's
Leuven, Belgium

Uncle Hubert rose early and left for Brussels before anyone other than Aunt Marie was awake. Michelle met her aunt in the hall at 7:30 and went to the kitchen for breakfast. While eating, the subject of Michelle's attitude toward Alan became a topic of discussion. *Aunt Marie asked her if she developed any serious intentions toward for him.*

"Why do you ask," responded Michelle?"

"You were talking about Claude last evening; I began thinking it was for Alan's benefit?"

Michelle mentioned the Paris restaurant and how he impressed her by his humble gestures. Then said; *"It think Uncle Hubere asked Claude and I to change chairs to make it appear he was my fiancé for the pilots' benefit. Now that I have been with him, on a friendly basis, and have talked much about each other, I think he is beginning to attract me. I have been thinking of kissing him to find how he would react toward me?"*

Aunt Marie questioned, *"Are you sure it is not infatuation that is overcoming you?"*

"Definitely not. I've been infatuated before and know what that feeling is."

"Then you do think you may have just fallen in love with him, but, not sure how he really feels?"

"I know I have not fallen in love. Do you think Uncle Hubere would be upset if I began spending time with him?"

"Not me, if you really desire to know if you love him. I am not sure how Uncle Hubere will react?"

"I really do not care how he would react. He has to know I must make my own decisions. It is I who has to know something before he leaves. He appears to be such a fine person and does attract me now. And...if I find I have fallen in love, after he leaves, I may never see him again responded Michelle?"

"Michelle it is after eight. Why don't you go upstairs and wake him. I said only wake him and nothing more. Do not try to determine if you have fallen in there!" Then she heartily laughed."

Yes, dear Aunt: I shall be a good girl." She went upstairs to his door and knocked. Receiving no answer, she entered his bedroom and saw him sleeping on his side facing her. He awoke up as she sat on his bed near his chest. When she bent over close to his face, he thought she was going to kiss him, but instead she softly said, "It is time for your bath and breakfast."

He sat up, she stood up and acted as though she was waiting for him to get out of bed. He didn't and she asked, "Aren't you going to get up and show me your wonderful body?"

"I am nude and who told you I had a beautiful body anyway?"

"Oh, I just thought you might have one," she said, laughing, as she walked out of the room.

He got out of bed and surveyed the room, then the bathroom before bathing. The rooms were the sizes of good hotel rooms with the equivalent conveniences. While bathing, he began to believe Uncle Hubere's questioning his status was right. He unknowingly buried that inferior opinion into his mind. On his way downstairs he began to believe, having Michelle as his fiancé would not be good or proper for her. As he entered the kitchen and sat down, he was very quiet.

Michelle could feel something was bothering him and smiled for a reaction, which she did not receive. Then a thought entered her mind, "He has some sort of a problem on his mind and wondered if he should not have come here or is it the social class thing, they discussed last night?" She dismissed those thoughts momentarily, turned to Aunt Marie and told of her plans for the day with Alan.

During breakfast Michelle mentioned they would initially go to the RCUL chapel and left shortly after breakfast on bicycles, riding north on the street headed for the chapel.

They arrived in time to attend the ten o'clock mass. They left immediately after mass and visited her former RCUL father's office, then, to the library and on to schools in various places of the city. During their encounters with Michelle's friends his depression did not go unnoticed. They returned to Aunt Marie's at noon. Alan was quiet all morning and also during lunch. His gloom lead Aunt Marie to ask, "Is something wrong, you are so quiet?"

He couldn't hold it back and responded, "I feel coming to Leuven was a mistake. I just don't fit in with anything you people have or do."

Marie senses Hubere's involvement surfaced again and asked, "Why do you say that?"

"Hubere was right, your house, your rooms, your servants. He told me he believed I'd never provide the environment nor the social life to keep Michelle happy."

Michelle burst out, "How could you," as she turned, looked at Aunt Marie and ran out of the kitchen and upstairs to her bedroom. Then Marie asked Alan if he was aware saying things like that could upset Michelle.

"Aunt Marie, "I'm sorry. Uncle Hubere pointed out how unfit I am for Michelle. It took all of last night and this morning thinking about it and just looking around before it all to sank into this slow brain of mine. You see, my parents are hardworking people, and, for all my twenty-one years, I only lived an everyday common life, no fancy balls, and no social affairs. Their friends were people like themselves. They had dances mostly related to their European heritage and played a lot of 'Pedro' and 'Pinnacle' when having house gatherings. Today, everyone we met, touring the university and Leuven, has so much respect for Michelle. They frequently asked, "Did you see him or her, have you been to this or that club yet and so on. Even though she introduced me as your guest to everyone, they all asked where Claude was. It made me feel so small."

"Alan, are you so fragile that people's words belittle you? Michelle has been brought to my attention, you were an outstanding athlete at a highly respected university and were highly honored by Sergeant Williams for something you did in combat. Is this all true?"

He was speechless, and shrugged his shoulders as though he wasn't sure of what she said. Marie continued, "You must not let anyone mess with your life, just mind your own life as you want it. That is all that should matter to you." Then, out of a clear blue sky she asked, "Do you have any emotional feelings for Michelle?"

"Naturally I do. How could anyone not. She is so beautiful, friendly, and sociable."

Marie had a good talk with Alan for a half hour about their lives, the kind of things they have in common and themselves before Michelle returned to the kitchen wiping tears from her eyes. Marie like a typical mother told her not to worry about anything uncle Hubere said or may do anymore. "Now do something for each other!" Alan looked at Michelle, they smiled as he chanced putting his arms out. As he did, she put her arms out and around his neck, then folded herself into his arms.

As they separated Alan thought of kissing her but lacked the confidence to do anything more than hold her. Neither said anything and Marie trying to be a matchmaker questioned, "Do the two of you have more than friendly feeling towards each other?"

They simultaneously, nodded, yes, they do. "Then for heaven's sake kiss," she added. Their embrace and kiss had love written all other them. Aunt Marie commented, "Now you two are acting normal. Please do not make me remind you again. Oh...you children! I shall never get used to the way you two act."

Monday Afternoon 15 January 1945:
Leuven Belgium - Bicycling Visits

Michelle initially led him to visit the Paul van Hooft family. On their way Michelle told him, "They were my parents' closest friends. Paul was and still is a RCUL Professor of philosophy. He teaches in four languages: Dutch, French, German and English. To keep homed in the languages the van Hooft's would visit my parents. Paul and my father would converse in all four languages, while my mother and Mrs. van

Hooft enjoyed each other's presence. Mrs. van Hooft had one child that she lost in childbirth and could not have any more. They are my God Parents. As a result, they bestowed on me the love they would have had for their own."

On their arrival at the van Hooft's Michelle and Alan parked their bicycles in a rack close to the house. He waited at the foot of the porch stairs while Michelle rang the doorbell. She rang several times with no answer and concluded they were not home. As Michelle began to descend the stairs she tripped, and he caught her in his arms. When they separated Michelle said, "Don't you like me enough to kiss again?"

He smiled, to hide the thought he really wanted to, as he held her in his arms. She put her arms around him and passionately kissed. Michelle separated, stepped back, looked directly into his eyes, and said, "You don't kiss like someone who appears to be so shy and innocent."

His face turned beet red as he responded, "I don't know how you mean that. No, no one ever said I was or wasn't. Would it bother you if I said I wasn't innocent?"

"Not at all. It would only prove your blushing is a deceiving act of innocence." As she said that, Alan turned stone white and being speechless nodded repeatedly no and stared at the ground. He felt so embarrassed he thought of leaving and going back to Brussels. Michelle realizing something was wrong and asked, "Did I say something that hurt you? When he didn't answer Michelle straddled her bicycle and said,

"Please let's go now." As she started down the driveway, he followed her. Michelle took him to her current home and family's residence to test him. Her maid Beatrix greeted her excitedly and asked who her gentleman was? She introduced him and asked Beatrix, a live in widowed housekeeper, to make them tea, then, she took his hand and lead him into the living room.

She sat him next to her in a love seat and smiling said, "If I said I could love you would you show me you could love me?"

"What do you mean?"

"Would you have me if I sent Beatrix on an errand?"

"Michelle, that's asking for a commitment. I have to return to combat, and I'd never make one I can't honor."

"What do you mean by commitments?"

"Commit myself to marry you! I don't believe in having an affair without a mutual desire for a lifelong commitment. A lot of pilots die every day of every week. Next week it could be me. I'll never commit myself and end up possibly having a child without a father. Would you want a child without a father?"

"You can't make me pregnant unless I wanted to. There is a doctor in Brussels...."

"Please Michelle lets drop this interest in a love affair. I'm not ready to risk anything like having a child, regardless of what doctors can do. There'll be no abortions in my family. Can't we discuss anything relating to this in your Brussels apartment?"

"All right, we shall return to Aunt Marie's house for supper, stated Michelle. When they arrived, it was near dinnertime. Before entering the dining room Michelle brought up the subject of love with Aunt Marie and told her, "*I entertained a love affair at my house to find how he would react?*"

"*Should I believe what I just heard? Did you really seek an affair with him?*"

"*I was only teasing him. He seems to blush so innocently but kisses very passionately. I cannot understand. He responded 'the war' keeps him from any affairs because he fears making me pregnant. I do not think he has ever had an affair.*"

"*I thought after your Parisian training you knew how to determine innocence.?*"

"*There was no mention of how to determine a man's innocence. We were only involved in an affair if the client was one exposed to valuable information. Remember, my affairs with the general and the colonel were professional, and love never entered my mind.*"

"*Do you think you could love Alan?*"

"I was told, in Paris, if at the end of an affair you feel euphoric and so devoted you do not want to separate it is very possible you love your mate. I could never experience that feeling with the Germans."

"Michelle; it seems you are as innocent as he may be about true love. Do not play with this. If you feel serious about him initiate a conversation about couples bedding together. If from what he says about commitments is true, you shall discover if he loves you and is innocent. If he is, I am sure, from your experience, you will know."

"Why are you discussing whatever it is in Dutch. "I know you're talking about me. I know a little German and understood enough of your words to make me the subject of the conversation. If I'm a problem, I'll leave."

"Alan, you do not know or understand Michelle. To be honest, our discussion was about you. We discussed how would she know if you are the man, she has waited for to enter her life. Neither of us wants to lead you into doing anything you do not want to do. We wonder if you are innocent of what an affair can reveal other than self-satisfaction. What Michelle wants is between you and her" ... and before she could say more the maid came to them to tell them dinner was ready. Marie then added, "We should eat before the food becomes cold."

During dinner Michelle and Alan discussed their post war desires. Michelle desired to go a medical school and he indicated he would like to change to an aeronautics program.

After dinner they returned to the sitting room and Marie intentionally had him sit next to her. Aunt Marie was testing Michelle's reaction. Michelle showed no reaction, she just sprawled out sitting in the armchair opposite them. Alan began the conversation asking Michelle when would she begin her next semester and, "When will you finish the undergraduate requirement for Medical school?"

"I am to begin my fourth and last year of a Biology degree with a minor in Pre-Med. next week. I remain unsure of where I would want to apply for a medical doctor's program other than Brussels University if and when this war ever ends."

Marie mentioned, "Brussels University is among the most reputable schools in Europe." Then after hesitating...added there are also several other good medical schools in England and France."

Alan interrupted several German universities were also mentioned, "Except, who knows when we all will return to an accepted relationship with Germany. I'm sure you are aware Germany has universities that have always excelled in all science programs".

After discussing several schools in France, England and Germany, Michelle asked, "Are there many universities in the United States that offer, both, Engineering and Medical schools?"

"Michelle, "Every state has a good university that offers

both Engineering and Medicine. A few are New York, Texas, California, Massachusetts, Ohio, and Michigan that have some of the finest in the country. In reality, every state offers a good medical program somewhere."

"Do you think I would be eligible for any of those good universities?"

"Michelle, with the grades you had in secondary schools and Biology, I don't believe you would have any difficulty being accepted in any university in the world," responded Marie.

"Aunt Marie would you understand, if I find I could love him enough to be his fiancée and attended the same university he chooses if both of our programs are available?"

"Do you believe you could love him enough to consider following him to his country?"

"I am not sure. Maybe, if we continue to see each other before this war ends, I will be?"

"My dear, do not make any brisk decisions. He has to return to combat and as much as I may wish him well, he may not survive. A hasty decision now may lead you into much stress."

"Do you really have to fly combat missions when you return to France?"

"I told you I have to. My obligation is not only to my country, but to the friends I fly with."

"Maybe Uncle Hubere can have your assignment changed to a non-combat one? He has a great deal of influence, and I am sure he could take care of you if I or we asked?"

He thought of Hubert's words with him when they were at the chapel and responded, "Michelle you are a very intelligent and wonderful person and friend. 'A friend' is all your uncle believes I should be. Please don't make me get into a discussion like we had this morning".

Marie agreed, "Michelle we should not spoil this wonderful evening we have had with any more of Hubere's attitudes now. When the time is proper, we can all get truly serious about any relationships you wish to pursue." She heard the hall clock chime ten thirty and said, "It is close to the time I usually retire. Please excuse me, I am going to bed." Then smiling she jested, "I hope you two will behave in my absence. And go to bed, in your own ones, that is, before midnight." Laughing softly, she left them in the hall.

After Marie went into her room and Michelle had Alan to lie on the rug next to her in front of the fireplace and attempted to excite him with passionate kisses. She became concerned after fifteen minutes of necking seemed like an hour, when he did not make an advance toward her. She wondered, "Was he not interested in sex with a women," then thought, "I think I should ask him if he has had an affair before. No. Best to use some philosophy on him.

"Alan," she asked, "I have taken anatomy courses. I learned about males, their hormones and how they respond. I am in a mood for love, and you are not responding to my passion for you. Do you still have those two girlfriends in your mind blocking a sexual advance?"

"No, they're not on my mind. I never thought of them that way. That doesn't mean I don't care enough to let you excite me. I am excited, but I gotta resist."

"Do you not think you could love me? I am asking you to physically show me if you do?"

He wasn't sure of what she was leading up to and asked, "I could easily fall, madly in love with you, if that's what you're leading up to? But I can't do anything to consummate a bond between us now, then after I leave, you find someone else, it would destroy me."

"You must never say that. Don't you remember what Aunt Marie said about how men pursued me after Brussels was liberated? So many men have made my life miserable, so miserable at times I wanted to go to Switzerland or to Sweden into hiding where no one could find me. Alan.... I.....I am attracted to you and if we have an affair, I think it would be for love and love alone. If we are meant for each other and we have an affair full of affection it could be an answer to a lifetime of happiness.

"Michelle...I have very strong feelings about that and must restrain from any love affair we might have. You know, when you don't have someone, you don't think of dying. If I made a commitment, I know I'll develop the fear of not being with you the rest of my life."

"Why should you fear dying because of me." She put her arm over his shoulder, drew him close and said, "I am... the one...who should fear losing you."

"I can't let myself be drawn into this; I can't be sure of how long I'll be around."

Michelle questioned, "Would you consider making love and sleeping with me when we get back to my apartment, or are you making all this up because you do not want me?"

"Michelle, give me some time to think this through, and at least until we're back in Brussels,"

"You are procrastinating. You can't imagine what love is like with the right person?"

He told her he didn't know and does not want to find out now. "Please wait?"

16 January 1945: Tuesday Leuven

After breakfast they visited a few schools located throughout city before going back to her father's office. There they met a Franciscan priest who recognized her, hugged, and told her, *"Everyone here misses your father as you do, but we know he is with the Lord."*

She introduced Alan to the Franciscan and had a short conversation before leaving. They had lunch in a restaurant favored by students where they met more of her friends. After returning, to Aunt Marie's house she asked, "Alan how much leave time do you have left?"

Alan hesitated and Michelle answered for him, "He could remain until Friday morning."

Marie, then asked, "Would you remain with Michelle and me for at least another day?"

"I am supposed to be in Paris at the Monmarte Red Cross Club. I left Paris on the first day of my leave. I've been here for three days and if someone, for some reason was looking for me and found me in Belgium, the Army could consider me to be AWOL or even a deserter. I don't know if you understand my situation. I must go back to Brussels tomorrow and then be back in Paris by tomorrow night.

Tuesday 18 January 1945:
Michelle and Alan's Return to Brussels, Belgium

Michelle and Alan left for Brussels, on bicycles, at 1430hrs and arrived at the cafe 1900hrs. On their arrival Phillipe had a note for him from U.S.A.F.E. signed, "Capt. Alfred E. Jacobs."

It read, "You are expected to be at the Paris Red Cross by 1730hrs, on Wednesday, 17 January 1945. If you do not comply, you will be listed as being AWOL."

Michelle cooked a beef stew dinner in the cafe kitchen while Phillipe and Alan remained at the bar talking about the impact of the note he received. They took the food up to her apartment, had dinner with red wine and cleaned up the dishes, utensils, and pans. Then, stoked up the sitting room heating coal stove Phillipe had started early that afternoon when she called and ask him from her aunt's house and said they were on their way.

She led him into the sitting room carrying a bottle of wine and glasses saying, "I would like to put on my nightgown and bathrobe to listen to good GI music while sipping a little bit of wine," and asked, "Would you join me? I have a pair of pajamas, not military, for you." Without an answer, she went into her bedroom and came out wearing her sheer robe over her light knee-high nightgown. On her arms, she held a bathrobe with a clean pair of Phillipe's pajamas and bathrobe with slippers and suggested he take a bath and put them on.

He went to the bathroom and got into the tub. There was soap and a washcloth on a small rack on the wall next to him. As he washed, she walked in with her robe open while he was in the tub, and he found himself unable to resist looking at her in the garments revealing her beautiful body. She asked, "You have not washed your back since who knows when. Will you let me wash it now? I swear it will not hurt you and you will feel much cleaner."

He responded, "OK, but you gotta stay out of the tub while I'm in it."

She came to him, took his washcloth, and gave his back a good scrubbing, then, leaned over and kissed him after saying, "I shall be waiting for you in the sitting room," and left. He finished bathing and while drying he thought, "She is ready for me, but I'm not sure if I want to do this?" As he put on his pajamas, bathrobe, and slippers he wondered, "How hard was it for her to get these for me?" While walking through the kitchen and into the sitting room he heard the radio was playing big band music. Entering he saw her sitting in the middle of the couch such that which either side of her he sat would be quite close to her. So, he sat down on the left side of her.

She picked up a wine glass half full of red wine and asked him to do the same. Then turned had him wrap his right arm around her left and they sipped some wine. He asked her what that was all about, and she said, "You really are naive. Haven't you seen that before, it is something two people do when in love?"

She sat back and asked, "Would you be willing to discuss a couple of things seriously?"

"Sure; what do you have in mind?"

She put her glass down and moved close enough to him to make their thighs touch. He began to feel uneasy when she put her right hand on his thigh and said with a very attracting look in her eyes, "You are blushing. Are you still shy in my presence? You should not be, I do care for you as much as if I was your fiancée. Don't you care for me at all?"

"I feel the blushing and can't help it when you look at me like that. You are so beautiful you make me shiver whenever you touch me."

"Remember, you promised, in my Leuven home, to discuss our relationship when we returned," and added, "This night may be 'the one' we shall remember forever."

He felt her blue, warm eyes penetrating him as they sipped their wine, and he was unable to control his natural instincts and had to hear her out. She talked about being married here, then, return to the U.S. after the war. Then we could both attend the same Ivy League university, you for three years and I for three in a medical program."

"Hold it! Where would I get the money for tuition and to live on for both of us?"

"I will acquire control of my assets including a large amount of money when I graduate next January. There is more than enough to support us for the rest of our lives."

"How did you come by the assets and all the money?"

"I told you! Remember the fabric mill in Liege? Half of it became mine after my mother died." She had to stop for a moment as she thought about her mother. She continued, "Her half of the fabric mill and all her money became mine with half of the mill remaining with Aunt Marie. The fabric demand for clothing, furniture, etc. has increased as other countries have been liberated. Our over-all plant manager, of the fabric mill, has projected our production would double or triple with the end of the war. When Uncle Hubere heard of this he suggested I sell my half of the fabric mill to Aunt Marie. Before I could deny it, he told me the money would be more useful now rather in the future when the mill sales may decline. I looked directly into his eyes and emphatically said I could never sell. That's for me, whoever my future mate is and my children."

Then changed the subject as she usually does when she has something serious on her mind. She laid her head in his lap and turned to face him. He looked down at her and she pulled his head down to kiss him. She wanted to make him seal their love and ask, "Why don't we drink our wine," and asked him, "Would you permit me to talk to my uncle Hubere about a non-combat assignment for you." Then before he could answer asked herself, "What am I doing? I have not done anything with him. I think I have fallen in love with this American without an affair?"

He seriously insisted, "I have no options and must leave by Wednesday noon and didn't feel this was the time to put a final cap on that subject. Can't we put all this off for a while, I don't feel like getting into a long discussion about not returning to my group, OK?"

Michelle leaned over, put her right arm around his shoulder and settled down in his go to bed together," and questioned; "How do you think two people truly in love might react in an affair?"

"I don't know, like I said, all my relationships were platonic. I've been told women take longer to be ready than men and a guy should not rush things. If he does the girl may know he is together doing it for himself, and love has nothing to do with it. I imagine when they're in love and joined together, both would feel so euphoric they'd never want it to end. At least, that's what I think I'd do if I were one of the couples who were sincere in a relationship. I don't know what she would do, OK? Now tell me what you think?"

"You sound like you have learned carefully or is it experience? You know I've been in bed with men. My experience with those occurrences did make me wonder how it could be with someone you really love. I hated what I had to do so much I never had a desire to think about this before. I can say this, I would feel so euphoric if I found someone, I knew really loved me, I agree it could be as you said, "One would wish it never ended."

"I've wondered, how would you know, no one else could make you feel more euphoric?"

"You have made me think, if you were in love and it was so wonderful with one person why would you care to even think of anyone else. I think real love will bind you together?"

Alan's resistance finally weakened and against his better judgment and he thought, "I do feel I could really love her and only her! I don't remember of ever feeling this much for Mary Lou, who I thought I liked so much. That was my problem I guess, I liked her a lot, but not enough to want an immediate affair with her!"

"Why are you so quiet? I thought your mind took a trip somewhere?"

"It did! I was thinking if you are serious about this I should," he hesitated, I should try, but let's not risk making a child. I have two condoms in my wallet because everyone, from my base, who went off base over one night had to take more than one if they went on leave. We were even told if we needed more where to go to get them, like, any base and your leave orders. Would you mind if I used one with you?"

She told him he could, but it would feel better without one, then, began kissing him and proceeded to softly chew on his ear lobe. They ended up in bed, he just laid on his side facing her. Michelle immediately began kissing him passionately with her body pressing to his. She rolled him on his back and was on top of him before he knew it. She slid her arms under his neck, and he wrapped his arms around her back. Michelle had to hold back her laughter; he was so innocent she had to encourage him to proceed to do what he said. She guided him through the entire episode, then, relaxed with a deep sigh while they were still together. Then, smiling with tears of joy she asked, "I believe I was your first, was I not?"

Alan admitted, "Yes, this was my first time. And her tears had made him wonder if he satisfied her and asked, "Was I a disappointment?"

"Oh... Alan for someone's first time you were wonderful." He could feel her trembling while she kissed him again, and added, "I had this strange feeling, I felt so wonderful and did not know why?" She rambled on, "I have never felt the passion that remains with me now! You are the one I have waited for!" Then, finally rolled off of him onto her back and lay motionless looking at the ceiling for several moments. She turned toward him and whispered softly, "Are you aware of how much you have made me love you? Remember, I said I would feel like I was in heaven with the right man, well someone had a hand in this and saved you for me, on this night, for this wonderful moment together. Who ever thought love could be like it has been with you."

They lay facing each other for several minutes kissing

passionately. Michelle broke the silence saying, "You go first, get rid of that thing, and clean up on the bidet. When you return, I will go to the bathroom."

After both had cleaned up Michelle wanted to continue necking in bed. Alan obliged and Michelle stated, "Alan.... be honest with me. If you experienced what I have, you cannot deny me a commitment now?"

"Yes, I did feel so euphoric with you. But there are so many pilots I have known the last two years who made commitments and got married. When I was home on my last leave one of them, from my hometown, married a girl he knew through high school. I heard she was pregnant three months later. He was killed on his first mission. If you love me as much as you say I don't want to risk anything like that happening to you."

"That is precisely why I want your permission to talk to Uncle Hubere. I know from his position in the Belgian government, he can get you relieved from combat duty. "

"Do you really think he would? He didn't talk to me like he would do anything for me the last time I saw him. He'd more likely want to get rid of me. I don't want you to ask him for anything for me. Please don't ask your Uncle Hubere to have me relieved from my combat duty and complicate matters more than they already are."

"I know Aunt Marie would ask and have Uncle Hubere

relieve you of any combat duty if I asked. He could arrange an assignment, possibly, in your Group's administration offices or if you preferred, with the 9th Air Force."

"If he has that much power and you involve him, I will never see or speak to you again."

She began to cry, and Alan quickly added, "Don't do that, can't you understand I couldn't live with the knowledge of a pilot dying because I wasn't there to fly a mission I would have been assigned." He leaned forward, with head in his hands, and said, "I can't! I have to fly 'my' missions.

Lying on his back with his arm under her neck when she said, "I know you shall live and return for me, and we will make a child."

He just answered, "Yes my dear," as he rolled on his right side. She snuggled against him on her right side and pulled his left arm around her with his hand in hers. Several quiet minutes later they both fell asleep.

Nine

NINTH TO EIGHTH AIR FORCE

Wednesday 17 January 1945:
Brussels, Belgium and Paris, France

Michelle woke up in the middle of the night. She wanted him again and thought, "He is leaving tomorrow, I may never see him again. I should get over him and wake him. But, on a second thought he is sleeping so soundly I must let him sleep.

Michelle was up early Wednesday morning, telephoned Hubert's office and his secretary told her he left for Paris, early Monday morning, and had not returned. She thought, "I'll ask him as soon as he returns to do something. Best I not. If Alan discovered, I did" ... She was getting so confused she did not want to think of that anymore now, so when he woke, she asked him to bathe with her.

"It would be better if we washed separately," he answered.

And she responded, "We have made love! What is wrong now?"

"Your uncle Hubere keeps popping up in my mind. I know he will try to manipulate a relationship for you to get together with someone he likes after I leave."

The mention of Uncle Hubere infuriated her, and she made her mind up to settle with him for belittling Alan in his attempt to destroy their relationship. When calm she said, "Please forget Uncle Hubere. If he attempts to persuade me to get involved in any kind of a relationship, I shall leave Belgium and contract a 'Manager to look after my Fabric Mill interests. She hesitated and added, "Make me happy; bathe with me?" He yielded and agreed on the condition there would be no love affair and smiling she said, "Anything you want dear," with her fingers crossed behind her.

It didn't take long to excite him and when it was over, he said, "You promised? You lied?"

Smiling, she said, "You did not resist! And if it is love you can't trust me anymore." She then put on a lovely pink, sheer, chenille bathrobe over her short thin nightgown. Then stood very close to him as he dressed, toying with and hugging him frequently. She pressed her warm body against his and aroused him again as he was trying to dress. Her body language and occasional kisses made him think she wanted to have another affair. Disturbed, he attempted to remain calm and indifferent and asked where could they go for breakfast.

Michelle apologized saying, "You distract me so easily I forgot about that," and still in her bathrobe, got out the eggs, bacon, and potatoes to make breakfast.

Alan suggested she not make a breakfast and dress to go out to a nice restaurant. She disagreed saying, "I love making a good breakfast for you. So, he found a place and sat on the long side of the table. Then leaned against the wall watching her cook moving around the kitchen so gracefully her body hypnotized him. His mind wandered with inferior thoughts, "Gosh, she's so perfect and beautiful, I know she's capable of having someone better than me."

The breakfasts were ready and broke his reflections as she put the plates on the table. She sat next to him and after a few mouths full she stood up and said, "Excuse me, "and went to her bedroom. She had retrieved a small mahogany box from her bedroom, brought it to the table and moved her chair close to him and put the box in front of her plate. She noticed Alan had been very quiet all this time and appeared to be thinking. Before beginning to eat she asked, "Something is on your mind? Do you want to talk about it?"

Being caught with that thought he responded, "I 'm wondering if I'll ever see you again?"

"That's a foolish question! I shall be here or in Leuven waiting for your return," she said as they began eating. She hadn't eaten much when she opened the mahogany box. The box revealed a huge diamond ring and a jewel rosary.

Alan gulped when he saw the ring and asked, "Where did you get those? Are they real?"

"They were my mother's engagement ring and rosary made with diamonds and rubies. Aren't they something? Especially, how each diamond and ruby are retained by specially designed thin elliptical surrounding, gold settings. Alan, would you mind if I wore this ring as though we were engaged and if anyone asked, I could say, I'm engaged to an American pilot?"

"You will not if the pilot's me! When we get engaged, if you'll still have me, I'll buy you one!"

She responded, "Whatever you want dear, but would you at least consider permitting me to wear it on my right hand as a symbol of our love until you buy one?"

"Why do you want to appear engaged? People would want to know who your fiancé is?"

"I will tell everyone you proposed when you were here, and I began wearing the ring. It will provide me with some protection and a good reason for refusing all these ridiculous date requests. Then she put her face in his hands and told him, “I shall pray the rosary for you every day after you leave,” and threw her arms around his neck and began kissing him. She was still kissing him passionately when they relaxed and silently looked into each other’s eyes.

“Will you always love me because you were my first,” he suddenly spoke up?

Michelle, slightly upset responded,” What made you have to say that! What in heaven’s name do you really think I am. I have fallen in love with you! And what do you do? You come to me with this questioning attitude. I believe you are the man I have waited for. You can be more than I ever imagined if you would only believe in yourself in the presence of women. When you do that, you shall discover how wonderful life can be for you and ‘only’ me. Now lean over and give me a kiss. Our time together is waning, and you are wasting it.” He obliged and she held his face in her hands and after kissing him several times asked, “Is this not better than your insecurity?”

They finished eating and dressed. Before leaving she mentions, “If you would accept Uncle Hubere’s help he could find some way for you stay. Michelle please let’s not get into that again! You know I must go. I’m obligated.”

They went downstairs and into the café and Alan thanked Phillipe for everything. They left shortly after for the train station at 11:40 and arrived there before the train did. Twenty minutes later the train was there, and Alan put his bag in a compartment and came back out on to the platform to kiss her. She didn't want to let go of him when the train whistled for its departure.

He gently separated from her, kissed her on both checks, her forehead, then, her lips, with a long passionate kiss. He got on the train as it started moving seconds later. Michelle walked faster alongside his compartment to keep up with the train as it accelerated. She was crying as she began to run, then, she stopped when she and his car reached the end of the platform. He had his face against the window and saw her put a handkerchief on her face as she was disappearing from his sight.

He sat back, holding his tears and began wondering if he would ever see her again.

Wednesday 17 January 1945: Paris, Return to Ninth Air Force Group

-

The train arrived in Paris at 1650hrs. A sergeant met Alan there at 1650hrs holding a B-4 bag. On the way out to a jeep He asked the sergeant, "How did you get my B-4 bag?"

"I had orders and the Red Cross people got it from your room when I checked you out."

"How much do I owe you for that?"

"Nothing, Colonel Bennett took care of that with a letter."

"If I remember correctly it took about four and a half-hours to get here from the base. It's now five o'clock; think you can make it to the base by nine thirty?"

They reached the base at 2145hrs, and he was dropped off at his tent. His tent-mates were waiting for him with a bottle of scotch. Cooper greeted him as he entered the tent with, "We heard you were found in Brussels instead of Paris, is that right?"

Cooper poured scotch into their mess kit cups and Bauer toasted Alan, "Here's to our traveling tent-mate, and are you going to tell us all about your what we've come to understand was, a one time in the world, Belgian adventure?"

"How did you get to Brussels in the first place," asked Benson?

"What's going on? What have you guys heard," a confused Alan asked?

"We heard you were in Brussels with a blond who had big time connections," stated Cooper.

"I'm tired. Jeees...guys, I'll tell you about it tomorrow morning. I have to get some sleep."

"We heard you didn't get much in Brussels did you," added a laughing Benson.

"Much what?"

"Never mind. We're going to the club for a while, "Wanna come," asked Bauer?

Alan finished his scotch and said, "I'm really tired," then; laid down on his cot.

"OK, we'll let you rest. Come on you guys, let him have his dreams," Cooper responded.

They walked out and he fell sound asleep in a few minutes.

Thursday 18 January 1945: Base Headquarters 378th Fighter Group - France

-

Alan had breakfast with, Cliff, his flight leader. Naturally the other men at the table asked him to tell them a little about what he did to cause such a fuss. Cliff interrupted and told him, "You have to get to base headquarters before 1000hrs."

He finished his breakfast, returned to his tent, washed up and Cliff drove him to headquarters. Two sergeants greeted them, with a snappy salute, at the entrance of base headquarters, then directed them to the CO's office where he saw, several officers sitting against the back wall. They, who all wanted in on this session, were Group Operations officer, Squadron CO, Major Cassidy and Captain Clancy, his Operations officer.

Colonel Bennett, toying with Alan, initiated the questioning with, "Did you read or have anyone tell you the destination of your leave orders?"

"Yes sir; they were for Paris."

"Did your orders include Brussels?" "No sir."

"Then, would you be so kind and tell us why and how you ended up in Brussels."

"Well, you see sir, I met these paratroopers," background snickering interrupted him.
"Come now, lieutenant continue," directed Bennett!

He hesitated, then began, "Saturday night, I went to a café with a couple of my friends and met three paratroopers there who asked me if I would go to Brussels with them that night and return on Sunday night or no later than Monday morning."

"If they asked you to go with them tomorrow and jump with them, would you."

"Well sir I couldn't do that, I don't have any jump training.

Would you sir?" Now there was hysterical laughing in the background.

"I wasn't with them, you were." Someone laughed so hard he fell off his chair and when he turned to see what happened a voice said, "What are you looking for now?"

Bennett had to laugh and asked, "Who fell off a chair."

"I did," said, Clancy, Alan's Operations Officer.

"Just a few more questions Lieutenant, "How did you meet this girl?"

"The girl sir?"

"Yes, the girl in Brussels."

Well sir some friendly paratroopers took me to....". He was interrupted again by someone who couldn't hold back his laughter and continued, "They took me to this cafe in Brussels and it was so late we couldn't find..."

"Bennett interrupted with, "We heard, quarters for you that night, right?"

"You knew about the quarters, sir?"

"Yes, we do."

Now Alan's mind was beginning to spin, and he had trouble thinking clearly.

"Tell us about this girl," a familiar voice behind him asked?

He looked at Colonel Bennett and stammered, "The, the, the girl, sir?"

"Yes, the girl who was nice to you. Do you always answer a question with a question?"

"Well, ah...sir, I don't know exactly how to tell you, except she was very kind to me...."

When Bennett said, "You shack up with all girls who are kind to you?" A roar came out of the background.

The laughing stopped Alan for a moment and said, "This one was special sir."

Bennett laughing asked, "Was she so special because she wanted you to sleep with her?"
"Not the first day, sir."

"Not the first day!" He paused then continued, "Relax, tell us how you got on top of Belgium? Of all girls in Belgium, how did you find this Mimi or was it Michelle," said Bennett?

"You know her name sir?" She was just there and let me sleep in her apartment on Saturday."

"Now you want us to believe you slept in her apartment and didn't do anything."

"No sir, like I said not at first. She talked me into it after a couple of days, sir."

The roar now could be heard throughout the entire Headquarters building and Bennett, laughing could hardly talk and stammered, "Oh...oh I... I see! She had to talk you into it?"

The walls were vibrating now because the CO's staff had their ear to the door. It took a few minutes for all the laughing to stop. When it quieted the colonel asked, "Alan, as I understand, at first you didn't know who this girl was? When did you realize she was from Belgian high society?"

He answered. "Yes Sir, I figured it out after meeting her father, no, I mean her uncle."

"Which was it her father or her uncle," asked the CO. Then there was some more laughter. Disturbed by that, he couldn't help turning and said, "That's not funny," in an upset tone! "Her father was in the Belgian underground and killed by the Gestapo!" Now, he began talking too fast and had to stop momentarily to catch his breath. Then he continued, "She tried to talk me out of returning to combat telling me her uncle could do something to have me transferred to a non-combat assignment if her Aunt Marie asked him? I told her not to even think of that and not to dare try!" Then, added,

"I told her, I didn't think her uncle would, after the one-sided conversation I had with him."

"Yeah; he could transfer you, but not out of combat," answered the CO. Then added "Everyone in 9th Air Force now knows who you are and where you were." He needled him more with, "Wing informed me you were found staying with a Belgian Government Official's niece by USAFE."

He attempted to apologize for being in Louvian when USAFE looked for him. Being really concerned he asked, "Sir; did my being in Brussels create a problem for you?"

"No! You had the problem and had a friend, in 9th headquarters who took care of it."

His Squadron CO, behind him, suggested and they all toast him and wished him well. While drinking, they forced him to tell them of the 'entire Brussels incident'. And when he finished Colonel Bennett asked, "Are you aware you are to be transferred to the 8th Air Force. Wing would not tell us more than that. All they said was, 'It was directed by USAFE through a 9th Air Force general and wouldn't tell us which one. But we know why and by whom! Do you have any idea who it was? Lieutenant Jim Keane is also on the orders. Did he ever meet or know this girl?"

He answered, "Keene never met her."

And Bennet said, "I' just wondered why he is on the same

9th Air Force orders with you. We protested for your CO, Cassidy, through Wing to keep you and they asked 9th Air Force if we could keep you, but, they 'nixed' our request."

On the last drink in the bottle, the C.O. said, "You have quite a Belgian experience to tell, someone someday...lover boy."

Then Alan's Squadron CO, Cassidy, added, "Yeah, and I can say, he was in my Squadron."

Everyone was feeling pretty good when they left. Alan went to his tent and immediately, fully clothed, fell asleep. He woke up at 0600hrs the next morning and his tent-mates were waiting for him to wash and dress. They walked to the mess hall with him, and he told him what he knew. Also, why, and how he suspected Michelle's uncle was probably at the root of the transfer."

Thursday, 19 January 1945

At breakfast Jim Keane and Alan, were told 'be prepared by 0930hrs' for transfer to the 8th Air Force. Both went to their tents after breakfast and turned in everything required by supply at 0820hrs. Then returned to their respective Ready Rooms to say good-bye. Cliff met Alan at the door and escorted him into their ready room where CO, Cassidy, and Operations Officer, Clancy, were waiting with the guys who all wished him luck.

He was picked up with his B-4 Bag and footlocker by a sergeant who drove him from his tent to group headquarters where Jim was waiting. They received their transfer orders, then, he and Jim plus his footlocker and B-4 bags left for Paris in a six-by-six truck at 1000hrs.

Five hours and fifteen minutes later they arrived at the Replacement Depot gate and went to headquarters to check in. They met seven of the thirteen pilots who were assigned to the 9th Air Force with them in November. Four of the missing were believed to be POW's and two were listed as KIA. That afternoon they were checked in a hotel a block away from the depot.

He and Jim wandered around that evening and ended up in the restaurant where he first saw Michelle. This time the matre d' recognized Alan, was overwhelmingly courteous and pleasantly seated them. Jim noticing asked why they were given VIP attention and Alan told him whom Michelle's uncle was when he was there in November.

After a generous serving of, real, steak they returned to the hotel. Before going to bed, he sat down at the room's desk and wrote a letter to Michelle.

He informed her he was being transferred to the 8th Air Force in England. And he would also write a letter to her after he arrives to provide her with his APO address.

Friday Morning, 19 January 1945

The next morning a Captain met the pilots after breakfast with their assignment orders. Obviously very jealous he asked who they knew to have been given the hotel rooms? He overheard one of the pilots suggest he envied them because they had rooms in the hotel. Attempting to intimidated them he addressed them with, "OK 'fly boys' listen up!' I have your orders."

A Lt. Colonel, included for transfer, appeared, heard, recognized the Captain's attitude and said, "These pilots earned their hotel rooms last night, if that's your problem."

He received no answer and told the Captain to get on with the arrangements he was to prepare. He arranged for a six-by-six truck to pick them up and take them to Le Bourge airport. The pilots including the Lt. Colonel boarded a C-47 for transfer to 8th Air Force bases. The transport aircraft left at 1100, crossed the English Channel and made an English landfall at 1145hrs. They were vectored around London, a restricted zone, and landed at the 389th Fighter Group Base.

Ten

EIGHTH AIR FORCE MISSIONS

Friday 19 January 1945:
Headquarters, 358th Fighter Group - England

En route the Lt. Colonel introduced himself as Jacob Herrington and told them he also was a transfer from the 9th Air Force. On disembarking they were picked up by a jeep and taken to Group Headquarters where they reported and met Colonel Carl Randolf, Commanding Officer.

In the short conversation Alan and Jim found the Lt. Colonel was a highly decorated, ex-RAF, British double ace pilot. He was recently grounded after recovering from severe head injuries from a P-47 crash landing. Alan and Jim learned the Lt. Colonel knew them from their records in the

Replacement Depot Headquarters office. CO Randolf welcomed the Lt. Colonel as the new Group Executive Officer. A little later they were informed they were assigned to the 385th and 386th fighter squadrons respectively. Before they left the headquarters, the CO took all three to meet Dale Jerrett, Group Operations Officer.

Jim and Alan were taken to their respective squadron Ready Rooms where Alan met his CO, Jay Duneforte and Operations Officer, Captain Carl Morrow. Thirty minutes later they were picked up and taken to the base supply building. There they were supposed to receive their flight suits, bedding, handguns etc. Jim received everything, including an A-2 Flight Jacket. Alan received everything except the pilot's leather Flight Jacket.

When he asked the supply sergeant, why he didn't get an A-2 flight jacket, the sergeant told him, "Lieutenant Keane received the last one, sir."

He saw the sergeant wearing one that looked new he asked, "I thought they were for flight personnel only? Why do you have one?"

He responded, "My supply Officer issued this one to me."

After he was taken to his quarters with his sheets, pillows, fight suits etc. he returned to his squadron ready room and immediately went to his CO's office. He walked into the office unannounced, amazed Dunforte simply saying, "No A-2 Flight Jacket-no fly."

The CO then asked, "What is this all about?"

"I thought A-2 jackets were flight personnel issue only. I didn't get one."

Let me guess, "They told you they didn't have any, right?"

"How did you know that? Did somebody call you about the jacket?"

"Lieutenant this is not the first time this has happened. The people in supply always seem to have pilot equipment problems and always are short or out of something."

"But sir, the base supply sergeant said they were out of them and was wearing one."

Alan saluted, turned to leave and Dunforte asked, "Where do you think you're going?"

"I'm going to Group Headquarters and ask for a transfer back to my 9th AF squadron."

"No, you're not. You're going back to base supply and get a Jacket! Don't leave, wait!"

Dunforte called and told the base Supply Officer, "One of

my new pilots needs an A-2 jacket. Your sergeant, in supply, gave one to a 385th pilot and told my pilot you were out of them while he was wearing one. I understand it appeared to be fairly new. My pilot is going back to supply. Call your sergeant and tell him to take his off and if it fits my pilot give it to him! If it doesn't, find a 'new' one within the next five days." Then he told Alan, "Take my jeep and go back to the supply building. If they don't have a jacket that fits, they'll have one for you within five days." After he left, the CO called Morrow and told him about the flight jacket problem, and they laughed so hard one would think they had a fit.

When Alan arrived, the sergeant saluted him and said, "Lieutenant try this one on for a fit. If it fits take it, if it doesn't come back in five days and we'll have one for you."

It fit and he returned to the Ready Room and Morrow met him there. They had to laugh when he told him about the jacket. Then, had the sergeant with the jeep, who had been waiting all this time, to take him, his, footlocker, B-4 bag, bedding, etc. to his room.

Alan met Morrow, at dinner, who introduced him to several squadron pilots. Three of them began to tell him how many air victories they had. Two of them, lieutenants, said they had two and one, a captain, had three. He asked them how long have they been here. They all said they came together from the U.S. "Five months ago in August."

He responded, with a tilted nod of his head and said,

"That's pretty good," to give them recognition. Then each told him what they shot down and what kind they were, with Alan nodding, good, as they told him Me-109s and FW-190s. Morrow changed the subject and began talking about the base. He told him it was an RAF base evacuated for their group, that's why he saw all the nice brick buildings, including this officers club and quarters building. Alan asked if anybody knew if it was possible to get a leave to the continent. When asked why, he told them, "I thought it would be nice if one could get to see Paris or maybe Brussels."

"Why would you want to go to Paris or Brussels someone asked?"

He hesitated before answering..., "I heard Brussels is pretty city, a lot of middle age type buildings and some guys told me the girls there were as fine as any in Paris. They supposedly don't dress as fancy and use less make up, but are naturally prettier," then stopped and wondered why his room was not in this building before asking Morrow, "Why is Keane's and my room a couple of blocks from here?"

Morrow answered, "We're full up here. First room opening we have, you'll get one."

"Will Jim Keane, who came with me be my roommate?"

"Jim will get his when there's a room opening in his squadron area."

"Is my flight leader anywhere in here? I'd like to meet him?"

"I don't see him anywhere." He then asked the pilots if anyone saw Schueler at dinner?

"No, he was here. He just left before you came in," answered a pilot at the table."

After dinner Alan went back to his room and Jim was there, reading a book. He told Jim about the room arrangements and Jim told him his squadron guys told him the same thing, then, they talked about their conversations with the squadron pilots. After several minutes he asked Jim to excuse him, he had to write a couple of letters. Jim continued reading and Alan sat at the room's desk, got a sheet of paper from those he put in the drawer and began:

19 January 1945

Dear Michelle:

I arrived here today about, noon. I never realized know how much I could miss you. And how much I enjoyed every minute with you. Our visit with Aunt Marie was so pleasant, but your Uncle Hubere caused me much distress. He insinuated I'm not good enough for you. In your opinion, am I? etc... act. etc..." Then closed with his new APO address.

I Love and miss you so much,

Alan

He went to Group Headquarters and mailed the two letters. The next day Alan met his 'A' Flight officer, Capt., Jack Schueler, at the 0630hrs morning mission briefing. And met 'A' Flight pilot's 1st. Lieutenants Fred Beane and Andy Harris. The days flight schedule briefing ended at 0725 and all pilots returned to their respective squadrons. There Alan was introduced to four more 'A' flight pilots after the squadron briefing. This briefing included, weather, type of flak, number of guns, and locations in route to target.

After the briefing several additional pilots, not aware he had flown in combat, again boasted of air victories. He told no one anything about his combat time. The only persons, on the base at the present time, aware of his combat time were the Group CO, Randolf, Lt. Colonel Harrington, Alan's squadron Commander and the Operations Officer.

At the conclusion of this briefing major Dunforte instructed Alan to go to the hospital after lunch for a Medical Flight Check. There Capt. Joel McCarthy MD, the squadron doctor, discovered Alan flew in combat from personal records he was given for the medical check.

On the CO's return from the day's mission Doc McCarthy informed him of Alan's 9th AF missions. Dunforte informed him he and Operations officer Morrow were aware of his combat time in the 9th Air Force. He told McCarthy to call Morrow and Alan into his office to discuss the flight positions he flew in, i.e., flight leader, element leader, etc. He found Alan buried deep in the pilot's handbook on the P-51. He interrupted his study and told him he was wanted in the CO's office. At the end of the informative discussion Morrow took Alan aside and told him he was scheduled to attend ground school beginning Monday morning in the large group hanger.

The next morning Alan sat in the back row seats, with Jim Keane, of the group's mission. He noticed the mission's lines, on a wall sized European map, entering the continent a little south of Antwerp and passed just a bit north of Brussels. He began daydreaming of being on the mission. He visualized his flight flying escorting, on the right side of B-24's and seeing Brussels a bit further south. And imagined, as they approached the city, he dropped out of formation into steep dive from 25,000 feet and leveled out at 100, with an airspeed just under 500 mph over Brussels University. He looked back as he buzzed over it and as he circled, he saw Michelle run out of a building waving at his P-51. "She knows it's me," he imagined and suddenly found himself circling Phillipe's and seeing her outside there. An elbow dug into his right rib area that snapped out of his daydream saying, "What...what's the matter?"

Jim said, "You were dozing and began mumbling something."

He put a hand over his mouth. Jim held back his laughter and said, "What a character?"

Alan met his flight leader captain Schueler outside of the building and they walked to the squadron ready room with several other squadron pilots. As they walked into their ready room, captain Morrow approached and informed him, "You only have to attend the ground school sessions pertaining to the P-51's description. Now, go meet Jim Keens and two other pilots in the main hanger with your instructor."

Monday, 22 – 29 January 1945:
Ground school and P-51 Transition

Alan had six days of Ground School on P-51 B's C's and D's. New arrival pilots were scheduled for 15 days of Ground School including, hydraulic, electrical, instrumentation, fuel, 50 caliber gun systems etc. Then, learned all cockpit operations and how to pre-flight the aircraft. Several of the session's pertained only to the K-14-gun sight and its use in air-to-air combat, strafing and dive-bombing. Between the days classes he studied and learned everything about the P-51D from manuals and updated information.

He passed the blindfold cockpit check, then was scheduled to fly twelve transition flights averaging two hours each. He diligently practiced all designated stalls and recoveries from various conditions. His final transition flights consisted of acrobatics and formation flying.

He received two letters from Michelle and one from Aunt Marie on Friday 2 February. His roommate, Keane, intercepted another letter on the following Wednesday. He smelled perfumed envelopes and broadcast it all over the club and made it a point to bring this to anyone's attention that was willing to listen. That resulted in Alan being asked all sorts of questions, most respectable and a few slanderous.

One letter from Michelle told of uncle Hubere's plans for Claude and her future with him. Alan wrote back, he knew in his absence Hubere would bring Claude out of the closet.

Saturday, 24 February to Wednesday, 04 April 1945
8th. Air Force Combat - Escort

-

Alan's first mission, 24 February, was the escorting of B-24's to Nuremburg and bringing them back, to an area well behind our friendly lines. Subsequently each of three squadrons, separated to find their own individual German targets of opportunity. These escort missions averaged four and a half-hours. The loss of men and P-51s was negligible on most missions. By the end of February 1945, he had mailed eight and received eight letters from Michelle.

The target on the 27 February was Berlin. At the group briefing, it was strongly stressed not to chase any Me-262 jets, that dove at their bombers, for more than a few thousand feet below bomber altitude. The general order was stay with the bombers. The group put up forty-eight P-51s, sixteen in each of three squadrons. Schueler lead "B" flight, in their squadron, and Alan was the element leader with Andy Morisson as his wingman.

About twenty minutes from the target, they encountered more than sixteen Me-262 jets that were at least five to eight thousand feet above them. Eight jets dove simultaneously on the B-24s. They attacked in groups of two on the front, center, and rear sections of the box of bombers. The entire group dove after the diving jets with his CO, Dunforte leading the squadron. Several thousand feet below their box of B-24s he ordered his squadron to break off their chase and return to their altitude. The other two squadrons chased the jets until they were out of their sight.

Dunforte ordered 'A' and 'B' flights, with four P-51s each, to fly top cover over a few boxes of B-24s. 'A' flight covered a few of the forward and 'B' flight covered a few of the rear boxes of B-24 bombers. 'C' and 'D' flights flew at the bombers level, on each side of the several boxes. Top cover was a couple thousand feet above them.

A couple minutes after each flight was set in their positions and began patrolling a gaggle of boggies (unidentified aircraft) were spotted. As they came closer, they were identified as approximately thirty or more Me-109s and ten or more FW-190s. They split up into groups of two or four aircraft and attacked our B-24s at four locations.

They dove making a firing pass at the bombers, then, climbed back to altitude and made more passes. All sixteen P-51s, of Dunforte's squadron, were so busy trying to intercept the enemy and keep others off their tails no one had an opportunity to fire. There were so many airplanes in a small section of the sky one had to pay attention to keep from intercepting or being shot at from behind. Aside from being shot down, everyone had to keep their wits sharp to evade a collision with a 109, a 190 or one of their own 51's. After five minutes the German fighters broke off their attacks and dove for the deck. It looked like those Me-109s and FW-190s were all that were to 'show up' and the CO ordered us to chase them.

They were probably low on ammunition. Alan lost his wingman, in the previous skirmish and ended up alone at two thousand feet separated from his flight with no wingman chasing Me-109s. Alone, he caught up with six of the Me-109's and ended up in a Luftberry circle with them. He never had a chance to shoot at anybody, but two of the six, Me-109's, collided and crashed. And the other four left on the deck heading due south. There wasn't a witness to the mid-air collision and Alan hadn't fired his guns, thus, there was nothing on his gun films to confirm his two Me-109's destroyed. Thus, 'No Pictures No Credits.'

Shortly after, while climbing on a heading in the direction of the bomber stream's flight direction, Alan spotted three Me-109s attacking a crippled B-17, on two engines, headed back toward England, several thousand feet below him. He dove on them and occupied them trying for a few minutes to get at him. They broke off the skirmish and headed southeast.

He stayed with the bomber for a half hour at five thousand

feet. Alan thought he saved them, when suddenly they were hit from a field of anti-aircraft that looked like 88 mm. proximity fused bombs going off close to the B-17. He was a couple thousand feet above the bomber and the flak rarely got close to him. One of the B-17's running engines was hit, it caught fire and it lost altitude rapidly. Alan saw five parachutes come out of the distressed bomber and felt bad that he couldn't have done more for them.

He began a steep climb doing evasive action when he saw flak around him and became sick to his stomach seeing, from his altitude of fifteen thousand feet, see the bomber crash and burn.

He found at the debriefing, three Me-109s and one FW-190 were shot down. Dunforte claimed two Me-109s. Schueler claimed a FW-190 and Sanders, 'D' flight leader, the other 109. No one in Dunforte's squadron was seriously hit.

Alan flew three uneventful B-24 escort missions during the next two weeks. The group escorted B-24s on twelve of the fourteen-day period. The Luftwaffe did not appear in their group's bomber escort area. Each squadron after escorting the bombers back to our friendly lines, returned to Germany separated and looked for air or ground targets of opportunity. Dunforte's squadron only found a small convoy and a freight train they severely shot up. They found three Luftwaffe bases of which two appeared abandoned and the one they tested for anti-aircraft had too many guns to challenge at this stage of the war.

The other two squadrons were more fortunate during this two-week period. One day Major Henley's 385th squadron met twelve Me-109s attacking their bomber escort area. They split into flights of four and went after the 109s. A 385th flight leader got behind four Me-109s and firing hit two and his wingman hit one. All three went straight in. Shortly after he successfully broke off, he saw two 109s at ninety degrees from him behind two of their P-51s. He maneuvered to get them in his gun sight. He hit one and his wingman came in and got the other 109. The first began burning and the other went into a spin and spun out of sight at a low altitude.

The 384th was the other fortunate squadron, lead by Major Paterson's sixteen P-51s. They returned into Germany to find targets of opportunity after escorting the bombers out safely. They flew east for about ten or fifteen minutes then turned to a northeast heading at ten thousand feet and found an active Luftwaffe base that threw a lot of 20 mm flak at them. A few minutes later, now out of the sight of the Luftwaffe base, a gaggle of about thirty Me-109s heading for that air base were spotted at a low altitude. Paterson posted his P-51s to attack the Me-109s. They shot down twelve and broke off heading for England when they got down to their tracer bullets indicating they only had fifty to seventy bullets left in each gun.

Also, during this two-week period the group had a "Stand Down" relieving them from flying missions on Saturday the 10th and Sunday the 11th of March. This was Party Time, Alan received four letters, before party time, from Michelle telling him how much she missed him and poured out her heart with her love for him.

A party time dance was held at the club. Girls were trucked to the base from adjacent towns and city for the party. Occasionally a pilot here and there escorted girls to play dens. The Group CO posted an order that all girls had to be off the base by noon Thursday. And any pilots scheduled to fly missions better not be caught with a girl in his nest the night before his scheduled mission.

Alan was a wallflower during the party not wanting to do anything with any girl, not even dance. He engaged himself in bridge card games and a poker card game. Lost a little but had fun anyway. When talking to Captain Schueler, also a wallflower, he told him he wouldn't expose himself to a possible VD exposure. Supposedly the girls were selected, but he would not do anything anyway, Michelle's letters, full of love, were always on his mind.

On the 15 March Berlin raid Alan was C flight's element leader's wingman. They escorted B-24s at twenty-five thousand feet. Dunforte had sixteen P-51s with two flights of four, top cover, at twenty-eight thousand feet over a box of bombers. It was very humid at their altitude and the bombers contrails became so dense they formed clouds with a top level very high above them. His element leader lost sight of their flight leader and began climbing from twenty-six thousand feet in the contrail formed clouds.

They broke out of the clouds at thirty thousand feet heading east, the direction toward Berlin for a half hour hoping to find their group or the bombers. Alternating wing fuel tanks every fifteen minutes Alan noticed it was 1230hrs. He figured they flew past Berlin for more than thirty minutes and estimated from their airspeed, of two hundred and ten mph at thirty thousand feet, they had a ground speed of well over three hundred miles per hour compared to the bombers speed at maybe two hundred and fifty mph. tops.

His plastic thigh pocket mission schedule indicated the bombers were to drop their bombs on Berlin at noon. He radioed his element leader who ignored his supposition and wanted to keep on an eastern heading. Alan wished him well and did a 180-degree turn back to a west heading. A few minutes later the element leader came up to him and flew his wing. Forty-five minutes later they found the bombers heading west and their group at twenty thousand feet flying through what now was a broken cloud sky.

Encounter with Me-262 jets

Alan was 'A' flight leader's wingman on Thursday's 5 April. Captain Schueler had 'C' flight on this mission. Twenty minutes from the target, twelve Me-262 German jets appeared high above the B-24s. The jets dove by twos attacking the box of bombers. His flight leader initiated a right-hand diving turn and began chasing them. He suddenly, pulled up in a high 'G' turn simultaneously dropping his external tanks, then. Alan attempting to stay with him, had to pull his aircraft's nose up and to the right, with the same 'G' force. In this high 'G' condition he could not reach his drop tank switches. Struggling, he reached and lifted the tank switch covers and attempted to drop his tanks, but only one came off and the other hung up. The P-51 rolled so fast it did a two and a half (2&1/2), snap roll to the right before he could recover. The sudden recovery from the snap roll, made the other tank come off and fly over his canopy.

Now in a climbing left bank he called his flight leader to tell him he was not with him and warn him that he had no rear cover. Receiving no response to his several radio calls to his flight leader he thought the snap roll somehow damaged it. Then, he felt a strong tapping on his right shoulder. He instinctively turned to look behind him and saw a Me-262 jet firing at him and immediately pulled into a tight left, 4 G, banking turn.

Alan was so engaged attempting to stay with his flight leader and recovering from a snap roll, he hadn't turned on his gun switches. Then, the Me 262 suddenly appeared in front of him and filled his windshield less than 600 feet in from of him as he recovered from his snap-roll. The 262-pilot looking up at him. Alan pulled the gun switch, but the guns did not fire and within the next second or two the Me-262 rolled over into a dive! In less than a second, he rolled the P-51 into a dive to chase him with guns switches now on. Shortly he was at the maximum controllable air speed of the P-51 at Mach 0.8. The airplane began buffeting and he throttled back slightly to slow his air speed enough to regain flight control.

He increased his airspeed to full throttle again as the aircraft came out of compression to a controllable airspeed and quickly maneuvered to get the Jet in his gun sight. He fired again at a range of approximately 1200 feet and fired and saw incendiary flashes on the 262's rudder. His second firing was from an eighteen-hundred-foot range. His tracers were below the jet due to their separation. He repeated the compressibility recovery cycle once more and at a range of twenty-five hundred feet saw his incendiaries flash on the ME-262's canopy and it's dive suddenly increased from fifty to seventy-five degrees and entered the clouds.

Alan leveled off at the top of the clouds and he looked at his altimeter that read just under two thousand feet. He knew this altimeter reading, due to different air pressure set in England could be in error a plus or minus (+ or -) two hundred (200) feet and also knew he was in the Kaltenkirchen area where the hills below the clouds were from five to fifteen hundred (500 to 1500) feet above the lowest terrain level. He circled around the area for a few seconds thinking if the jet didn't reappear, he had to assume the Me-262 didn't make it. He thought, "The jets ground speed had to be over five hundred miles (500) mph or more when he entered the clouds at an approximate seventy-five-degree angle. The jet only had at the very most, three thousand (3000) feet for a safe pull out. At his dive angle and at airspeed over 500 mph, Alan assumed the jet had to crash.

He turned to the west heading they were on before the

Me-262's appeared and began a steady climb back to twenty-six thousand (26000) feet. As he was climbing, he realized that when the Me-262 appeared in his windshield and had he been able to fire his guns he might not be here anymore. He thought, "If my gun switches were on, I had plenty of time to hit that 262 in my windshield. Hitting him with six all fifty caliber guns may have either made him explode or break up a second later. Either way I would have been hit by his debris and gone down with him. That would have been a costly victory if whoever tapped me on the shoulder hadn't been there and also make sure my gun switches were not on."

Alan reached the bomber stream heading northwest back toward England, flew along side of them, and luckily found his squadron and flight leader. When he pulled into formation on his right side, his flight leader turned and nodded his head several times while looking directly at him. The remainder of the mission was uneventful.

He parked on the 'A' Flight ramp next Schueler. Alan's mission flight leader parked in the next ramp and was standing next to his plane, in the adjacent ramp, waiting for him. Alan climbed out of his cockpit and walked toward his flight leader. Before he reached him, he shouted, "Where the hell were you? Why didn't you call me when you left me?"

He wouldn't let Alan explain anything about his snap roll or calling him on the radio. He angrily climbed into the line truck that took them to the ready room. Schueler heard all the shouting on the flight line and the flight leader again questioning him in a commanding tone.

Schueler approached Alan's flight leader and said, "Look, you didn't announce you were going to attack. We have to wait for your command that would have included telling us to drop our tanks. We, not concentrating on your flight, saw you drop your tanks, and I could see Alan didn't have a chance to drop his when you pulled up sharply. That's when he did a two and a half snap roll and lost sight of him below us. Two other pilots saw his snap roll and were too occupied to see what happened to him and thought he was a goner.

Alan's flight leader became embarrassed for climbing all over him when he realized there were a reasonable explanation. Thus, he didn't comment when Alan filed his Me-262 claim at the end of the debriefing. The Intelligence officer received a denial, a week later, for the claim because there wasn't any pilot witness and his gun film did not sufficiently define any hits, also, no one was aware of any pilot being able to confirm the altitude of the cloud level in the area. The Me-262's angle of entry was the only thing confirmed.

Ten days later the 385th squadron CO heard of Alan's claim and of it being denied. He verified the cloud level was 2000 feet in that general area on the day of Alan's claim and he notified his CO. The claim was resubmitted with the confirming altitude level of two thousand feet and a week later Alan's claim was awarded as a probable.

England 8th AF - Ceases Bombing Germany
Sunday, 20 May 1945

He mailed ten letters and received sixteen from Michelle by 6 May 1945. One letter told of Aunt Marie having a long discussion about her life with Uncle Hubere. She changed his mind about Alan and made him realize Alan was not one of those boasting American soldiers he encountered after the liberation. He then ceased pushing Claude on Michelle. All her letters were filled with love, marriage and occasionally her desire for their child. She didn't answer his question, 'why a child now' under the existing circumstances? That evening he wrote a letter attempting to convince her he wanted her and their child, but not necessarily now.

6 May 1945

My Dearest Michelle,

I've told you and you know we can't think of a child as long as I have to face combat conditions. It does appear the war in Europe will end soon, but that does not give me much freedom. I talked to our Operations officer and was told it was very likely I would be sent to the Pacific because it doesn't appear that war will end soon. I do not have enough combat time in the European Theater to be immune from an assignment to fly in the Pacific Theater and that makes it mentally, impossible to think of having a child etc... etc... etc.

I love you and will truly enjoy our creating, not yours or mine, but 'our' child and be there to watch he or she grow with a couple others who will follow. I want a family filled with happiness with a wife like you giving us children to love and raise...etc.

When the wars are finally settled, and if I survive, I'll be there waiting for your response to my marriage proposal, if your still available for me. My greatest fear is that you won't believe me and by the time I'm in a position to return to civilian life you may have found someone else. As long as you live there will be no one other than you I want to grow old with.

I love you, there is no one else,

Your Alan forever.

Alan was hospitalized with the flu for 11 days, (Monday 7 to Tuesday 17 May). He flew both of the last two missions in Europe on Thursday. 19 and Friday 20 May 1945. All missions ceased as flown by 8th AF from Sat. 21st April to May 7th (end of war in Europe). He flew 20 total missions with the 8th AF from 24 Feb. to 20 Apr. 1945. There were two pilot losses during the last eight escort missions he flew.

Eleven

PACIFIC ASSIGNMENT

June thru September 1945
Alan's remaining time in England

Alan asked his CO, on Friday 1 June, if it was possible to get a leave to Brussels or Paris? He informed him that no leaves to the continent were permitted until future notice. On 12 June, a Monday, the CO began interviewing each pilot assigned to the squadron. When he got to Alan, he asked him if he would like to remain with the Squadron for the Pacific Theater? Alan asked if there were any other options available for him? The CO informed him any pilots not selected would return to the United States. These pilots would be assigned to a Pacific squadron as new replacements. "That could put you on the bottom of the priority list and maybe you will end up flying as green sixteen again."

He then asked, "What will happen if I stay with your squadron?"

"I promise you this one, I made you a flight leader in May before this war came to an end. When we get back to the states, we all will receive a ninety-day rest and recuperation and leave. I'll put tracks on you and make you a captain as soon as I can before you go home on a thirty-day leave. After the leaves we'll go to a base in California and check out in P-51Hs that have been modified for escorting B-29s on long flights, like Okinawa to Japan.

That offer was enough for him to decide to remain with his squadron. The CO seemed happy, and Alan asked, "Do you have any idea when we will leave England for the States?"

"Sometime between the end of July and the middle of August as things stand right now."

"If we are here through the month of July, do you think I could have a leave to Brussels or even Paris sometime during the month?'

"Alan; I will do what I can to get you a leave, but I can't promise anything. All I can tell you right now is; Division froze all leaves until further notice. I have no idea what Division has in store for us. I imagine a lot of groups have people wanting leaves and I'm sure they are aware of this. They know we among other Groups waiting to hear something about permissible leaves. So, just wait like everyone else and, I can't promise, but they should be able to permit leaves after the first of July. If they open up, there shouldn't be a problem for a five-to-seven-day leave, not to Brussels, but, maybe seven days to London? I feel fairly sure something like that might be available."

That evening, 15 June, he had to think about which of Michelle's two addresses to mail a letter. He couldn't make up his mind, then, decided to mail two letters, one to Phillipe's apartment in Brussels, and the other to her home address in Leuven explaining the existing conditions. 'The letter explained he couldn't get a leave to Brussels, but, if he can get one to London in July could she meet him there?' He mailed the letter at Group Headquarters, as soon as he could, early the next morning.

Leuven, 21 June 1945, Aunt Marie's House

Michelle rode to Brussels with her uncle from her Leuven home, Thursday afternoon, to serve at the Brussels Red Cross Club that evening plus the weekend. On her arrival at the café, Phillipe told her, "You received a letter addressed here from Alan this morning." She thanked him, took the letter, sat at a table, and had to calm her trembling so she could open it. Phillipe noticing, she didn't open the letter asked, "What is the matter, Michelle?"

"I am too frightened to open it. I fear he is being sent home and cannot come to see me before leaving." He came over to her with two small glasses of red wine, sat down with her and asked, "Shall I open it for you?"

She again thanked him, this time for his compassion and the wine. She used a knife from the table setting to open the letter. She held it up and closed her eyes for a moment, then opened the letter and began reading:

15 June 1945

My lovely Michelle,

My dear Michelle, I love you. I can't get a leave to anyplace on the continent. That is, not to Paris, Brussels...or wherever. I may be able to have a leave to London in July. If possible, it would be the second or third week of July. I will send you a letter as soon as I know any dates. I'm going to ask for seven days." She stopped reading aloud and continued reading about his arrangement to stay with his Group if they go to the Pacific Theater after the end of July." He included telling her how much he loved and missed her. Then, closed with, "I will never forget the last night and morning in her apartment...etc... etc.

With Love to my dearest Michelle,

Alan

When the Red Cross Club closed at 2300hrs that night, she went directly to her café apartment, slept there and, after a fast breakfast, left for Leuven at 0839hrs the next morning. It was Friday and she used Mimi's bicycle, which was still there. She rode directly, without stopping, to her Aunt Marie's house. There she approached her with the critical question, "Aunt Marie do you think uncle Hubere would be willing to make an arrangement for me to visit London in July?"

"May I ask why?"

"To see Alan before he leaves for the United States. They refused his request to come here, since he is on a schedule to possibly fly in the Pacific for the remainder of the war."

"I do not think Hubere would. You know his attitude toward Alan."

"Would you please try?"

"He will be home this evening for the weekend. Do you want to have dinner with us? We could address him at dinner and if necessary, maybe he would permit us to go if I went with you as a chaperon. Our chauffeur will take you, if it is too dark to ride your bicycle, when you want to go home to Beatrix. Why not phone her now and tell her where you are."

"Aunt Marie you are so brilliant and so caring, I love you."

They sat in the sitting room and spent the remainder of the afternoon talking about Alan and what her intentions with him were until Hubere arrived at 1845hrs. They ate dinner quietly with a very few exchanges of words. Hubere was suspicious of Michelle's being there and felt she was up to something instead of being in Brussels at the Red Cross Club.

As he finished his dinner, he saw both Marie and Michelle were not completely finishing their dinner and asked Marie, "All right, you two are up to something? I recommend we go to the sitting room and discuss whatever is on your minds."

Marie and Michelle sat in the love seat facing Hubere on the armchair and Marie asked, "Hubere could you get a travel voucher and arrange for Michelle to stay London?"

"It is that American pilot is it not! Michelle, I can read that all over your face. You want me to do something for you and that American pilot to promote your relationship. I will not do anything that may prolong your relationship until the Atlantic separates you!"

"Uncle, you don't understand. I love him and that means more than all the money in the world to me. There are people who lived their entire life not knowing what love is. I have fallen in love and understand the joy that comes with it."

"You know he cannot provide for you as you live here. And the status of the people he associates with is beneath you. It will ultimately separate you and you deserve more than anything he can provide. Here you have friends of your social class that you have known and schooled with. You have enjoyed each other's company and grown with them through the years. If you do not wish to marry Claude, I am sure there are numerous successful men, I know, from families you grew up with who would love your attention."

Michelle gave some thought of what could persuade him and asked, "What if Aunt Marie comes with me as my chaperone? She would be with me at all times, and I could find if I really love him as much as I think I now do. Maybe I will not after seeing him for a week."

"Yes Hubere, I think Michelle has a very good possible solution. They only knew each other for three days. A week with him and us together, every day, could resolve knowing him much better to convince her 'he is not the man she thinks she wants' for a lifetime."

"All right! Let me think about this over night and decide in the morning."

That made Michelle so happy she threw her arms around his body and hugged him as tight as she could and said, "I knew you were a wonderful understanding uncle who would provide me with the opportunity to see him one last time," and thinking she had to say more added, "And give me the time to make up my mind and possibly end our relationship instead of going through life not knowing if he was or was not the man for me."

Michelle was the first one in the kitchen, at 7:30am, the next morning. Hubere and Marie arrived for breakfast at

8:15am. The words flowed from Michelle, "Uncle Hubere have you decided about London yet?"

"Your aunt and I talked about this later last night, and she convinced me she would not let you out of her sight if she was with you. I accept her promise and will arrange for two good rooms at the Ritz for you. Do you have the dates you plan to meet him?"

"I shall write to him immediately and have him provide the days he can be in London."

Four days later, 27 June he received Michelle's letter answer, "Yes! I can be with you in London as you asked. A good room shall be reserved for you at the Ritz Hotel for you leave, just tell me on the day you want to meet and the days you will be there, and I will be there?"

That afternoon Alan asked his CO if he could have a seven day leave for London in July as he said may be possible. On Thursday morning, 28 June, the CO said he would see if he could clear a July leave through Division that afternoon. He saw Alan at dinner and said he would be able to get him a leave 'after 1 July' and asked when did he want this leave?

"How about seven days beginning with 12 July?"

The CO's answer, "Consider it done, 12 July through 19 July?"

He asked no more questions and hurriedly finished his lunch and went to his room. When he left Schueler still eating said, "It looks like Alan is really hooked on that Belgian girl."

Everyone laughed and the CO said, "Maybe I'm going to be responsible for a problem?"

In the letter to Michelle he included, "Can you meet me in the Ritz lobby, in London at noon on 12 July? After we meet and I check in I'll take you somewhere for lunch."

Saturday, 7 July, he received her answer,

"I should be at Ritz Hotel, Thursday, 12 July at noon. Please do not be late. I shall be on pins and needles until I have my arms around you! If for some reason I'm delayed, please check at the desk. I will have a message for you."

12 July 1945: Thursday: London, England

~

Michelle and her aunt checked in the Ritz Hotel at ten fifteen (10:15 AM) on 12 July. The manager, who was waiting for her appearance, immediately recognized, and greeted Marie as they entered with, "How is your husband, Minister Petremont. Is he not to be with you on this visit?"

Her response was, "No he is not. We want to register two rooms for us, if possibly the bridal suite for my niece and her fiancée. He is an American pilot." The manager complied, registered them with the bridal suite and a good room on the same floor. He gave them two keys, one for the suite and the other for the good room. She followed that with "We shall go to our rooms, brush up a bit and return to the lobby and wait for his arrival. Please have a bell boy handle our luggage." And, if he should arrive before we return to the lobby have him sit in that chair, pointing to it, and tell him Michele shall be here shortly. I would appreciate your welcoming him with dignity. You do understand what I am asking?"

He assured her he would notify his counter clerks to watch for and treat him accordingly. They took the keys and had a bellboy carry their bags. They arrived on the fourth floor and first went to Marie's room. *On the Way Michelle asked her aunt, "You only reserved two rooms. Where will Alan stay? "*

"With you in the Bridal Suite. I shall leave you two alone and shall arrange to visit the numerous friends we have here. Just leave a note at the desk for me telling when you will possibly leave, and we shall get together for our departure."

"With a room and the suite will Uncle Hubere be suspicious of where Alan roomed?"

"We shall tell him we arranged the room for him, and we occupied the suite. How do you expect to determine if he is the man you want for a lifetime if you do not sleep with him? Do not concern yourself on how we cover for our meals. You charge all your needs here to the hotel and I will pay for all of the expenses."

"Aunt Marie you are so wonderful and understanding!"

Alan walked in the Ritz Hotel at 1215hrs. He was amazed by the interior of the lobby. It was luxurious, like one of the French Louis' interior designs and walked to the long check in counter. He wasn't sure where to stand to get the attention of one of the three clerks talking to two people. No one approached him and he stood there several minutes. Then, suddenly one of the clerks left the person he was talking to and looked like he was going to Alan. He walked passed him and he heard the clerk ask," Can I help you Mademoiselle?"

Alan turned around to see who he was talking to and saw Michelle standing there smiling from ear to ear. Then as he came close to her, she threw her arms around him and passionately kissed him. The clerk lost for words, stumbling said, "You know this man? Is...is...this the Monsieur you have been waiting for."

Michelle told the clerk, "Please get the manager for me!"

He dashed off and into a room behind the long counter and brought out the manager. He came to Michelle, and she told him, "I did not appreciate the way my fiancé was ignored and had to stand at this counter for several minutes and was not recognized after my aunt described him as an American pilot. I do not see any other American pilot in the lobby?"

The manager apologized promising her he will assure everyone in the hotel will know who her fiancé is and shall treat him accordingly. She graciously and in an upset manner said she would accept that apology and remain in the hotel if he does not waver from his promise. Michelle took him to their room. When she opened the door he asked, "What is this?"

"It is a Bridal Suite. The grandeur you see is for us. I am not forcing you into a marriage, but I want this to be something we shall never forget if you have to leave me, to go to the Pacific and I have to wait, for heaven knows how long."

"Michelle I can't afford this. A couple days here will cost more that I earn in a month."

"Do not be concerned about the charges. They were taken care of by Aunt Marie. I wrote you that Uncle Hubere has not changed his attitude toward you as a person, but Aunt Marie who is here with me had him accept you as a friend of the family! He lectured her and me about you before we left Brussels. You did not receive that letter?"

"Aunt Marie is with you? I didn't get any letter like that. Anyway, how does that pay our bills here. I don't want to sign a hotel bill I will have to pay for later. Why don't we check out and go to a Red Cross Club and get rooms I can afford?"

"Alan...Alan you do not understand European social society. This room was arranged by...Aunt Marie. You are now a guest of the Belgian Government, and I am supposedly your fiancée and escort. Do not feel obligated for anything. Please enjoy this with me. Aunt Marie will meet you at lunch and is going to go her separate way from us while we are here. We shall meet together again on our last day. That is the way she desires it to be. This is our opportunity to be with each other without any interference."

"OK, I don't understand. Where do we go for lunch?"

"We, you, Aunt Marie, and I shall eat here, all I need is something light. Are you hungry?"

"All I want is a good salad if they have that and a cup of real coffee, no more chicory."

During lunch Aunt Marie and Michelle asked him if he had seen the London Bridge, the Big Ben clock, Buckingham Palace and the Changing of the Guard or Saint Paul's Cathedral. He said he was only familiar with Piccadilly Circus and a theater near there because both were near the Red Cross club where he roomed with friends on a three-day leave in May.

"You never wrote you were in London and what were you doing in Piccadilly Circus. I know what goes on there. You promised you would always be faithful to me, were you?"

"Michelle don't get this all distorted out of proportion. I went there with two pilots from my squadron who wanted to show me what takes place there. My God! Those damn girls thought they were the pick of the world. They wanted twenty or thirty pounds for a night with them. I told one of them, no girl is worth that much for even a week."

"NO GIRL? How long have you believed 'no girl' is worth that?"

His face turned beet red as he said, "M...M... Michelle; I...I... didn't.... mean really no girl. I... I wasn't directing that at you. I...m...m...meant the prostitutes parading around there."

"So?"

"Jees..., I don't think I know what I'm talking about now. Could we forget this?"

She broke out with a big smile and said, "I understand, you don't have to say anything more. I do know about those girls. Some of them were pretty, were they not?"

She had him trapped. He felt he couldn't say anything without getting in trouble. Thus, he smiled at her and nodded his head yes, a couple of times, then changed to some no's. She came close to him, still smiling, kissed him and said, "I think I know what you meant."

Aunt Marie never said a word, she just enjoyed what Michelle put Alan though and said, "I shall leave you love birds now. Alan, please take care of Michelle. I shall see you again before we leave." She kissed both of them and left to a waiting limousine.

That afternoon Michelle took him to numerous places around London mentioned at lunch. They walked to some places and took a taxi to others when needed, like to Saint Paul's. They were back in the hotel at 1830hrs, washed and went to dinner. At dinner, Alan was hesitant to order because of the high prices for soup, salads, and a la carte dinners. The dining room food prices seemed so expensive he didn't know what to order. He asked Michelle if there was a, not to exceed price, limit on what he ordered. Michelle said, "The food here is expensive, but the food you receive is pre-war quality. Do not be concerned of what you order, I told you we, you and I are guests of the Belgian Government. Then, Michelle proceeded to order lobster tails a la carte for both of them.

He was so elated after they finished their dinner he had to say, "I never knew anything could taste so good. Where did you find out about the taste of lobster tails?"

"Alan, you lived too far from the oceans to admire some of the food that it provides. I have so much to teach you about the better things in life."

"You are the only good thing I need in my life. Everything wonderful will flow from that." Michelle signed for the dinner, and they stopped in the lobby where Michelle asked, "Would you care to go to a movie theater tonight? There is one near and only a few blocks walking distance. The theater is showing the movie 'His Girl Friday' with Howard Hawks and Cary Grant. The critics claim it is a splendid comedy."

Alan said that was fine with him and they left the hotel at 1830hrs. They got out of the theater just before 2130hrs and walked for a half hour talking about Ivy League universities. Arriving at the hotel they went directly to their room. Got in their pajamas, he wore the one she gave him, and they sat on a long soft couch listening to the radio playing the late 30's and 40's tunes for an hour while they were petting on the davenport. The night was another one of a Michelle special, trying and hoping she would get pregnant. She told him not to use any condoms he would enjoy their union so much more. He agreed, but couldn't understand why she was so insistent?

The next day, Friday 13 July, was Alan's birthday. Michelle woke up early, then, woke him at eight thirty and made him stay in bed. He was going to get out of bed, and she told him to just sit up. She placed a bed tray over his groin and thighs containing a plate with bacon, eggs, potatoes, toast, and a cup of good coffee.

Michelle led Alan directly to the bathtub when he got out of bed. She tried, but, he pleaded, "After all that...last night, I didn't get much sleep. I'm really tired. Won't you let me recuperate during the day light hours?"

She agreed saying, "All right now you store up some for me that is potent." He knew what that was all about, and they both dressed, went down to the dining room where Michelle, ordered her breakfast and had waiters bring out a birthday cake and everyone sang 'Happy Birthday Alan. He was always so easy to embarrass he sat there blushing the entire time they sang to him, and she is standing next to him topped that off by leaning down to him and giving him a long passionate kiss. Everyone applauded and when things settled down, they brought out her breakfast. He sat quietly while drinking a couple cups of coffee while she had her breakfast.

They walked to nearby Green Park, sat a little and eventually to Buckingham Palace. They watched the 'Changing of the Guard' at noon and returned to the hotel. After washing up and having lunch Michelle asked him if would like to see some of the finer structures in London. Alan hadn't and she took him to the nearby Tower of London, then, back toward and to Saint Paul's Cathedral that afternoon. That evening Michelle enticed him to see a ballet with her in Sadler's Wells Theater. Later that evening Michelle asked, "How did you like the ballet?"

He told her, "It was OK, I don't think I would care for another one."

"I had lessons in dance as a teen-ager and I once had a bit part in a school ballet."

"I'm sorry. I didn't mean it wasn't good, I just don't appreciate that kind of dancing."

The rest of the days, the 15th through the 18th they went to Private Schools and watched a 'Cricket' match. In the afternoon she took him to watch a Rugby Football team practice. They spent a couple of evenings at a movie theater. On another, she took him to the partially reconditioned Covet Garden Theater where they saw an hour and a half of excerpts from Broadway shows including the now popular 'Oklahoma' that was wonderfully presented. They left shortly after nine o'clock and returned to their hotel and took a seat in the dining room where both men and women could be served alcohol and had two glasses of dry red wine before retiring.

That night Alan asked, "Are you trying to get pregnant by me not using condoms."

"Don't be silly! I menstruated just before coming to London. Nothing will happen."

That was all a big lie, she knew she was ready. Then every night was the same as the first and she let Alan rest all day.

The 18th and last full day, after breakfast she took him to Stratford-on-Avon and a visit to Shakespeare's home. They toured the site of his home that was demolished in the eighth century by an eccentric owner because of the magnitude of visitations.

During the six days they were together Michelle did everything she could to become pregnant. On Wednesday evening, Alan's sixth day after they had an affair Michelle acted strangely. First, she passionately kissed him every few minutes saying, "I love you, but never knew I could love you so much." Then, she waited on his every desire or need every moment for the rest of that day. He couldn't do anything without her at his side saying, "I can do this or that. You rest,

I shall do anything that needs to be done. I do not want you to tire yourself."

And Alan did everything he could do from the very beginning of the first night there to that moment before he fell asleep that night to discourage her from becoming pregnant. 'They made love as often as Michelle could get him to co-operate,' Alan was truly naive. He talked about them both going to an Ivy League University together as often as possible to stress the need to not get pregnant so they could both graduate approximately at the same time. He typically said, "When we go to the university together, you in Med. school and I in engineering. If we have a child I'll drop out of my program and get a job to support us, until you complete your education. Then you. ....." She stopped him there putting her hand over his mouth.

"You are so concerned about children and expenses. I shall try not to become pregnant, and we shall not have any financial problems. I have told you more than once, I will have an income more than enough for the rest of our lives."

Alan didn't feel the same way, but to avoid any further misunderstanding he said, "Please forgive me I'm sure you know about that much better than I do. Mon precieux-aime, I couldn't think of being with you and not wanting all the love we have for each other." Then laughing said, "Just give me some time to rest occasionally?"

Aunt Marie made an appearance at lunch before Alan had

to catch a train to his base. The three had lunch and Aunt Marie was aware they were in love and told Alan she was happy for them. "If you are the man Michelle feels she wants for a lifetime, who am I to judge differently? I hope this occasion has settled your relationship once and for all!"

They had a sad parting and Michelle cried again as Alan got on the train and she watched until it was out of site, then, returned to the Ritz and Aunt Marie. They remained another night and, on the way to Brussels, Marie asked Michele if she took all the proper measures to avoid getting pregnant and Michelle said she did. Later in their discussions about the week their Aunt Marie suggested they tell Hubere that she was undecided and believe there may be someone else for you in Belgium.

Sizing of his squadron to technical order strength was completed shortly after his return to his base. A few days later CO Duneforte confirmed he was the 'E' Flight Leader, a position, specified in the tech orders. A week later, the last in July, the Group was scheduled to participate in a mock air to air battle. The opponents were Czechoslovakian pilots in RAF Spitfires versus the 378th stripped down P-51s to simulate air to air against a Jap Zero.

Alan led 'D' flight for the engagement, and they encountered the Spitfires over southern Scotland. The Czechs' were the attackers and came at 378th in singles and two at a time. After a few minutes of maneuvering Alan was in position for a camera kill on a Spitfire and the Mock Battle was canceled and the CO's voice came over their radios, "Let's go home."

After landing and getting debriefed he informed his squadron two Czech Spitfires trying to make a pass on the same P-51 had a mid air collision with their Spitfires.

The first week in August the 378th prepared for shipment to the United States for their 90-day R & R. The pilots' foot-lockers were sent to Blackball on 8 August. Pilots had only a small supply of clothes, those they were wearing and those packed in their B-4 Bags. They were getting anxious as the tenth day of August approached and they were to ship for the States on the fifteenth.

The Pacific War abruptly ended 15 August 1945 by the nuclear bombing of Japan. On the morning of 20 August Alan's CO interviewed him again. He asked, "Would you want to return to the US or take a short German Occupation assignment and travel around Europe. Go to Paris, Switzerland and, smiling, maybe Brussels."

"How long of an occupation tour are we talking about."

"Six to eight months at the most. You will be back home by April."

"Could I think about this for a day or two?"

"Sure, but let me know by Thursday the 23rd."

He went to the club for lunch and while eating thought, "Maybe occupation duty is the wrong thing to do?" But then, there's Michelle waiting for me, I think? And I promised I'd come for her when or before I knew I'm going home." Questioning himself confused him, so, he went to his room and laid on his bunk to think about all and any other factors to help make a decision.

He knew he would never get home in time to register for the fall semester, even if he left England next week, which was very unlikely. Then thought, "By the time I'd be processed out of some separation base it would be mid September and too late to register at any Ivy League University, besides Michelle won't graduate until January 1946.

All the guys released from the squadron to go to the Pacific were on the US probably out by August and have probably loaded the universities by now. Well, that's it, I'll go to Germany and see what the CO can do to get me a decent assignment."

Later that afternoon he met his CO and said accept the Occupation assignment. His CO told him he'd try to get him a good assignment, so, all Alan could do was wait.

Twelve

ASSIGNMENT: OCCUPATION

Friday 31 August 1945
358th Fighter Group - Germany

Alan was not aware, until that Friday, how much the CO had gone out of his way to have him reassigned to his 9th Air Force Group. He and 357th squadron fighter pilot, Lieutenant Thom Robertson, was also assigned to the same Fighter Group. They had their footlockers returned and were prepared to be taken by C-47 to the 358th's German Air Base by Wednesday, 5 September.

Friday, 7 September to Monday 31 December 1945
Germany and France

Alan and Tom left England at 0830hrs and arrived at the 358th Fighter Group base at 1055hrs. They met their Squadron CO, Major Jim Cayhill, in his line hanger who arranged to take them to Base Headquarters after greeting Alan back and welcoming Tom with him. A line truck picked them up a half hour later while Cayhill was updating himself on what Alan did in the 8th.

At Base Headquarters Alan found 1st Lt. Jonathon Roberts (fighter pilot), who greeted them and now was assigned as the Base Personnel Officer. Roberts ask for and they gave him their records and he had them fill out a few new ones, then filed everything.

Alan asked Roberts, "What's with this Base this stuff, where's Group Headquarters?"

Jon told him, "They are one and the same. They just refer to it as Base because our P-51s are almost gone. We'll get into all this later. The line truck that brought you is waiting for you. He knows and will take you and Tom to the 357th barracks.

There, a pilot, Ray Londre, who Alan didn't know met them and lead them down the long hall to a room in the northeast corner of the barracks. Ray pointed out the door to his room and told them he'd wait and to knock when they're ready for lunch. Their room was big with two beds, two clothes lockers and two desks. Pillows and cases, two sheets and two blankets were stacked on their beds. They were quite happy with their new home. After they were settled in their room, they went to Ray's room, and he led them to the Officer's Dining Room for lunch.

He took them to a table of pilots, and they met, Bob Andrews, and Nick Towers who were also 357th pilots. After having lunch and a cognac with coke Alan returned to his room and wrote Michelle a letter including his new APO address.

Two days after his arrival, Sunday, he met Ivy League friend, Harvey Daniels at dinner. Still there, he was about to be shipped home. Typically, Daniels, had to tell everyone at dinner about Alan's Ivy League athletics. The base Special Services officer, 1st Lt. Claire Strait sitting with Henry James and Joe Notaro, football player, were at the same table. They overheard everything Daniels said. Claire invited Alan to the club, next to the dining room, for a drink after dinner.

In the club Alan asked him, "Is there anything else to drink beside cognac and/or coke?"

Claire said he was sorry to inform him that was all they could get and told him, "Maybe the Club Officer can answer any of your questions."

He got around to asking Alan about football at his Ivy League university. He told him he wasn't first string but was fortunate enough to be his back up. He explained that position as being a relief man and above a second-string position man.

Claire said, “You mean, you were as good as the first stringer, but not better than him?”

“Well sort of. The first-string guy had good credentials. He was an All American the previous year and at the other guard position was an Honorable Mention guy. The team was loaded. The coach made the team National Champions a year before I got there.”

Then, Claire knew he was more than qualified and asked him to join the base football team. He agreed and played his first game, at their base, on Saturday 15 September 1945.

That afternoon he had the biggest shock of his life. He received a letter from Michelle smelling as if doused in passionate, bath powder and bubbling over with exalted joy and love.

September 6, 1945

Oh, My Alan,

“I have been waiting to hear from you. We did it, you wonderful lover, I am pregnant. Remember that great second last day, Wednesday the 16th, of your leave in London with me? I felt that might have been ‘my day’. Oh...yes it was and now I am so happy, next April my Aunt will become a grand Aunt.

I thought, that when this event would really occur, she would not be elated, but be angry. I was so wrong to worry! She's exalted and seems to be so more than I am. We plan to keep this from Uncle Hubere until I become noticeable. Etc..... etc.

She closed with, "When can you come to Brussels for me? I need and want you more than ever right now!"

Forever your Lover,

Michelle

Alan told Strait about the letter. He said, "Talk to Jim Watson, Club Officer if you want to go to Brussels. He takes a week to go there and back at the end of each month for liquor rations. From that moment on he discussed everything with Claire Strait who was five years older than him and also a very settled person. He was always under complete control of himself despite the many verbal jabs he received because he was a pilot and had to meet with base Ground Officers every Monday morning in the roll of Base Armament Officer.

He and Alan became close friends and thereafter did many things together. They began rabbit (hare) hunting in the morning that fall. After the first week of hunting and getting a hare, children began following them all over the fields. As neither Strait nor Alan liked to eat rabbits, they agreed to give any hosen (German for hare) they shot to the kids. Everyone in the local village knew when they were hunting. Soon numerous children, ages 5 to 16, followed them all the while they hunted, and the bigger and older ones wanted to take all the hosen shot. For each hare shot they had to control the kids. Claire suggested that they select which child would get the kill.

In a few weeks, over twenty-five children were following them. Many had not received hosen. Seeing the ones that did get a rabbit run home shouting 'Hosen, Hosen, Hosen' gave Strait and Alan an emotional high. These kids were running home to put meat on the table. Soon the surrounding farmers knew the hunters and treated them as friends.

These were humble people who couldn't have done anything about Hitler who had lured some of their children into Nazi-ism and lost most in the war and now began to appreciate these American pilots. They were not permitted to have any kind of weapon thus, through this gesture of putting meat on their table they were gratefully accepted. Shortly they invited Claire and Alan and a few others to come to their fall Saturday night dances.

They planned to hunt every day possible until the first snow of December. On two days early in that month they shot four deer and had some kids bring their parents to get them the kids ran so fast their feet were almost off the ground and in five minutes they returned with a dozen adult men. In their best English they proclaimed their adulation that overwhelmed Alan. Accepting their grateful gesture brought tears of joy into his eyes.

The deeper snow came, and Claire took Alan to the indoor range shooting. He had armament men oiling weapons to keep them in good working order. There, Claire showed Alan how to disassemble the M1, the .45 machine gun, the carbine and the .45 automatic for cleaning. Claire was really good with the .45 automatic. He put seven shots in a twelve-inch circle on the target torso of a man-sized cardboard target from one seven shot clip. Claire taught Alan the best way to hold an automatic to increase his accuracy enough for him to put five bullets in the twelve- inch circle on the torso target.

Jon Roberts, an avid bridge card player, heard about Alan being fairly good at bridge, but never played with him. One evening after dinner Roberts asked Alan to play a few bridge hands as his partner one evening. Roberts asked him if he would be his permanent bridge partner after recognizing he knew how to bid very well and made almost all of his bids. Alan accepted the invitation, and they played most evenings together. As partners they became very well fitted and eventually became the base bridge team to beat.

The undesirable thing about the club was the limited kind of alcohol available. The club bar was supplied with only Cognac and Coca Cola; thus, a Cognac and Coke became the occupation's Martini. One could also drink a plain cognac or plain Coca Cola, that was it. Alan met the Officers Club officer, Jim Watson, at dinner on Sunday 30 September. He soon became aware that Alan was receiving letters from a girl in Brussels via club conversations started by Tom. During their conversations Alan asked Watson if he made scheduled trips, Liquor Runs, to Paris and Brussels at the end of each month?

During the first weekend of October Watson approached Alan for a favor and would reciprocate by including him on a Paris and Brussels Liquor Run. He received his requested favor and promised Alan he would be on the 27 October Liquor Run. Watson had to make arrangements to get him included on the orders for the Liquor Run. As soon as he knew their travel dates, he informed Alan.

Sunday the 7th he immediately wrote Michelle saying, "I will be in Brussels approximately on the 28th of October. I hope you're still my fiancée."

He got a letter back from her ten days later dated 12 October. Her entire letter related to, "I suffered a miscarriage on Wednesday the fifth of October. We lost our daughter. Now you don't have to worry about me being pregnant anymore. You never seemed to want our child and now you received your wish. Will I ever see you again? I still love you anyway."

The more times he reread the letter the worst he felt. He weakened so much and finally broke down and cried. He kneeled and prayed asking, "LORD why? She was a good person. She always wanted the baby. Why did she lose it? And why does she think I'm so happy about it. Maybe YOU shouldn't have permitted us to meet, and this would never have happened. How can I tell her how hurt I am for her?"

He talked to the Roman Catholic Chaplain about his relationship with Michelle and how worried he was about her miscarriage. The Chaplain told him, he accepted the conversation as a confession and would give him communion on Sunday if he came to their mass. On Sunday 14 October Alan was there for communion and talked to the Chaplain, after mass, who asked, "Do you feel better now?" You should, our LORD understands you."

"Michelle is Catholic. How do I tell her? She thinks I'm happy over her losing our child."

"Write and tell her you came to me, told me everything and I gave you our communion and we talked. I believe she still loves you and didn't mean anything bad in her letter. Go write her right now while this is all fresh in your mind."

He hurriedly walked to his barracks room and sat right down to write her a letter.

14 October 1945

Dearest Michelle,

You may not want to believe how devastated I was when

I received your letter. I always told you we shouldn't have a child now. That never meant I would be happy if you lost a child. I was so distraught about the whole thing I didn't know what to do. Well…I went to our Catholic Chaplain and told him about us. I'm not Roman Catholic, as you know, but he accepted my telling about us as a confession and gave me communion this morning. I feel better now. I hope you understand how much you mean to me and find this letter makes you feel a little better too? I want our children as much as much as you want one from me. That time will come soon too.

How did this all happen? Did you fall down some steps at the apartment? Or did you have an accident with a car on your bicycle. I hope you didn't eat something bad and get some sort of food poisoning. Are you all right now please let me know as soon as possible. I won't stop worrying about you until I hear everything with you is all right."

He closed with, "Did Aunt Marie know you were pregnant? Did uncle Hubere find out? If he did, was he happy about it? You take good care of yourself while you're recovering. I'll be with you as soon as I'm able! Again, I ask you please take special care of yourself. I just don't know how to tell you, and please believe me. I feel so bad I can't even think straight anymore. I do love you more than you want to believe! Please understand me.

Forever your love,

Alan

Thirteen

LIQUOR RUN to BRUSSELS

Saturday, 27 October to Friday, 02 November 1945:
Liquor Run

At 0745 AM two tech. sergeants Walter Zelinski with George Sabol driving a Six-by-Six truck stopped at the Officers Club to pick up Watson and Alan. They were waiting for them while drinking their morning coffee after breakfast. They came out of the dining room and Sobol was to drive the initial leg to the Rhine River. Watson and Alan rode in the cab and Zelinski was in back laying on a mattress in a sleeping bag to stay warm.

They left the club at 0830hrs, Saturday, 27 October, and scheduled a return to begin between 0830hrs and 0900hrs, on

Friday, 2 November, from Brussels. By 1510hrs they crossed the Rhine River, that is about two thirds of the way to Metz. They stopped, got out, and stretched a bit, switched drivers with Zelinski driving and Sabol riding in back.

They arrived at the Metz O' Club at 1750hrs. Alan got out of the truck while Jim gave his men some instructions. Five minutes later, Jim led Alan into the Club and found the Club Officer had been waiting for them. He knew they were coming and kept the kitchen open to feed them. Watson introduced Alan to Kenneth Illand as the Metz Club Officer.

Ken took them upstairs, showed them their rooms and returned to the dining room. They were served a good baked chicken dinner. Mid-way though dinner the conversation turned to girls. Ken and Jim discussed French and Belgian girls and admitted they had girls they always stayed with on liquor runs. The conversations became lengthy and Illand suggested they go into the club if they wanted to talk about girls. In the club, Jim brought up the subject about Alan knowing a girl in Brussels he seemed anxious to see.

Ken asked why he wanted to see this girl. He simply answered, "She's a good friend."

"Yeah; I know all about good friends in Brussels, especially girls," commented Jim. Then added, "We go to Brussels regularly to see our girl friends who take good care of us."

That led Illand to ask, "When did you last see this Belgian girl?"

"I haven't seen her since July when we met in London on my seven-day leave."

Curiously Jim asked, "You talked about her at our base, but never mentioned her name?"

"Her name is Michelle Odette van Bortonne."

Which led Illand to say, "Michelle was a common Belgian name, but I never heard of anyone with that last name. Then questioned, "In what in part of Brussels did she live?"

"Not far from the Grand Place in an apartment above a café off one of the side streets."

This led Jim to ask, "By any chance, would its name be the 'Cafe de Amite Gai'?"

When Jim asked that Ken continued with, "Did she have a nick name like Mimi?"

"Well, some called her Mimi, but her real name was Michelle. She picked up the name Mimi during the German occupation. I don't know if she uses that name anymore?"

Both club officers were shocked when Alan mentioned his Michelle was the girl, they called Mimi. That led to her mother's engagement ring entering the conversation. When they asked, "Does this Mimi or Michelle as you call her ever wear a big diamond ring?"

"I don't think she does. She had one that was her mother's. I told her not to wear it when she was alone. I didn't think she wore it much after that. The diamond must weigh at least a karat. I don't think she was aware the stone was a real diamond and didn't think anyone would violently 'roll her' for it."

lland said, "she told everyone who asked, she got it from her fiancé, an American pilot, for their engagement. "Are you the pilot who gave it to her?"

"Hell no, I just saw the ring! If you're talking about Michele, I just told you it was her mother's. How would I ever get the money to buy something like that?"

"You could buy one cheap from a GI who stole it from a German home. A lot of GI's stole jewels as they rolled through Germany near the end of the war," commented Watson.

"All right," added Iland and continued, "Now let's have the truth, are you the American pilot she tells everyone she's engaged to?"

"Jees... can't you guys understand, I've never asked my Michelle!"

Watson, looked at his watch, it was eleven o'clock and he

said, "OK, we'll have just one more drink, then, we got to go to bed for an early start tomorrow morning."

Illand met them at 0700 eating breakfast and asked, "You made up your mind yet to tell us the truth yet? I have gone to Brussels regularly since the end of the war for liquor. You are the first American pilot I am aware of who ever said he knew her."

"You want to know if I'm engaged to her? I can't answer that. Maybe some other guy did or it's some other girl? There's no way I could know whether or not she's really engaged. I was somewhat familiar with the family. I understood her uncle, by marriage, wanted her to get engaged to his nephew."

It was 0715 and Jim said, "We don't have time to keep this up. I'll find out in Brussels."

They left Metz shortly after that and arrived in Paris at 1320hrs. They ate lunch quickly at the cognac supply base and left for Brussels. A little more than five hours later, over rough roads, they parked in front of the Brussels' USO club.

They walked into the club and Michelle noticed Alan with Jim. She ran across the room, threw her arms around Alan's neck, and began kissing him, which shocked everyone in the club. She was wearing the diamond ring and held up her hand with the other arm around Alan. None of the girls working there believed she was really engaged. They all believed, as she told them, she used the ring as an engagement to ward off advances and dates.

A Jim Watson, in shock, said, "I should have known this, just wait till I tell Ken!"

As Michelle led Alan out of the club, "Jim asked, "Are you leaving for your treatment?"

On the way to her apartment, they talked about her miscarriage. Michelle suddenly broke into tears. "I wanted her so much. When I lost her, I wished I had died instead of her, and I saw you there with me. I told this image, of you, I'm sorry I lost our child."

She stopped and just stood silent for a moment, then, asked Alan to hug her. Her face against is revealed he too took this very seriously. She knew when she felt his cheeks wet with tears. Through tears she told him, "The last letter I received from you meant so much to me. I will save this letter for the rest of my life. and, how sorry I am if my letter made you feel guilty.

You're not catholic, are you?"

"No, I'm Episcopalian."

Then she paused and asked, "Did you really talk about this with the priest on your base?

And did he really give you a catholic communion?"

"Yes, he did, and he said he would pray for us."

"What a wonderful person he must be!"

They walked slowly at times and arrived at the café at 10:15 after forty minutes of crying, hugging, then, petting on the way there. Michelle told Phillipe he was coming, and he met them halfway to the bar. When they met Phillipe shook his hand and hugged him with the other arm. Alan was surprised how Phillipe acted so happy to see him.

Catching his breath he asked Alan, "Have you ever seen Bert again.? He stopped here to say good-bye in July. He said he was going home the following week. We spent the evening with him before he left for the Red Cross Club. That was the last either of us saw of him,"

Shortly after they completed their greeting, Michelle asked for two pork dinners, which Phillipe had prepared for them. Alan wanted to pay, and Michelle insisted she pay for the dinners, but Phillipe having the last word refused to accept anything for the meals.

The plates were hot, and they took them up to Michelle's apartment. While eating their dinners he asked, "Michelle, when did we become engaged?"

"After someone left London experiencing expressions of love with you and giving me..."

she hesitated and tears began flowing again, a child."

He took a fork full of pork and potatoes, chewed and swallowed them, then asked, "What did Aunt Marie think of this? Was she upset with you?"

"You know, I always confided in Aunt Marie and told her about being pregnant, but nothing about the miscarriage, yet? Uncle Hubere doesn't know anything about the pregnancy or the miscarriage."

"You mean you told no one. You had the miscarriage all by yourself?"

Michelle picked at her plate and ate a little, looked at Alan and said, "I did. Phillipe knew. He took care of me like a daughter. He was a great father there for me when I needed him. I told you of the doctor who took care me during the Occupation, he took care of this also."

"Did you ask him if he knew what happened? Did he say you could still have children," Ubere?

"He told me to rest a few months, abstain, and see him after each menstruation. He will tell me after a few months when it will be all right for you and me to try again."

"You mean you told him we were trying and not married yet?"

"Yes, I told him we didn't want to wait and if we had a child together the Army would send you, with me and our child, back to the United States."

"Who told you that? I never heard anything like that?"

"Uncle Hubere told me when he talked about me not associating with you anymore."

They stopped talking and he began eating while Michelle, being upset hardly ate. He finished most of his dinner and Michelle hadn't eaten half of hers. He assisted in the washing and drying the dinner settings. He felt guilty and cleaned the table where he made a mess. Michelle suggested they put pajamas and robes on. Alan didn't object, remembering how wonderful it was to be with her in London.

She went to her bedroom without saying a word. A few minutes later she came out wearing, a new shear nightgown and robe, also, carrying a pair of pajamas and slippers he never saw before. The pajamas were royal blue with wide pin stripes.

She knew by the look in his eyes he was wondering about them and announced, "When your letter told me that you would be in the Army of Occupation, I had an opportunity to go to Sweden and there I purchased a few bedtime clothes for us. These are a pair I had hand made for you. The slippers came out of a shoe store. Surprised? I know all of your sizes?"

Your trousers are 34 by 32 long and shirts are 15 and 1/2 by 32 sleeves!"

"Man, this is a surprise. I'm glad I don't have to use your uncle's stuff anymore!"

They went into the sitting room, sat close to each other on the couch. Michelle picked up his right arm and put it around her neck and snuggled a little closer and put her head on his chest. He then turned a little to his left so their faces were near each other and kissed her.

Then asked, "Now, what were we talking about when we stopped to eat?"

"I said something like if we had a child we could go to the United States. Remember?"

Suddenly Michelle lifted her head from Alan's shoulder and began crying, and said, "What are we going to do now?"

"Well, I think you should eventually tell your Aunt and maybe your uncle? No...just tell Aunt Marie, maybe by the time Hubere hears about it he'll be cool enough not to say much."

"You came here for me, and we can't do anything, I'll try if you want?"

"Michelle what do you think I am? I'm happy just to be

here with you, can't you believe I love you so much, just being with you makes me happy. Can't I just love you?"

She threw her arms around his neck and said, "You know what to say at the right time. I love you so much. When we can, I want another child from you. Are you willing?"

"I want to be sincere and hope you believe what I'm about to say to you. It's now near the end of October. You shouldn't even think about trying for another child for three or four months. Let everything inside of you get right. By then, it will be around the beginning of March before we should think of trying again. The Army will probably send me home no later than May. If I get you pregnant in March or April, you will have to marry me if you want to go home with me. Count nine months if we are going to do this thing right, it should be January or maybe February 1947 when our child would be born."

"Yes...I shall try. You said when our child will be born. Yes... yes, I understand, but, what if they want to send you home before I get pregnant?"

"Then I'll try to arrange a marriage here, Uncle Hubere willing, and take you home with me."

"I knew you were wonderful. You have acted insecure so often. I think I know you now. When things are bad you are at your best. That is why you are still here with me; you were a good pilot I knew they could not kill you! I love you! And we shall do exactly as you have said."

He questioned further, "What will happen if we really get engaged and Aunt Marie and Uncle Hubere hear we did that without ever mentioning anything to them?"

"Do not concern yourself about them. You are here for me, are you not?" He didn't have to answer that.

He put his arm back around her neck and she snuggled up, so their faces were very close. He kissed her again and asked, "Why don't we just sit here and smooch while listening to the GI station and some good soft music." Over an hour passed without them saying hardly a word other than loving each other.

Being tired from his long ride he began to doze on and off. The clock stuck eleven thirty and Michelle suggested they should go to bed. Fifteen minutes later they were hugging in bed. Shortly, Michelle rolled on her right side. She reached behind her and across his chest and grabbed Alan's right arm to have him snuggle up close behind her. In a few minutes both were sound asleep.

The next day, Sunday, Michelle woke up, was out of bed making breakfast. She was frying bacon strips, eggs, and toast with a pot of coffee brewing. When they were ready, she woke him, and he came out to a breakfast all laid out on the table for him. A tablecloth with about a three-inch crocheted edge, two candles burning with no lights on. She sat across from him now and while eating he looked up several times before he said, "You are something again and again."

"What do you mean by that?"

"You're special! You always do the right things to make me love you. You make my breakfast and let me sleep, then, if my clothes are worn a day or so you wash them."

"That is not being special! I love doing that for you!"

"One thing bothers me, this time if Uncle Hubere finds me here I don't think he can kick me off the continent, but he could kick me out of Belgium again."

Michelle repeated several times, "He will never do that again."

Aunt Marie said she told him I want to stay out of his life until he treats me as an adult and permits me make my own decisions. Since then, whenever I visited Aunt Marie, and he was home I ignored him and never talked to him. I was surprised, when Aunt Marie and I were alone, she told me my silence hurt him."

After breakfast she talked Alan into taking a bath. This time she didn't ask to join him. When he finished washing, he dried himself and had his clean underwear on, Michelle took her bath and by the time she finished Alan was completely dressed wearing an Ike Jacket.

When Michelle got out of the tub and was dressing, she asked him if he would like to take a walk around the Grand Place to see some places such as the Palais des Congres, Theatre Royal du Parc, and some others, then, spend a little time in a park area near the old opera house, the Theatre Royal de la Monnaie.

She talked as she dressed and put on a lovely, just below the knees, floral dress. The shade of pink background accented her skin coloring. "God she was beautiful," Alan thought! They went downstairs and told Phillipe they would be out and about most of the morning. They left, went up the street a little over three short blocks to the Grand Place. They walked to a few places Michelle mentioned and settled in a park like area and sat on a bench surrounded by shade trees.

Being near the old Opera House she asked Alan if he liked operas and he told her he used to listen to operas on the radio from the Metropolitan in New York City, every Saturday when he was in his early teens." And added, "Two of my favorites were the Barber of Seville and La Boheme.

They got off the bench at 1230hrsand walked about a thousand meters down the street and entered a café. They had a glass of beer with their fried slab bacon, lettuce, and tomato on a toasted bread sandwich.

They left the café at 1335hrs and Michelle took Alan to the two o'clock opera where they enjoyed The Merry Widow. After the opera they walked to the Grand Place, entered the Café de Louis, where Michelle said they had good food and especially wonderful large dinner sized Spanish Omelets; it was like she said, 'delicious'; especially the sauce. They went back to Phillipe's and talked to him for more than an hour about their future plans while having a glass of their red wine.

As soon as they got into Michelle's apartment, she suggested pajamas and he put on his new Swedish ones with his slippers and she her sheer ones. They sat close on the couch listening to the GI station playing big band music. Michelle became attached to, I'll Never Smile Again, and knowing the words, began singing softly with the radio.

When the song ended, he had to say, "You have a terrific voice! Where did you get it?"

"My parents purchased it when I was in my late teens, with a laugh. I began having voice lessons when I was thirteen and was taking them right up to May 1940 when the war broke out. My voice teacher was a tenor with the Brussels Opera and went to war. I never saw him again. I don't know what happened to him, maybe he was killed. When Brussels was liberated, I tried to find him, I asked people he sang with at the opera, they had not seen him either. I felt very sad, his voice was more than good, it was astounding."

Moon Light Serenade was on next while she was telling

Alan about her voice teacher. Without stopping, she asked him, "Shall we dance?" After they danced to 'I'll Never Smile Again' and then, 'What's New.' Michelle asked him, "Could we make one of these our song?"

Alan answered, "They're both really good. Let's make them both our songs." They danced to other songs until midnight when Michelle said, "We better go to bed, it is Midnight."

When they got in bed, Alan suddenly became the aggressive one. He turned on his side facing her and slid his arm under her neck, drew her close with his other hand on her lower back and they began kissing. Michelle asked, "How about some exercise early tomorrow?"

"OK, where and what kind?"

"I had a bicycle ride to Louvain in mind. It is going to be a nice day and we could ride there, visit Aunt Marie, and stay overnight."

"I'd like that except what about uncle Hubere?"

"I shall call Aunt Marie from Phillipe's and see if he is home and find if she will have us."

Michelle woke Alan up early on Monday the 29th and prepared another great breakfast. While he was eating, she went to the café and called her Aunt who was happy to hear from her. She pleased Michelle by saying she would be happy to have Alan and her overnight.

Michelle ran up stairs and told him to hurry, Aunt Marie was waiting. She gulped down her breakfast, had Alan help her with the dishes, cleaned up the kitchen and dressed, then, packed her spare clothes, and took clothes from Alan's B-4 bag and put them in separate bags made for bike carriers. As they walked down the back stairs carrying their bike bags Michelle told him, "We are going to get our exercise now, bicycling to Aunt Marie's house."

They started out and when they came to the stream where they first kissed, Michelle had to stop. They got off their bikes parked them well off the road, then, walked to the tree they first sat on. "I shall never...never ever forget this place. This is the place where we had our first kiss, and I began to fall in love. This tree is blessed and has blessed us," she commented.

They sat in the tree with Michelle on Alan's lap, then, hugged, kissed, and talked for fifteen or twenty minutes before leaving. They arrived at Aunt Marie's at 1130hrs and she was at the door and open it as they peddled up the long driveway. She told them, "Take the bicycles around to the back and the chauffeur will take care of them.

They entered by the rear door, walked through the kitchen and to the lobby entrance where Michelle tried to look into the one-way window to Hubere's home office. Marie told her, "You will not see him there, he is not home. The chauffeur took him to Brussels early this morning. Come in and we shall sit in the sitting room, I have something to tell you."

Michelle and Alan settled in the love seat and Marie in the armchair. Marie rang for the maid and had some tea prepared while they chit chatted about things in general. The tea arrived, the maid filled the three cups and left. Aunt Marie then told them, "Parliament and the King discussed a change in the administration that effects Hubere."

Michelle injected she heard, "Phillipe told me that some of Uncle Hubere's supporters favored someone to replace him and have him assigned to a lesser responsible position. Has he said anything of possibly being completely eliminated from the parliament?"

"I doubt that very much. He is an excellent politician, but, you see, a new political group has captured the minds of parliament and many men in Hubere's party may be replaced."

"But Will he survive despite the changes," asked Michelle?

"He feels he has enough friends in both parties who respect him and would not want to eliminate him as they feel he still has much to contribute. If nothing more, as a consultant."

She took a couple of long sips of her tea and said, "I do not wish to dwell on that. Please tell me how the two of you are. Any new plans or directions for you Alan?"

Michelle took over and asked Aunt Marie, "Do you think

Uncle Hubere would still object if I formally announced Alan is to be my fiancé?"

Marie answered, "Hubere is your legal guardian. He should know and approve of him."

Alan looked at Aunt Marie and said, "If I have to ask Hubere for approval forget it."

When Aunt Marie asked 'why', he responded, "I don't want another encounter with him? He told me, in specific terms, on Saturday the 13th, Michelle's birthday, when I was first here 'I was not one of you for many reasons! I do not want to go through that again."

Michelle answered, "I do not care what uncle Hubere thinks or told you."

"Michelle, I can't and won't destroy any relationship and create havoc in your family!"

Michelle then said everything will be different after January 1946. Alan asked, "Why?"

And Michelle responded, "I shall graduate, in January, everything willed to me becomes mine. Uncle Hubere will no longer have any control of me and my parent's possessions."

Alan responded, "Listen! I said I don't want to be any part of destroying a relationship!"

When he said that, Michelle sat up and said, "There I see! Now you can rid yourself of me," then, ran she to her bedroom and threw herself on the bed in tears.

Marie said to Alan, "She has been on edge ever since her miscarriage."

"I've told her I will marry her, with or without Hubere's blessings, when I'm sent home. I do not want to drive a wedge between her and her uncle any sooner than it has to be."

"Do not worry. She will calm down shortly and return. If she does not, you can get her."

A few minutes later Aunt Marie said, "Go to Michelle's bedroom and comfort her."

Alan entered her room and sat on the bed next to her. She was laying on her stomach and he put his hand on her back and slowly and softly rubbed it up and down.

She rolled on her back and fighting tears told him, "You will not destroy a relationship. And anything you might do 'for us' now shall make me happy. All I want from this second on is to be your lover, wife, and the mother of your children."

As she sat up Alan took out his handkerchief and dabbed her eyes. She stood up, put her arms around his neck asking,

"You wouldn't let anything interfere with our desire to marry, would you?"

He kissed her and answered, "Not really. I would just like everyone to be in agreement."

He put his arm around her waist and said, "Let's go downstairs and talk to Aunt Marie."

They returned to Marie and Michelle repeated what she told Alan in her bedroom and concluded with, "That is exactly the way I want it to be and nothing else."

Marie startled by her determination responded, "You two do what you want. Be happy!"

Alan now interrupted, "Aunt Marie would it bother you to talk about Mimi?"

"No, I do not believe it would. I have accepted that and of course, I still have Michelle. You would be surprised if you ever saw them separately on the same day with them dressed in similar color dresses. One could not tell them apart. And at times their own fathers also could not."

"Please tell him about the town picnic when we were, I think, thirteen years old."

"Michelle, I don't think anyone at that picnic will ever forget that day. Alan, you have to understand these two girls. My Mimi was always very conscious of her appearance, avoided dirt like the plague. It seemed she had a phobia of dirt. Now, Michelle was the opposite. She essentially was a 'Tom Boy'. That is why she developed as a strong-willed person of fortitude who will face any adverse governing factors of things or people, which does not exactly relate to the incident that occurred at the picnic.

Michelle thought up this devious plan. It began when she asked Mimi if she would like to try her new dress, she was wearing, to see how it looked on her. Mimi thought that would be very kind and accepted the offer. They went to a secluded locale, and they exchanged dresses. Michelle then paraded her around the entire area and had numerous friends tell her how gorgeous she looked in the dress. Michelle told her she did not care for the dress and could keep it. Mimi told her it would be asking too much, and Michelle talked her into accepting the dress by a long-drawn-out conversation mentioning all the things she gave her. You have to understand this was a plan by Michelle to get Mimi dirty and see how she reacted. It also confused all of us. She paraded Mimi around some more attempting to occupy her mind to make her forget she had her new dress on.

An hour later Michelle asked Mimi if she would take a canoe ride with her. Mimi said she would, but Michelle had to paddle, and they walked to the dock. Mimi carefully got in the front of the canoe and Michelle, paddling, took the canoe out about one hundred feet from the dock to water she knew was only three or four feet deep. Then, she deliberately tipped the boat over and both fell into the muddy creek. They walked out with muddy water all over them including their dresses, now muddy, revealed much of their difference. The two girls looked very much alike with all the muddy water it was difficult for one to tell who was who, between them. Michelle took advantage of the situation to confuse everyone and went to her, Mimi's, father and said, "Look what Michelle did to me and my dress," while Mimi was attempting to tell him she was Mimi, but, Michelle, in Mimi's dress, would not let her get a word in. She began screaming and Michelle's father began to scold Mimi wearing Michelle's dress, thinking she was his daughter while Michelle who stood there laughing. This caused Hubere go after Michelle thinking she was Mimi and began scolding her for laughing so hysterically.

Annette came to the rescue. She recognized them by their shoes and asked when they changed their dresses. Hubere and Jacques hearing this began arguing about scolding each other's daughters. Of course, our friends were listening and absorbing all this, and they became engrossed in the entire situation. Then, when Annette interrupted the arguing and told them who was who and what was what with the dresses, both Hubere and Jacques threw up their hands. That is how much the cousins looked alike, with mud on, their fathers did not recognize who was who. I do not think anyone still alive in Leuven ever forgot that day. Michelle was something!" This story of her past made her chuckle and she felt better now.

After lunch she took Alan on a bicycle ride around Leuven, stopping occasionally and talking to her friends, but now Michelle would not let anyone continue conversations in Dutch. The conversations were all in English to include Alan in the dialogue. This sent him the message, "Her love was sincere, as she forced all of her friends to speak English for him."

That evening he asked Marie to tell him about Michelle's father and mother. She showed him pictures of both families from the birth of the girls to the beginning of the war.

That night, he lay in his bedroom visualizing these Belgian families as the girls grew and became aware of the social status Hubere alluded to that was obvious in the photographs. He fell asleep thinking maybe everything Hubere told him was the way it was.

Michelle in her bedroom was aware how much their social positions were revealed by the photos and lay awake, for an hour, worrying how they affected Alan before she fell asleep.

They arose late the next morning and came to the kitchen a few minutes apart. Marie was waiting and had the cook prepare breakfast. Alan was quiet all morning and did not show his concern of the social life the photographs displayed that Michelle must leave if she married him and went to the United States.

Tuesday, 30 October 1945: Brussels

After one evening with Aunt Marie, without Hubere, they happily returned to Brussels on Tuesday and spent a quiet time sitting in the park and watching pedestrians, a few joggers, and bicyclists. They saw people dressed in all kinds of clothes. Several wore trousers so large the crotch came down to their knees and the chuffs had several folds. The clothes were probably all they could find. Even though they looked funny; it also was sad it was all some people could afford. Another couple passed by dressed up for a formal affair in the area.

They really didn't notice much as they concentrated on each other more than any other of the activities around them. It was a beautiful day for the end of October. There wasn't a cloud shading the sky and the slight breeze they felt, was warm and comforting. At noon they strolled through the park and to the Grand Place, now in peacetime, bustling full of people. They entered a restaurant Alan said looked similar to the one in Paris, then, asked Michelle if they would toss him out and let her in. "You will never forget the Paris incident, will you?"

"How could I? That's when you captured me and then made everyone, I ever saw seem insignificant. I was not aware of it until I got back to my tent and went to bed. You hid in my subconscious mind. When you came out, I was your prisoner, I couldn't erase you!"

After lunch they walked (toured) the Grand Place area where cafés were alive, full of people, for several blocks in all directions. She led him around the area to show him the several directions to Phillipes' café. Arriving there about eight fifteen they entered and spent the early evening drinking wine while singing with customers.

At 2245hrs they returned to the apartment, put on their pajamas, snuggled, listen to the GI radio station, and relaxed on the couch until 2230hrs. They had one glass of their wine, went to bed, Alan against Michelle's back, and snuggling when they fell asleep.

The next morning, she made Alan's breakfast, went into the bedroom, and jumped on him. He woke up wondering what was going on, she said, "You gave me a child last night."

Oh yeah! Please tell me what kind of trick magician artist, do you think I am?"

"I am only fooling. I dreamt we were fooling around again all evening, then, jump in bed and really enjoy ourselves. It seemed so real, and I was so happy."

Alan changed the subject and asked, "If you graduate this January and we go to the same university together, how are we going to raise a couple of children while attempting to get our degrees. You will be in Medical School. I'll have to take care of the children and will never be able to complete an engineer program to gain the respect of your uncle."

She said. "It shall not be a problem. God will be with us. He made us a perfect match for each other. Remember? Aunt Marie said that last January."

Alan finally gave in and said, "OK, we'll do what you want, but we should be careful and not have children if we are attending the university at the same time."

Fourteen

LETTER OF CONFLICT

Thursday, 01 November 1945
Trip Back to Base from Brussels

Alan was at Phillipe's, where he spent, his last, Wednesday night with Michelle. Watson and his sergeants picked up the whiskeys at 0730hrs Thursday morning and Michelle hung on Alan's arm while they were talking about the journey back in front of the café. When he was about to get in the truck Michelle threw her arms around his neck and began passionately kissing him. She was pinned to Alan's body, and he had to break from her kiss. As she let go and his fingertips slid out of hers, he turned and got in the truck's cab. The six by six with Sabol driving left at 0710hrs. As it rolled away Michelle began crying and Alan continued waving to her until they turned the corner at the far end of the street.

On the way Alan and Michelle were the subject of their conversation. They wanted to know how he met her and why she picked him out of the many who approached her?

To all questions Alan's lone answer was, "Your guess is as good as any!"

They reached Paris at 1335hrs, in time to have Watson pick up the Cognac before a quick lunch and left Paris for Metz at 1450hrs. The road to Metz was as rough as the road from Brussels. It took just under five hours to get to Metz.

The Officers club at 1945hrs

Watson, Illand and Alan had a go around about the girl with the big diamond, during the late dinner saved for them, and was never seen on a date with anyone since she was first seen during the liberation of Brussels. Ken broke the ice with the question, "How the hell did you manage to break through the wall she had around her all that time."

"What you call a 'wall' was her shield from predators, guys that labeled her an ex-prostitute. She had several dates after the liberation of Belgium, all were catastrophic. She wasn't behind a wall. I understood, she had several dates after Belgium was liberated with guys who practically raped her. She is, without question, truly a fine lady. Her reputation stemmed from her obligation to be a Resistance Mistress for a German General and later a Gestapo Colonel. Believe it or not she got out of them a lot of high-tech missile information, for the Resistance to sabotage.

"That's not the way we heard she was," said Illand.

"I know one of their underground's Cell Leader and he told me in addition to the sabotage info she dug out of those officers the German strategy believed the allied invasion would be in two areas, other than where the allied command planned and had it been passed on to the allies. Anyway, because she used her irresistible body and beauty to extract this information, she was labeled a Rexist, a German collaborator. I accidentally learned about all this and treated her as a lady. You see, I didn't break down any walls, I just treated her as the real lady she came out of what you might call a gate and eventually we mutually wanted to be together."

"That doesn't tell me much. Does she really want to marry you and are you willing?"

"Bet your last dollar on it, I am if she still wants me when I get my call to go home."

"There are still a lot of guys out there trying to get her. Aren't you afraid she may find someone who will interest her more or be a better lover than you," Ken continued asking?

"I tell you how it is with me. I love her more than you can imagine, but, if some day she finds and wants someone else before I marry her, good luck to the guy she takes. I'd rather have it happen now; it would really hurt. But if it happened after we were married, I may go mad and need a loony bin."

"No one ever verified all the rumors about her. She's been labeled a con artist among other things. You may be in over your head and then you find out she may destroy you."

"You want to know something, no one has had the experience with her relatives I've had. They are legitimate, upper society and associated with the Belgium Government. I know that from my personal experience with her, her aunt, and her uncle. Just all rumors you have heard. I have nothing more to say, I'm going to my room."

"I didn't think he'd get up tight about her, did you?"

"I don't know Ken! He has quite a good reputation. Maybe he does know everything he has said about her. I'll work on him on the way to our base and see what I can find out. It is getting late and I'm tired from the drive from Brussels to here. I'm going to bed too, see ya in the morning." He got up from the table and left for his room.

Alan was the first in the dining room for breakfast. Illand came in just as Alan sat down at a table. He got a cup of coffee and joined him. Alan didn't respond to his "Good morning" received and just kept eating. Then Tom added, "Alan if I upset you last night I apologize. Will you accept my apology?" Alan still didn't acknowledge his presence and he continued, "You taught me something last night. From now on I'll support your position about your girl. Do you understand how stupid I feel?"

As Alan was about to say something, Jim arrived and said a jolly, "Good morning. Did you guys sleep well last night, I did. I fell asleep so fast I can't remember getting undressed. Why is everyone so quiet?"

"Ken and I had a discussion about last night and now we have a better understanding."

"Yeah, I apologized to Alan, and I really mean it."

"OK. So, Alan are you ready to go. I'll have a little breakfast and we'll leave."

He and Ken did all the talking and avoided saying anything about Alan and Michelle while Casey and Sabol were at the door chomping at the bit, anxious to leave. Jim and Alan said good-bye to Ken, and they started out for their base at 0955hrs. They stopped for a brief stretch at the Rhine again and Zelinski drove the rest of the way with Sabol riding in the back with the supplies. Five minutes later they started for their base and arrived at their home base on Friday, (the 2nd) at 1830hrs. On the way Jim tried to talk to Alan about Michelle and he was non-responsive.

Saturday through Friday, 30 November 1945

Alan returned to hunting with Strait, mornings, played football Saturday afternoons, and bridge most nights, with

Roberts. During the weekday mornings the kids came, they got the hosens from Claire and Alan and on bad cold or rainy days they practiced firing at the indoor range. Things became pretty boring during November for most men on the base.

Alan kept in touch with Michelle with two letters a week each way. One letter read,

5 November 1945

My dearest Alan,

Uncle Hubere heard, I had been pregnant and had a miscarriage a couple of days after you left. He confronted Aunt Marie and demanded to know who the father of the child was I lost, and, when she confirmed it was you, he ranted and raved about that 'No Good, so and so, American Pilot'. He asked Aunt Marie for your APO address, and she told him she did not know what it was. He became very upset when neither she nor I would admit we knew your APO. He went through his diplomatic services and had the new premier confirm you APO address. Then, I understand he wrote you a letter. Did you get one?

Your Michelle

Two days later he entered his Belgian office and was inwardly so furious he had difficulty controlling his temper. His anger was evident to his secretary, and she meekly asked him if she did anything to upset him. He told her it was not her and sat at his desk to write the following letter to Alan.

07 November 1945

Alan,

I recently received notice that Michelle had a miscarriage. That must have been the result of some male having sick sperm. I immediately confronted Marie and she confirmed you were the father of the lost child. Maybe I did not make myself clear when we met. Your relationship with Michelle was out of order! You are not from an accepted social class of people when I spoke to you about her and future relationships. Because of you not heeding my notice you made her pregnant with a child she could not carry. She was very ill during the miscarriage, and we were afraid of losing her. Fortunately, she knew someone able to provide excellent medical attention to her needs, because we are of good social stature.

Now to deal with you, did no one inform you Michelle was to be engaged when you encouraged her to have you and became pregnant? I am contemplating having you accused of forcing her to succumb to you by a condition labeled 'RAPE'. I do not want to hear you are ever in Brussels again, let alone 'I repeat' if you are ever seen in Brussels, I will have a bulletin published that you are the person who raped Michelle. If I so much as suspect or hear you are in Brussels or Leuven again, I will have you accused of being a rapist and did threaten to cut Michelle's throat if she did not cooperate with you.

Are you aware that if you commit a Belgian felony, Belgian Law will prosecute you?

Hubere

Alan couldn't believe anyone could lie and hate so much to write such a letter. He was sure Hubere didn't know about her being pregnant nor the miscarriage well after it all happened from the way Michelle described it.

That letter made him more distraught than he was for several years. He looked for Jim in the dining room and met him a few days later to tell him he couldn't go on the November Liquor Run and thanked him for the offer before he made one.

Hubere's letter so depressed him, he rarely left his room except for meals and when he did, he didn't associate with anyone. He rarely saw his roommate, Robertson, who spent a lot of time with pilots from another squadron. They had something going in the local and nearby villages with German girls. They were together mostly at bedtime and meals when Tom was on the base.

Strait was first to approach Alan looking so depressed and asked, "What's the matter?

You've looked down in the dumps for several days. Did you get bad news from home?"

He answered, "I just want to be left alone until I can get something out of this brain."

At dinner a few days before Watson was going on the November Run, he looked for and found Alan at dinner and asked if he was sure he didn't want to go with the upcoming Liquor Run? He thought for a moment and said, "It would be best if I do not go this time."

"If there is a problem, needing your attention, you should come along."

"Forget it. You just go and have a good time."

"If I see Michelle and she asks for you, what do you want me to tell her?"

"Just tell her I've been sick, or I've had a demanding assignment."

"I don't think she will believe that?"

"Tell her anyway or whatever you can come up with."

Watson left at 0800hrs on Saturday the 24th and scheduled return on Friday the 30th. On the way he stopped at Metz. Michelle and Alan were the subject of their conversation.

Illand asked and Watson told him, "I don't know what's going on between them."

When Watson arrived in Brussels, Michelle asked, "What happened to Alan?"

To save him from embarrassment, he told her, "I was not able to get him on the orders. It was my fault for not going to our wing to put him on it as an aid."

Michelle did not accept that answer and pressed for more of what he knew. She asked, "Did he mention anything of avoiding a confrontation with anyone?"

"He didn't say anything. I do apologize for not being able to get him on our orders."

Michelle ran from the club and bicycled directly to Leuven and Aunt Marie, in tears. She pleaded, "Has uncle Hubere somehow reached Alan to change his mind about me. If he has, please help me find a way to have uncle Hubere accept Alan once and for all.

Aunt Marie answered, "I don't believe Hubere did anything."

On Monday Michelle received a letter from Alan about his not coming to Brussels with a return address of the Brussels Government Offices on it. She feared opening it, and sincerely thought that he got to him and talked him out of ever seeing her again. She just looked at the letter for several minutes before finally opening it.

26 November 1945

My dearest Michelle,

I did not come with Watson. I didn't want another conflict with your Uncle Hubere. Please write to me as soon as you finish reading this letter and tell me if anything is not true.

Hubere claimed, in his letter, you came to your senses about Claude and me, would not be accepted by your social class of people and, thus you plan to get engaged to Claude. He threatened to accuse me of raping and making you pregnant and added that Belgian courts would try me for Belgian crimes. Then closed with, "I love you enough to wish you happiness if I am not the person to get old with you. Please make sure who you chose really loves you and you are sure he will make and keep you happy.

Your ever loving,

Alan

Watson left Brussels on the 24th and arrived at his home base at 1600hrs on Friday, the 30th. He told Alan, "She was all broke up because you didn't show up."

Five days later Alan received a letter from Michelle. The letter scolded him. The basic content was, "I am angry. I have not had the slightest thought of anyone, least of all Claude, only you! My doctor said I am all right and will be able to bear children in the future. If any discontent exists between you and Uncle Hubere, I shall resolve everything! Please come, see, and tell me, I love only you.

Your Michelle...always"

30 November 1945 – 04 January 1946

On 30 November 1945, Group headquarters received notice that Alan, Henry James, and Joe Vetrano were selected for the European Theater Air Force All Star Football Team. Alan was selected for a guard position to play on both offensive and defensive teams. James and Vetrano were selected as backs on the offensive team. Everyone on base was aware Alan played at for an Ivy League university through Daniels. James claimed he played at Michigan and Vetrano claimed Penn. State, but no one was sure of their credentials.

Alan missed Michelle so much and wrote her that he was to play in the Riviera Bowl in Nice, France on 1 January she might come to see him play and spend time together.

Group headquarters received their All-Star orders 7 December for the assignment to Nice, France from 14 December to 2 January 1946 to play in the Rivera Bowl. The orders included travel that would be provided by C-47 aircraft from their base to Nice and return.

Alan received Michelle's answer to his All-Star letter on 12 December. The root of the message in the letter read,

"I and Aunt Marie shall definitely visit Nice when you are there. We cannot be in Nice before Thursday the 27th because my grandmother will not be in her villa there until then."

Alan, Joe, and Henry arrived by C-47 to Nice airport at 1100hrs and most of the players were there by 1700hrs. A few others arrived late, 1930hrs at the hotel they were booked for. Tech. Sergeant Ivan Parrsavich the team coach remained in the lobby and personally greeted every player as they arrived. The next morning, Alan met All Americans Tom Jones (Tackle) Notre Dame, Mero Spandos (End) Alabama and Martin Clayburn (Center) Tulane. Most of the twenty-seven players represented several large well-known universities such as the Univ. of Southern California, University of Ohio State, Michigan, Georgia, and others of that class.

Ivan had them begin a two a day, two hour-long practice sessions on 17 December. Michelle and Aunt Marie arrived in Nice Wednesday, afternoon, the 27th of December. They went to Marie's mother's Villa and she was out somewhere. Aunt Marie knew where the door key was hidden, found it, unlocked the door, and relaxed in the living room. Louise, mother, and grandmother arrived later that evening and was extremely happy to have them. Grandmother Louise had heard so much about Alan. She told Michelle and Marie she wanted to know all about him and insisted Michelle bring him to the villa to meet him.

Michelle went to the boardwalk on Friday the 28th and

found where the team's hotel was situated. She arrived in the mid afternoon while the team was practicing. She returned to the villa then back to hotel that evening and encountered some players in the lobby. Because she was there giving them enough reason to make advances on her. The strong-willed Michelle brushed them off and asked the desk clerk for Alan's room number. He called Alan's room, and he came to the lobby. Michelle noticed and asked, "Where are your lieutenant bars? You look like a private." He informed her, Nice was an enlisted men's city, so, he had to look like one. He hesitated, for a moment, thinking about Hubere and asked if anything had been settled with Hubere. She lied, telling him all is settled. Alan spent Friday night alone with Michelle at the villa. Aunt Marie and Grandmother Louise were conveniently at her sister's villa overnight.

The next day he had problems with friendly players. They needled him, asking how he ever got to 'shack up' with such an attractive babe. Coach Parrsavich didn't think this was so funny and declared Michelle off-limits on Saturday morning, the 29th of December through (after) the game on 1 January. He called Alan aside and told him if he didn't abide by the off limit notice he'd be off the team. "We came to play football...........only!"

During practices Jones (Notre Dame) took a liking to Alan and taught him some very effective offensive physical tactics and mental attitudes. The two teams and the few subs were established, and they had one a day practices on 30 and 31 December. Alan impressed the coach so much, using Jones's tips, he had him play half the game at Left Guard. James and Vetrano didn't do too well in practice with what the backs were put through. Thus, they only played a few minutes during the last five minutes of the game. They won the Riviera Bowl game against the Mediterranean Theater All Stars 27 to 7.

After the game Michelle introduced Alan to her grandmother, Louise Hartmann. Marie and Louise made up their mind to ask him to stay with them for a few days. When he and Michelle arrived, they asked him and he called his base for a three-day extension, 2 through Saturday 5 January 1946. Personnel Officer, Roberts, extended his leave after explaining all about Michelle and her grandmother having a villa in Nice.

He spent that evening with Michelle, Marie, and her grandmother. The next day Marie and Louise shopped for additional food for Alan's three-day stay. While shopping, Marie revealed to her mother that Michelle wanted to marry this pilot. Louise, knew a little about Hubere's feelings and asked Marie, *"How he felt about Alan at the present time?"*

Marie answered, "He continues to strongly object to them seeing each other."

When they returned, Michelle and Alan were found lying in front of a roaring fireplace. Louise said, "Michelle, your aunt, you and I have to discuss something serious, privately" and asked Alan to excuse them? They left Alan in the living room and went into the kitchen. There, Louise asked Marie,

"How did Hubere permit to you to come when he is strongly against the marriage. Hasn't he said Alan would never be socially accepted and belittled him unfit for his social class. This is very upsetting. Did Hubere have any knowledge of the American football game here and that he might be one of the players?"

"We don't think he is aware of anything other than we went to Paris. My only fears are he may check with the few hotels where we regularly stay and wonder where we really are, then finds we are not in any of them," was Marie's opinion?

Louise said, *"If he only was in our family, I could easily take care of him."*

They stopped and went back into the living room, and he greeted them with, "Have you figured out yet if I would ever be good enough for Michelle?" He hesitated for a moment and added, "I feel so rejected I don't know why I'm here with you and her. I have a problem trying to feel comfortable in the presence of any of you since my conversation with Hubere. I've seen his kind in the United States. I 've met many of their children at the university. Their children had mixed attitudes and never accepted people like me in their social class and probably never will. That's not my greatest problem, Michelle is. I feel so tread on, I don't want this for her. I love her, but if I must leave for her sake, consider it done. I'd rather see her happy with someone else, than be an outcast with me. I won't say any more."

They, Louise, Marie, and Michelle told him never to

believe, think or ever say that again. None of that is true. You are a fine gentleman. Michelle deserves to have a man like you!"

Michelle asked her grandmother if she can do something to resolve the problem. She said she will try, but, Hubere does not have to listen to her, he is not from our family.

Michelle began crying and said, the problem is plaguing her and Alan's life. Aunt Marie said she thought Hubere would do nothing if Grandmother Louise interfered, "I understand how you feel after everything that has happened in your life. If you love him and really want to marry him do not let anything, get in your way," Louise added.

Then Michelle asked Aunt Marie, "What do you believe and how do you feel about this."

"I agree with everything mother said. But I have to live with Hubere," she answered.

Aunt Marie hugged both of them and Michelle asked, "Can we go to the boardwalk? "I want to give Alan a tour of the Riviera Area, also, Grandmother, can I also use your auto?"

Louise jokingly said, "Don't damage it," attempting to make them feel better.

They went on the tour, attended a stage show that evening and 'necked' before returning. The days passed so quickly for Michelle she asked Alan to get another extension. He told her he doesn't want to press his relationship with Roberts.

"He had problems getting me this three-day extension. He couldn't do it, the extension had to come through Wing."

Hubere called the villa looking for Marie and Michelle. Michelle accidentally answered the phone. Hubere had now zeroed in on them and asked one thing, "Is that American there? I know he is and want you to rid yourselves of him immediately. I do not want him prying on you anymore. Is that clear!"

Alan got ready to leave, he had to catch the 1300hrs train. Michelle went with him and was there when the train was about to leave. Alan held her and he sadly asked, "Michelle, do you believe you will ever be able to see me again?"

She told him, "My love, don't think of that. Everything has to be and shall be worked out. I take my exams next week and have done so well it is impossible for me not to graduate. On that day 'I will be my own self with my own assets and responsibilities."

The train began moving at 1530hrs and she cried again as the train left the station.

When Michelle returned to Brussels, she wrote a letter to him not to fear she will be there for him to see, meet and love any time he wants.

They began a regular twice a week letter to each other after his return. Michelle wrote when she completes her exams, she might sell out everything, leave Belgium and wait for and meet him at his home in the United States. "I have your parents' address. Please tell me if they are still living there in the event I arrive before you do."

Fifteen

CHAMONIX

Friday, 11 January to Sunday, 27 January 1946

During the evening of 11 January 1946, Bob Andrews sat at a small square table in the club bar reading the Stars and Stripes paper. Someone called to him and asked," Hey Bob did you see the article about Chamonix on the back page, of the paper, in the lower right corner?" Bob closed the paper, turned it over and saw the article. It read,

"The French government is disappointed at the response to their open invitation to all allied military forces for a 10 day all expense paid holiday, at the Chamonix Ski Resort. All necessary equipment will be provided. If interested contact your Personnel Officer."

Bob saw Ray Longe and Nick Tower, his good friends at

the bar. He called them over to his table and had them both read the Chamonix article, then asked, "What do you guys think? Both read it carefully, then; thought and Ray said, "Go for it! We should get a fourth?"

Alan Manston was sipping cognac and coke with Don Coates and Jim Turner in the club's anteroom waiting to play bridge with Jon Roberts, the Group Personnel Officer to show up. They knew Alan was a good friend of Roberts and would ease the process of getting orders for Chamonix and called him over to their table and showed him the Chamonix notice and asked if he was be interested?

He said he would be more than interested and will ask Roberts to check it out for them. "I'll ask him if he knows anything about this and if he doesn't, I know he'll find out for us, on Monday or maybe by Wednesday."

Monday morning, Roberts contacted Wing and they phoned back with details requiring the names of the personnel, and a date they would prefer to go. He told Alan all this and he got together with Bob, Ray, and Nick at lunch to talk about the names and dates. They discussed this briefly and they agreed on the third week of January and after lunch they went to Group Headquarters with Roberts and gave him their names and desired dates being the fourth week because the third week was too close to the request.

Wing called Roberts a couple days later. He informed Alan he received approval to cut their orders for Tuesday,

22nd through Thursday, 31st of January 1946 for four men. Roberts met with the other three and, at lunch, told them of their Chamonix dates. After lunch Alan went immediately to his room and wrote to Michelle.

Two important sentences in his letter were, "I'll be skiing, for ten days, in Chamonix from late Tuesday the 22nd and not leave before noon on Sunday the 31st. Can you come?"

They left the base after 8:00 o'clock Tuesday morning by truck for Erlangen in enough time to catch the 0900hrs train to Strasbourg located on the French side of the Rhine River. From there they took another train to a small town at the base of the mountain on which Chamonix was situated. They transferred to a train, pulled by a short mountain climbing engine. It arrived in Chamonix in the late afternoon.

They were initially directed to a five-story hotel and saw civilians all over the place. Two sergeants sitting at a military table next to the registration desk welcomed Bob's group. They had told them the hotel was for enlisted men only and only five enlisted men had registered. The first floor with twenty rooms was now all that was available for the enlisted personnel and the other four floors were available for civilians. "That's why you see European civilians running around all over the place to keep the hotel doors open."

The sergeants took a map out of the table drawer; unfolded it and showed them the hotel for officers was located on the edge of town and showed them how to go there. They arrived at a three-story hotel in the dark and behind it they were surprised to see a giant hill behind all lit up. There were numerous skiers going up a ski tow and skiing down the long slope.

While they were checking in at the hotel the absence of military personnel was quite apparent. The desk clerk told them only two French officers were registered. And military officer personnel were restricted to the first floor. The second and third floors were for civilian occupants only. He then casually assigned two each to rooms with two double beds, a desk, chest of drawers, closet, and a full bathroom, including a bidet. It was very neat and clean and obviously a first-class hotel.

They passed the dining room on the way to their rooms and noticed there were not many civilians, in there. Diners were only served until 7:30, so they hurried to their rooms, next to each other, and put their clothes away and came back to the dining room. A matre d' seated them at a table next to two young girls who were maybe nineteen or twenty years old. Noticing no menus Ray asked for one and was told everyone was served the same meal at each sitting throughout each day because all food was rationed to them.

Ray commented, "There had to be a catch to why nobody was there. They must have a limited amount and type of foods." Sure, enough they were served a pure GI dinner of baked Spam and potatoes with corn. During dinner Ray, from

Maine who spoke sufficient French began a conversation with the girls at the next table. They were from Paris.

After one or two sentences, in French, the girls said, "We want to talk to all of you, so; we shall speak in English. They spoke with a French /British accent. After dinner they joined with the girls, at one table, and had some wine together while getting aquatinted. The girls introduced themselves as Jacqueline and Margaret Darnay and said their father owned a ship building company. They talked themselves out about each other by 11:00 o'clock. Everyone thought it was time to go to bed; before separating and all agreed to meet for breakfast.

Wednesday's breakfast consisted of bacon, powdered eggs, toast made from French bread and GI type coffee. The girls were waiting at the dining room entrance to have breakfast with the boys. During breakfast they said they had their own ski equipment, knew how to ski fairly well and had been there over a week. After breakfast the girls told the pilots where to find the instructor who would help them fit their ski equipment.

They guys went out the rear double door of the hotel to find their ski instructor. The girls knew who their instructor was and pointed to him waiting at the bottom of the stairs for them. Seeing the girls leading the pilots toward him he suspected they were his students. The girls introduced him as Jean Claude de Valour. The girls and the instructor knowing each better than suspected they all laughed while speaking French and amazed the pilots by their close alliance.

He took the new students out and around the corner of the building, a basement of the hotel that was laid out with all kinds of ski equipment. Each pilot was fitted with proper ski shoes, skis about seven feet long, ski poles and new ski gloves. When everyone was set up, they went to a Bunny Slope on the right side of the big 1420-meter ski slope to the uphill towrope power shack.

Jean asked the girls if they wanted to join the pilots and they were elated. They knew what he was about to teach the pilots. They didn't mind and he slyly smiled at them. Initially he taught the pilots to snowplow ski straight and to climb up a hill with their skis sideways, parallel to the slope. He worked with them all morning until he felt they knew how to do those fundamentals well. They took a lunch break about noon. The instructor did not eat in the hotel with them and after lunch they found him waiting at the bottom of the stairs near their skis and poles stuck in the snow.

He had them doing straight snow plowing down the 50-meter Bunny hill all afternoon. And made a strong point; you have to, "Bend zee knees!" By 5:00 o'clock he had them all doing the snow plowing well. The girls just tagged along all day even though they knew how to ski. The pilots and the girls had dinner together and while eating Margaret asked if anyone played bridge. Alan said he did, and Ray spoke up he also knew how to play. Jacqueline interceded saying, "That would not be right. We have to find something to include Nick and Bob." She paused a moment and brightly asked, "Do you know how to play pinnacle?"

The four guys knew so they got two decks from the hotel and played 'six handed' pinnacles. That made the evening special because they all relaxed and enjoyed a great evening together. Whenever someone made a bad error, no one became angry, they just laughed at each other and by the end of the evening they were talked and laughed out. They drank mostly coke and coffee all evening and everybody had a nightcap of red or white wine together.

Thursday morning, the 24th, Jean sat on the stone sidewall of the stairs waiting for them. He greeted them and said, "Today we learn to make snowplow turns on the 50-meter slope. They put on their skis and ski poled themselves to and climbed the hill as taught yesterday. He now emphasized they learn how much of a slight sitting position to assume and to lean forward on their skies. Ray knew how and Alan picked it up faster than Bob and Nick.

Jean was a determined teacher. He worked with Bob and Nick all afternoon teaching them how to snowplow straight and how widening and narrowing the spread of the back of the skis could make them go slow of faster and control one's speed. By the end of the afternoon, he had them doing fairly well at increasing and braking their speed without falling.

Before leaving he told them, I want all of you to practice

snowplow skiing and changing speeds with control. He recommended they try the bigger hill to the right of the long run as they improved because it was a little over 100 meters long. "That way you get to ski longer and can make more speed changes." When he left, they all did as he suggested and skied in the lights on the slopes until well after dark. The girls took the guys out on the town after a late dinner, that Thursday evening, and showed them a few nice restaurants if they wanted something to eat other than the GI meals. Everyone chose a knockwurst sandwich. They came back to the hotel at 9:45, got the cards out to play some more pinnacle and had a lot of laughs and fun until eleven o'clock that night.

Friday, the 25th, JeanClaude met them at the foot of the hotel steps, again, after they had their typical GI breakfast. They drew the made up and stored sets of ski equipment from the supply store and proceeded to the 100 + meter ski slope. He had them side climb the slope. The top of it was an extension around and behind the trees from a two-foot jump on the 1250-meter run. At the plateau he took the position with parallel skis for skiing downhill. He demonstrated about how much they should bend their knees and also how much to lean forward for parallel skiing.

He started with each one of them and had them start snowplow skiing, then slowly how to slowly bring the skis into a parallel position to slowly change and keep their speed under control. Ray was excellent; Alan was fairly good and picked the technique much faster than Bob and Nick. They made a climb, run, and climb, run, several times. They found they had to take a long rest after a couple consecutive side hill climbs.

After the lunch break, they met on top of the small plateau. Jean had them doing the same thing all afternoon. By dark he had Ray doing parallel ski runs extremely well and Alan doing them fairly well. Bob and Nick still had to snowplow, on and off a lot, all the way down the ski run to keep from falling. They stopped at the small jump to slowly snowplow going down that steep slope. Before Jean left, for the day, he said he would be late on Saturday and should continue practicing what they were doing that day.

After dinner they went to several cafés in town and began talking to some of the residents they saw on the slope. They took them to a café where they sang French and German beer songs. The guys couldn't join in but did enjoy the beer garden choruses. Bob and Nick had a couple beers too many by 2300hrs and staggered back to the hotel with Ray's and Alan's assistance who didn't drink half as much beer. Upon arrival Alan took Bob to their room and Ray did the same with Nick. Everyone really slept well that night.

On Saturday morning they had a bacon and scrambled egg breakfast and wondered where they came up with the bacon. They knew where their dehydrated scrambled eggs came from. We all ate, the girls left breakfast first, walked to the rear exit doors and saw Jean, at his usual station, waiting at the foot of the hotel stairs. The pilots met them at the bottom of the stairs to get their ski gear. While getting their skis

Jean told them he could only work with them until noon, and added he did not teach at all on Sundays.

Up on the 100+ meter slope he had them do more of the same thing they did on Friday and helped when they made mistakes. He also had them intentionally sit back and then lean forward on their skis to show them how to take little jumps.

Before he left at noon, he suggested they try the 1200-meter run and first use a lot of snowplow skiing until they got the feel of the longer run. Also, if they can, do as much parallel skiing as possible all-day Sunday. He left at noon and wished them well. Everyone used the hundred-meter slope and practiced what they were capable of doing the rest of the day. They had a good roast chicken dinner. A group at a table close to them, while having an apple pie desert, talked in French about a dance in the town hall by the Chamonix residents where everybody was welcome. Everyone in Alan's group went to their rooms after their apple pie to freshen up and the six met in the lobby before going to the dance.

Bob came up with an arrangement for Ray to escort Margaret and Alan with Jacqueline. Alan told them he was committed to a Belgian girl and would rather have someone else escort her. Then, Bob decided he would escort Jackie to the dance. That worked fine until they got to the hall because fifteen minutes later Margaret saw an American Army captain. He was her boy friend assigned to oversee the Chamonix ski package for the military men there, the pilots didn't know he existed before Margaret ran into him in the dance hall. Ray ended up with Jackie and everyone wanted to know about Alan's Belgian girlfriend.

Alan told them, "I hope you meet her tonight and no later than tomorrow. When and if she arrives, you'll be the first to be introduced. I can't say much more."

Michelle entered the hall at the entrance across the room from where Alan's group was standing, around 2045hrs. She ran into a several young French men and girls, near the entrance, she knew from Paris. They happily greeted and asked what brought her there. Several others who knew her also gathered around her. She knew that two of the girls who were in the French underground mistress school. It was obvious she received more recognition from the French, than the Belgians for being associated with the Resistance.

She told them her she came for her American pilot fiancé and hoped he would be there, as he said he would. Someone in the group, pointing, said, "There are four pilots across the room toward that corner." She looked around the room and seeing Alan, put up her arm and waved it. Her arm caught his attention and he saw her face between the people. On recognizing each other, they dashed across the room and met in the middle of the dance floor. An embrace was followed by a long kiss and when they separated, she took him to meet her French friends. Then, as he led her to his friends waiting across the room he asked, "Why did all your friends applaud?"

"Because I told them I hoped to meet you, my fiancé, and the applause indicated their joy for us.

He introduced her to Ray, Bob, and Nick. He stopped, as he was about to introduce her to the sisters. They apparently knew each other, hugged, and began talking in French.

Around 2200hrs Michelle suggested they return to the hotel. He shyly agreed and they left at 2210hrs. When she arrived at hotel she checked-in, asked if she had any messages and did not ask for keys; instead; she suggested they go to the dining room and have a glass or two of their red wine. They picked a table not too close to any one and ordered. They took a sip of their wine and Michelle paused and looked at him and told him, "I shall graduate from the University of Brussels on Sunday, 3 February, then; I shall be free of Uncle Hubere and gain control of my home, receive an income, that has been going into all my family's assets from my half of the fabric production company left to me by my mother." She put her arms around his neck and looked into his eyes and asked, "Can you come and be there for my commencement on the 4th of February? And after that; will you be willing to honestly discuss when and where we should marry? Aunt Marie said she couldn't wait."

He asked if she was willing to talk about that in private in one of their rooms? She believed that was a good suggestion and they went to the desk for her room keys. While Michelle waited for the desk clerk a French Captain entered and stood close to her. He had pilot wings and was decorated with numerous French military medals. He patted Michelle's butt, then; pinched it. Michelle jumped away and glared at him and Alan stepped between them to intercede. Michelle told him to step away; she could take care of the problem.

She loudly and angrily spoke, in French, with a long array of sentences at the Officer after which *he apologized and the desk clerk, shocked, couldn't believe what he heard.* Alan picked out a few words like *fiancé, faire, l'amour, se marier avec, s'excuser, moi* and asked her what he said. She responded with, "I told him, in no uncertain terms, you are my fiancé, my lover and we are about to marry, and he apologized."

They went to their rooms; Michelle's was on the second floor. She phoned to tell him where her room was located. She said, "Come up the stairs to the second floor. Take the hall to your right and walk to the end of that hall. My room is the last one on the right, number 329." She also suggested he come to her room either in or with pajamas.

Alan got his pajamas then went to and peeked out of his door. He cautiously searched the halls and the stairs. He ducked back in his room when someone approached. When no one was visible in the halls or on the stairs he walked silently and hurried up the staircase. Looked both ways through the halls at the top of the staircase, hurried down the hall and knocked on her door. She opened it and he went in.

They embraced with a passionate kiss as he entered the room, then; Michelle asked if he had an answer to her question? He informed her, "First I have to know if Uncle Hubere is aware you and I are making plans to be married?"

"I do not know. He talked about you recently and still complained of our relationship."

"I'll give you an answer when your uncle knows. Even if he disagrees." Hesitating...he asked, "Does your Uncle Hubere know you came to Chamonix to be with me?"

Michelle was going to lie, but; feared he may hear different and get upset with her. She admitted, "Aunt Marie knows, and she agreed, so she was to tell him I went to Paris."

"So; where do we stand on this issue? There will never be any peace if Hubere disagrees. You know that! We do need his acceptance. We have to have that if you want to be happy. If we don't have his acceptance your family will ultimately treat you as an outcast and you'll have no family and may become a miserable wreck. I don't want you to risk that. It could happen. I want you for life and be part of a happy family relationship."

"Why are you so concerned with what Uncle Hubere thinks. I said I'll be free!"

"How free? Your aunt and uncle are all you have. You are like their child now. They even treat you as if you were their child. Some day they will not only desire, but; want to be your children's grandparents."

"I know; I know; and that worries me. If we are in the United States, will it matter?"

"We have to get serious and talk about this seriously. I'm not avoiding an answer. "I understand. Aunt Marie, you and we have to get serious with him. I just feel there is no other way; Hubere ultimately has to be included in our relationship. You'll put Aunt Marie in a trap and precarious position. She has to live with him; remember when she said that?

She threw her arms around him and asked, "Enough! Will you sleep with me tonight?"

"Wait a minute? What about abstaining after your miscarriage? We can just go do that!"

"I visited my gynecologist a week ago. He examined me and said it would be safe now and be sure to use the cleansing kit as needed. And to see him immediately if I miss a period to assure there are no complications the next time."

"I don't care what he said. I'll have to go get a condom from my suitcase."

"Did you have something in mind if I didn't get here? I know how to take care of everything after we love together. You know we never use those anymore."

"I told you the medics make us take them if want to go off base. Remember?"

"All right will you sleep with me tonight? I want to love you and love you and love you!"

Alan was up at six o'clock in the morning and made it to his room without being seen.

Sunday, 27 January 1946 – Chamonix, France

They had breakfast together at 8:30 in the morning and went to the ski area and began skiing on lower end of slope. The 1500-meter slope had some small jumps and a three-foot high steep slope to jump halfway down. Michelle being an excellent skier worked with Alan on better downhill skiing and small jumps. Jacqueline and Margaret who also were excellent skiers worked on the other pilots. They skied until noon, had lunch and returned to ski slope until dinner. By 5:00 o'clock not everybody was skiing well. Nick and Bob couldn't go too fast without falling and had to make several stops on the runs they made.

All seven sat around and talked for almost an hour after dinner, then; Michelle decided to take Alan out on Chamonix, that evening. As they walked out of the hotel, she hooked her left arm around his right one and she made him inseparable all night. The other three guys went out with the Jacqueline. Margaret took off with her boyfriend. Michelle being familiar with entire area stopped in several clubs and proudly introduced Alan. He was amazed how well known she was by numerous people in the village. She seemed to bubble over love for him with each group of friends they spent time talking to.

A couple asked, "When did you take a fiancé? He is the first one we have seen you with over the past year and a half. And if you're not married, will you be, or doesn't it matter?"

She responded to those questions with," We are to marry in two months; in Brussels."

They returned to the hotel near mid-night, and she asked him up for a glass of wine. She wanted to talk about what they will do when they are both going to the university in the US. He put a shirt and his pants on over his pajamas to go to her room. When he entered, she had him strip to his pajamas and led him to the couch. "How did you come to know so many men and women in Chamonix cafés," Alan queried?

As she filled two glasses of red wine on the coffee table she answered, "Our families, my aunt's, and mine, spent many winter months here before the war. I last saw our ski instructor in the 1936 Winter Olympics. He was the coach of the French Olympic Ski Team. I was very young then; going on thirteen years old and he had difficulty remembering me. Enough of that now, "I will talk to Aunt Marie as soon as I can, and we, her and I, shall begin to soften Uncle Hubere into accepting us as a loving couple."

He finished drinking his wine, picked her up off the couch,

carried her to the bed where he put her on her side and laid down facing her. She put a leg around him, kissed him and had him excited in no time at all.

They had to relax, for a several minutes, in each other's arms before she got out of bed and cleaned up. She returned to the couch, then; he left to clean up. While he was gone, she refilled their wine glasses. As Alan approached the couch, she began singing her 'Ode to Brussels,' "How wonderful Brussels is when two found a sincere love exists; and learned together another day shall never be missed...They will forever be..."

Monday, 28th, Tuesday the 29th, and Wednesday 30th

The four pilots and two sisters met with Jean Claude, after breakfast, the next three days waiting in the lobby. At first Michelle didn't join the group. She stood off to the side and listened in on the conversation. Jean told the group, "I have arranged to take all of you skiing on a mountain run if you are willing."

Ray, the group's skier said, "We gotta do this guys and dolls. That is real skiing. No stopping every 100 yards and go at your own pace. What do you guys think.?"

Before anyone could say anything, Jean said, "If you want to do this, we have some very concentrated lessons you must learn to do well if you want to go up on a mountain."

Bob jumped in, "Am I good enough to go with you? I'll ski

day and night to learn if I have to." He was the first to ask, "What are the concentrated lessons you mentioned?"

"You will have to learn how to slalom, at least at a gentle speed on a gentle slope. Then do left and right turns at various speeds coming down the big slope if you do them slow it will be all right. It will just take longer to come down the mountain run."

When Jean looked at Bob and Nick; he noticed Michelle standing behind them in the background listening to everything. He asked the group to excuse him, "Would you mind if I talked to this young lady." Everyone said they knew her, and he should if he wanted to. In German he said, "*My dear young lady; I know you from somewhere,*"

"*Yes; we met some time ago. I am Michelle van Bortonne of Belgium. My family was in Paris after the 1936 Olympics, and we were introduced to you and your fiancée. We, my aunt, cousin, Mimi, and I were here for a month in January 1938. You gave us lessons.*"

"*Forgive me…now I remember! You both looked so much alike I thought you and Mimi were twins and how surprised I was to find you were not. You were cousins and were such fine girls. How old were you then?*"

"*We both were sixteen.*"

Yes, sixteen! Both of you were tall, developed enough to look like young ladies and were beautiful...and I see you still are. And your mothers who both skied so well? I remember Mimi's father was elected to the Belgian Ministry before the war, and your father was...was?"

"A Professor of Languages," responded Michelle.

"How are all of them...your parents, Mimi's parents and she?"

"We lost Mimi in May 1939 from a German shrapnel bomb. My parents were victims of the Gestapo. I would rather not talk about the incident, if you don't mind?

"I'm so sorry. I shouldn't have asked. Mimi's parents are all right?"

"Yes; they are very healthy."

He felt a little embarrassed for asking about her family, while hesitating, then; asked, "Do you know these girls and American officers?

"Yes; one of them, Alan is my fiancé. Jacqueline, Margaret, and I know each other's families from visits to Paris with my family."

Jean looked at the other six and apologized for leaving them out of the conversation. Margaret responded, "You did not leave everyone out of your conversation. Jacqueline and I understood everything the two of you said."

"I am apologizing to your young men; more than to you. We must get on with today's lesson. We will get your equipment, now." Having secured their ski equipment and while putting on their skis, Jean added, "This may be very difficult especially for you Nick and Bob. Come everyone; we shall go to the 100-meter slope. I have arranged to have slalom poles arranged early this morning on that slope."

He had them do controlled snowplow slalom runs all morning. Then, had them try to, under their control, increase their speed according to their learned abilities. He emphasized strongly, "Now you must learn how to ski leaning forward and bending your knees. You let them flex like so, and they act like shock absorbers.

That after noon he taught Ray and Alan to ski slowly down the slalom the course fairly well. In mid-afternoon Nick skied too fast, fell, and twisted his right knee. Alan and Bob helped him back to the hotel. The desk clerk called an ambulance and Bob went to the hospital with him. There he they wrapped it with tape and came back to the hotel on crutches.

Alan, Ray, and the girls continued practicing the slalom run. Jean watched very closely and continued giving, mostly the men, corrective instructions. They practiced on that slalom run continuously until six o'clock and that was enough. Climbing that hill was almost too much. They rested, occasionally, from being exhausted going up the slope so many times. On Tuesday, the 29th, they were out on the slope early and Jean met them, except Nick, at the rear entrance to the hotel. Ray told him they were out there early already and returned. He led them to the ski lift, and they were pulled by cable to the top of the 1420-meter run. there he said, "I think you ready for this. Bob, you do this with me. I'll watch and help you." He had them run the slope at a medium speed using right and left turns they learned from the slalom training. By that afternoon he had them going at a fairly good rate. Michelle was outstanding and the sisters were not far off of what she could do. The girls had this mastered; they have been doing this for several years. At 5:00 o'clock Jean told them, "Tomorrow we go to Mount Brevant and ski the mountain course. Be ready early and get your shoes, skis, and poles in time for the 8:00 o'clock bus.

Their dinner was a good baked chicken again. Only this time they put some kind of herb or something on it that gave it this, 'I can't eat enough to satisfy me" urge. Michelle again asked him, at dinner, if they could spend one more evening in town together.

As their group, of now seven, left the dining room they saw a young French pilot checking in. He appeared to be very young. Bob thought he looked too young to be a military pilot and Nick questioned his being a pilot saying, "He looks too young to really be a pilot." Alan suggested they not bother; "Who cares, anyway, what he is. Let him be."

Bob and Nick thinking the kid was an impostor went to the desk and asked for the manager. They said his authenticity of being a French pilot should be checked. While Bob and Nick talked to the hotel manager, Michelle and Alan left and went into town.

On the way down the hill from the hotel to the town he wondered, "Why she seemed so wrapped up in hitting all the cafés every night."

They met more of her friends, from prewar days, who arrived that afternoon. With her arm hooked to his she introduced him as her fiancé to all she knew. She seemed so elated when she met someone and told them about Alan. All the singing and dancing in cafés made him curious as to why, she was in town hitting cafés every night.

By 2230hrs they ended up in Michelle's room, on the couch, with the red wine. His curiosity surfaced when he asked, "Why do we have to be in cafés every night? And "Why is half of your conversations with your friends in French or Dutch?" Then, back in your room it's red wine, sweet talk and ultimately bed?" Before she answered he continued, "I can't believe you could possibly love me as much as you appear to do? I... "Do you really love me? I feel like your toy?"

"Stop! Stop! Stop feeling sorry and placing yourself in an inferior class of humanity.

I thought you were all over that after we talked about my miscarriage. Michelle stared at him finding it very difficult to control her temper. "You are not inferior to me. You are the only man I have ever truthfully loved. You are handsome and admired by everyone we have met. Has all this surfaced, because you cannot believe how much I could love you and only you? Don't you understand; I haven't gone out for such a long time and now with a fiancé we can go out and together enjoy ourselves. "Oh! Let's stop this discussion. It shall hurt more than help. We're here to enjoy each other and discuss this some other time." She being, an astonishing woman, regained control of her temper and in a few moments softly asked, "Whatever made you think you were my toy?

She held his hand and calmly asked, "Please...tell me what about me, is bothering you?"

He didn't answer and simply answered, "I'm OK; I feel it is best that I go now."

She did not try to stop him. She believed it best to let him go...tomorrow is another day. Peeking through her door, ajar, she watched Alan slowly walk down the hall. Halfway down he stopped, turned, looked at her room, and then proceeded. He disappeared around the corner of the floor. She sat down on the couch and began thinking, "This has to be a critical point in our relationship! I have to resolve his low esteem, inferior feeling and inadequacy of himself. Who would imagine a man excelling in everything could think he is so inferior; so shy among women and not believing anyone could love him as much as I do."

Wednesday morning the hotel manager contacted French

Air Command. Jean was at the desk asking for his students. He no sooner asked, and they walked out of the dining room and saw him. He told them to hurry the bus is waiting. It took several minutes for them to get their equipment and get it on the bus. The bus ride to Brevant was only a little over twenty-five minutes.

A cable car took them to the beginning of the ski runs on Mount Brevant. Jean explained there were three ski trails marked by, red, yellow, and green, flags. He informed them the red trail was very hazardous with narrow trails and jumps, in some places. Then added the Red was not for anyone of them. Then continued, the yellow trail, had small jumps for good skiers and this also not for them yet. And he said finally, "We are all to use only the green trail which challenges good new skiers all the way down. You girls do not mind staying back with us; do you?"

Knowing Michelle was an excellent skier he let her and Alan start, the 3+ mile run, first. Everyone else, in groups of two, with Ray leading started closely spaced and followed by the instructor, Jean, who watched over everyone; including Bob who was skiing with him. Alan asked Michelle what she thought about guiding him down the yellow runs. "I would prefer you establish yourself well on the green trail first. I have skied seven years before the war. I would not think of trying the red trail and not having skied since then I would hesitate trying the yellow trail also."

He said, “You know my limits better than I do; will you discuss our limits with me?”

He didn’t have to concentrate too much, skiing the green trail. He apparently learned more than she thought on the hotel ski trails. They cruised down to the chalet twenty minutes before the other six and ordered lunch.

While having a sandwich, Michelle asked, “What did you mean, will I discuss our limits?”

“Oh; it has to do with everything; all this stuff keeps creeping into my mind about you?”

They finished their glass of wine with a sandwich just before everyone else came in. The others had lunch of either a sandwich or a prepared meal with available wine. Michelle and Alan started twenty minutes before the others and reached the end of trail in thirty minutes. She kept track of the time and told him they completed the trail in fifty minutes.

“Is that good?”

“Yes; for your first mountain run it was very good, but do not try it alone.”

Michelle I am so happy when I think about getting married; then I get depressed?” He paused; then asked, “How are we ever going to get married? There are so many obstacles, like Uncle Hubere and his governmental powers.” And almost crying added, "Do you really think you can be happy with a dumb naive person like me."

Michelle responded, "Why are you torturing yourself over me? Then she teased him by spelling, I- l-o-v-e - y-o-u in the snow and asked, "Have you ever made love in the snow?"

"Michelle why did you ask that question. How could I? I've only been with you." Then, realized it was a suggestion; maybe a tease and responded, "Michelle not here. OK?"

She laughed at him for being so naive and said, "I did not intend to do anything; only because we do not have enough time. Anyway, I wanted to see your reaction."

The others arrived at the bottom on the mountain forty-five minutes later. After all, arrived and settled at base of Brevant; they put their ski equipment and themselves on the bus. Their bus left for the hotel at 1645hrs.They could see and admired Mt. Brevant from the bus all the way back to the hotel. It was then they became aware of the length of the ski run they had maneuvered down. They arrived at the hotel after 1725hrs, cleaned up and met in the dining room. During their dinner, Jacqueline and Michelle asked Ray and Alan if they would ask and receive a four- or five-day extension at Chamonix for all four of them. The guys said Alan knew Roberts best and thought he should call about an extension. He told them he would try.

They left the dining room, and he immediately went to

a pay phone and called their Base. He got a hold of Roberts and asked if he would find if it were possible to get them up to a five-day extension on their own time and costs. He said he would find out and call back as soon as he had an answer. As the others walked into the lobby Alan went to the desk to ask the hotel manager, could they stay, if they could get an extension since no one is using the facility as planned.

"He boldly responded; "I do not think you will be welcomed here again. I do not mean that for the girls; only you pilots."

Michelle quietly said, "Alan; I think, picking on the young pilot only created a problem."

They were not aware that the hotel manager had received affirmative information about the young French pilot. The manager motioned to Bob and Nick to come to the counter as the group entered the lobby from the dining room. Alan and the girls were near enough to hear the hotel manager tell them that the young French pilot was legitimate as were his orders.

Then, Michelle asked Alan, "After discussion last night and what we just overheard; are you willing to go into town for our last the evening together?"

The others lead by Ray and Jacqueline also had decided to go into town for their last night in Chamonix. Michelle and Alan left first; Ray and Jacqueline left later with Bob and Nick. He and Michelle separated from the others, at the first café.

Michelle and Alan met, Jean Claude, their ski instructor in the first café they entered. Jean said to Michelle, speaking in German, "I *have seen you in many cafés all week and you are always hanging on his arm.*"

She responded, "I love him! No one is to take him from me anyway you can think of."

Jean Claude and several others who knew Michelle laughed, then; got together and began a French songfest. That was when Alan discovered Jean was Austrian and half French as he joined in the songfest best, he could. Michelle led him out of the café and to their hotel at 2130hrs. On the way Michelle asked him if he would spend this last night in her room and be there by 10:00 o'clock? He was prompt and arrived with a bottle of red wine. Michelle took the bottle from him and placed on the coffee table in front of the couch and asked him to sit down and wait while she brought two wine glasses and an opener. She opened the bottle of wine, poured some in their glasses and sat very close to him.

"Where did you find that red wine? I thought of ordering a bottle of cold champagne."

He set the wine on the coffee table. "It's like red wine we always have. I brought it with me."

"Must you leave tomorrow with the others? Did your friend arrange an extension?"

"I should know tomorrow, but; I'm concerned of the complaining about that young French pilot might backfired on us as you said."

"If you must leave, we have to make, this night, a night to remember." Michelle noted. And I recall our meeting in the Parisian restaurant? Your hazel eyes captured me,"

Alan smiling said, "I don't know what happened after that first moment I saw you. I wanted to meet you but was too shy. I wanted to stop and talk to you on our way out, but; feared you would reject me."

"Then; you appeared in Phillipe's Cafe. I had you in my mind after first seeing you and had an opportunity to now know if my feelings were genuine. That was why I asked you to join us in the café," answered Michelle."

"I find it hard to understand 'why me' when many men in Europe were available to you?"

"Why you? I have been with many men who wanted me only for my beauty, in their beds. Remember our first night? You were one of the few men who treated me like a lady. You were the only man in my bed since the Gestapo left Brussels. I will not replace you."

"Did finding out you were my first to have affair influence you toward me in any way?"

"Alan, stop that now! I've never felt so much in love before. I had to come to see you. Did not my introducing you to my Aunt Marie and Uncle Hubere convince you I cared? Did not those days in Leuven, at the university, in the town, and my home tell you anything? Did not our love affair in my apartment before you first left Brussels mean anything to you?"

Michelle, I don't have any excuses. I'm just one confused person with a beautiful girl. She put her hands over his mouth, "Enough; Alan this is our night to remember."

Alan obeyed and embraced her as she passionately began kissing him. His heart was racing as she unbuttoned his pajama tops, then; he began removing her bathrobe. Standing next to the bed naked they passionately embraced with their heads buried in each others' shoulders kissing their necks. Michelle leaned toward the bed in this position and turned them as they fell with her landing on top of him. Later they fell asleep on their right sides with Alan behind and snuggled-up very close to her.

Thursday, 31 January 1946

The next morning Roberts phoned Alan and told him their request had been denied. And added, "The extension was denied by 9th Air Force Head Quarters and the French Government! What the hell is going on down there?"

Alan said he would explain it all when he gets back at their base. The hotel manager called Ray to the front desk after breakfast to inform him, "The four of you must leave today."

The pilots had breakfast with the girls before going to their rooms to pack. The girls waited to walk them to the train station at 1030hrs. They got to the station in plenty of time for their downhill mountain train to take them to the base station where, at noon, they were to board a train to Strasbourg. Hopefully catch the train there in enough time to make Erlangen by early morning.

Jacqueline and Michelle broke out in tears before Ray and Alan got on the train. "We will never see you again. You will be going back to America," cried Michelle.

He embraced Michelle kissed her, and whispered, "I promise to write to you often." And he couldn't understand why Ray hardly said anything to Jacqueline.

The train left Chamonix on time and arrived in Strasbourg at 1600hrs. They went to the local club. Their train was scheduled to leave at 1650hrs but didn't leave until 1855hrs. Dinner wasn't available and they waited in the officer's club for their train. Ray asked Alan if he called the base and told Roberts of their arrival time from Strasbourg.

"I called him this morning and I told him we would arrive at Erlangen at about 0400hrs in the morning." And Roberts first words were, "Do you have any idea why your request for an extension was denied?" Then, before Alan could explain he added, "What the hell did you guys do there besides stirring up a bag of worms? Not only Wing, but; 9th Air Force and the French Government were involved in denying your request."

He did not include that after some apologetic words, trying to get it across that he was not involved, Roberts calmed down and Alan said, "I really called to ask if we could have some transportation from Erlangen to the base? You wouldn't make us walk; would you?"

Roberts answered, "I should, but; I believe you weren't involved. Yeah, I'll have a six by six for you at the train station." And simply added, "The Base Commander doesn't know a thing about this yet. I'll do what I can short of getting myself in trouble. Then hung up. At that point, Alan didn't know what to think? He wondered, "Holy Jesus; did 9th Air Force know I was one of the idiot pilots who made this mess? I hope there's no one there, who remembers me from last January? Oh God if they know; help me."

Ray interrupted Alan's talking to himself asking, "Did Roberts say he'd have a ride for us from Erlangen to the base?"

He said Roberts would have a six by six at the train station for us. Then Alan thought. "If you have a good friend don't ask for anything; when you need him, he'll be there, to take care of you."

A band was playing dancing music in the club. They sat at a table close to the dance floor. A tall, pretty brunette girl was sitting alone at a table next to them. Ray asked her to dance. She said she was not involved with men in the club and was waiting for someone. Ray wondered how she got into the club and risked asking her if the club had an open-door policy for French ladies. She told Ray they did not permit women to enter without an escort; her father was her escort and a guest of the club since Strasbourg was liberated in 1944, and she was waiting for her him. He was to arrive soon.

Twenty minutes later, her father, a tall graying man, in a neat pin stripped suit walked into the club. He was surprised to see his daughter with an officer and asked who he was. She introduced her father as a professor at the University of Strasbourg and Ray told him, he and the three pilots with him at the next table were waiting for a train to Erlangen, Germany.

Ray asked him what he taught. He told Ray he is how teaching several undergraduate history courses and a few classes for graduate studies in European history,"

Ray responded, "I was in my second-year majoring in history before entering the service and will proceed to get a Ph.D. in history, if I can, and teach at my university, the University of Maine."

The girl's father tested him by asking some intricate

European history questions which he answered without hesitation. The grin in her father's face indicated he accepted him, and Ray asked if they wanted a drink. Her father wanted to buy, but Ray insisted. He made a good impression with the girl and her father.

When he asked her for a dance, she asked her father who gave her permission to dance with Ray if she so desired. But added, "Do not dance too close!"

Ray initially asked for only one dance. When that song ended, they sat down and talked about where each of them lived. They ended up dancing again to a couple of slow dances. When a fast score began Ray lead her back to her table. Before they left the girl told Ray her father said she could write to him if he was willing and asked for his address. They had to wait for Ray and the girl to exchange giving each other their addresses.

They left in time to catch their train, that left on time. On the train they asked Ray if he was going to communicate with the Strasbourg girl? Ray never gave him an answer and they thought maybe he and Jacqueline had something going together.

They arrived in Erlangen, several miles from their base, at 0415hrs and a six-by-six truck was at the station waiting for them. They reached the base by 0510hrs and they all were in bed and asleep by 0600hrs.

Friday, 1 February 1946

Alan asked Strait, at lunch if he knew where Jim Watson was? He told him he thought Jim was on his liquor run and left the previous Saturday morning. Roberts met Alan at dinner and sitting quietly next to him asked him, "You ready to tell me what really happened at Chamonix? You realize the French Government, USAFE, and 9th Air Force were involved?"

"I can believe that. What happened was, we just left the dining room as a young French pilot was about to check in at the desk. You know Bob Andrews who was with us? Roberts nodded yes. "Well; he and Nick filed a complained, to the hotel manager, that the young French pilot looked like an impostor."

Roberts asked, "What were their reason for bring this to the mangers attention?"

"Because they thought the guy looked too young to be legit and asked the hotel manager to check on him with the French Air Force; and the biggest boob of all; also told him, he shouldn't be there with us. Like he couldn't possibly be a pilot like us!"

I tried telling them to leave him alone because it's none of our business. He was French we've no right to question anything about him, but; they insisted. The next day as we were walking through the lobby from the dining room the hotel manager called Bob and Ray over to his desk and told him the young French pilot and his orders were legitimate."

Roberts said he had to go to headquarters and Alan returned to his room. There was mail on his bed. Michelle's letter dated 10 February was among his mail. It was a serious letter hat proposed a variety of marriage arrangements. It became very clear Michelle's major choice was to get married in the U:S. and attend a university together. She didn't mention anything about her aunt's or her uncle's position of a marriage.

On the 15th of February he answered her letter with a question about her uncle's current position on her marrying him. As he told her in Leuven, "I don't want to mess up a family relationship over me. It wasn't worth hurting you without his approval."

Her 20 February letter repeated the information she was free of her uncle's interference. And his control over her and all of her possessions ended on the day she graduated from Brussels University. He was no longer her guardian and had control of her inheritance. She reminded Alan, the inheritance was substantial, and will be all mine to do with as I please. She mentioned going out with her friends and celebrating her freedom." But she shouldn't have included, those supposed entitled men her uncle once mentioned were now approaching her for dates' again.

The letter deeply bothered him because he wasn't after her

estate, money or whatever her Uncle Hubere, thought. Alan's concern was, "She was now, in Belgium and one of the elites on her own. She was free of Uncle Hubere, but; was she free of her elite status obligations?" Among his other thoughts he wondered if she was free of her Belgium and possibly Claude. He was sort of a nice guy, seemingly a gentleman and well up in the Belgian society.

The hurdles confused him, and he thought, "Would his avoiding marriage be best for her?" He found it extremely difficult to write to Michelle of future marriage plans. He averaged sending two letters a week to Michelle after the week of 3 February. Michelle's letters were so upbeat he could feel her excitement and Alan never mentioned his insecurity again from the day she was free from Hubere. Despite Hubere's resentment and his fears he proposed marriage to Michelle in his 8 March letter. Then, for no reason Michelle's letters suddenly ceased after the last one dated 9 March 1946. Then, by Sunday morning 15 March Alan was a nervous wreck. He thought he wrote something to alienate Michelle.

He found Roberts and pleaded with him for a short leave to Brussels, who apologized because he couldn't get him a leave. He received information the previous morning that Alan and Strait were frozen at the base pending an assignment for returning to the US.

It was March 20th and he had still not received an answer to his letter of March 8th from Michelle. He became very depressed and thought Uncle Hubere got her to accept Claude or some other elite social class guy. He began to give up ever seeing her again.

By March 23rd, Alan had still not heard from Michelle and not receiving a letter hoped writing one more letter would get some sort of response from her. In it he said he would go to her and get married so she could return to the US with him. He also pleaded to her to forgive him for not making a decision to marry her sooner. And added, “I will never forget every moment with you. I will never have any more like them; ever! My problem has been, believing I am not good enough for you as Hubere said, but I am! You can’t imagine how much I love you. I will never forget you.

Sixteen

THE UNTHINKABLE

Monday, 25 March to 13 April 1946

Alan and Strait received orders to initiate a return to the United States on 25 March 1944. Alan became depressed over not hearing from Michelle since he never received an answer to his 08 March letter to her. He mailed one last letter to Michelle in an effort to hear from her containing.

"I am being sent to a port of deportation on the last week of March. I'll come to Brussels, if you still wish to marry me, before I'm scheduled to ship for the U.S. If you do not want to marry me anymore, tell me and release me from this depression I'm now in for not knowing what you think, feel, or want with or without me. Please tell me?"

They left by truck after breakfast 0830hrs, 28 March,

and arrived just before dinner at Furstenfeldbruck, Germany. Strait and Alan were quartered in a large room in a building formerly used by German Luftwaffe officers. Processing for the US began the next morning with a physical examination. It actually was a pre-separation physical to assure to any and all combat and/or non-combat injuries in the line of duty were properly documented. The paper path was sort of a personal historic trace. All the necessary processing was completed in five days: Wednesday, the 03 April 1944.

That next day was a do-nothing period, except for eating, sleeping, and waiting. That evening Strait found a six- or seven-year-old female German Shepard abandoned dog. The dog looked more like a wolf than dog but was extremely gentle and he named her Shasta. She gave both of them something to care about and turned out to be a wonderful companion. During the day she followed them everywhere and patiently waited when they entered buildings. At night she slept just outside of their quarters under the stoop and every morning she wagged her tail and looked so happy to see them. Claire took good care of her with scraps from every meal they had, including bacon from breakfast.

Alan still could not erase the thought of Michelle. He mentioned, to Strait, his depression over not hearing from her on several occasions. He suggested Alan should seek a seven or at least a five- day leave and go to Brussels and find out what your status is with her.

Friday morning, he made up his mind and went to

Headquarters to ask for a seven or at least five-day leave to Brussels, Belgium. He was refused, since; all transient personnel were frozen to the base awaiting transfer to LeHarve for shipment to the US.

They received orders on Wednesday 10 April transferring them to Le LeHarve, France on Friday 12 April. Strait immediately went to Headquarters and asked if he could take Shasta with them and was told animals could not be taken out of the area. They talked to many persons before finding a base assigned, sergeant who accepted Shasta. She looked so sad when she was left on a leash with the sergeant as they walked away. She just sat next to him and looked at Strait wondering why he was leaving her. Alan noticed Claire's face looked as sad as Shasta's, then; felt his own tears entering his eyes.

They boarded a train in the late morning of 12 April and arrived at LeHarve on Saturday morning before breakfast. The system never changes; they had physicals and completed more repetitious personal paperwork.

The following Wednesday Strait heard if anyone still having leave time available could ask for a leave to Paris prior to receiving a shipping date. Strait again suggested Alan should go to Base Headquarters and ask for his leave to Brussels. It seemed to be the right time to ask. At headquarters he found he had over thirty days of leave accumulated. When questioned why he wanted to go to Brussels in the British area and not Paris he explained, best he could, a future bride was waiting for him. He was surprised because that apparently was enough reason to warrant an immediate leave. The following day he received a Six Day Leave Order to Brussels for the period 13 through 18 April 1946.

Saturday, 13 thru Thursday, 18 April 1946

He caught the Saturday morning 0930hrs train for Paris and transferred to a Brussels train there. He arrived in Brussels at 1749hrs and waved down a taxi to take him directly to Phillipe's Cafe. He walked into café and found Phillipe's wife, Helena, and oldest daughter, Helga, the only ones there. They said Philippe was out on errands and expected back within the hour. While waiting Alan talked to his wife and oldest daughter. Both seemed uncomfortable by his questions about Michelle and avoided any direct answers his questions. He became desperate realizing by their silence everything was different now. His imagination carried him away wondering if Uncle Hubere got to her about maintaining her status and social life she had there. And despite him she ran off with some wealthy guy other than Claude to show him she could do what she wanted to do.

Phillipe entered the café an hour later and Alan came out of his depressing illusions. He was speechless and walked directly to Alan, hugged him, and didn't say anything. Then, he noticed Phillipe's wife and daughter looking at each other in a questioning manner. Catching those looks he asked, "What is it about Michelle that you seem to be hiding?"

Phillipe just shook his head no as his wife and daughter left the café. They all knew how much Michelle loved him and also, he loved her. Alan was initially bewildered by the sudden quietness, then; he realized something tragic must have happened? He took Phillipe's right hand and put his left on his forearm. Then softly asked, "Tell me, with who and where did she go?"

Phillipe hesitated, finding it difficult to tell Alan, "Michelle did not go anywhere with anyone. She was waiting for you and now...she...is...is...dead."

"She can't be! Tell me that's not true. Tell me she ran off with someone?"

"You are the only man she was seen with since the day you met her here. I remember so well; it was Friday, 12 January 1945, and it seems as though it was yesterday. From that moment on you two became so close to me I felt like you were part of my family."

Alan asked Phillipe to tell him what he knew, and Phillipe began, "She was murdered, on Sunday night March 10th; a terrible night; dark and raining. It happened the day after the Belgian Government exonerated her due to her Resistance activities. No one could imagine why she was shot after the honors and recognition she received. I was first to reach her. It happened close to midnight. She was coming here, home, from the USO. It was quiet and suddenly I heard and recognized three pistol shots. I ran out of the café and looked around and saw a body laying on the sidewalk three buildings from the café. I ran to it and it...it was Michelle. She was still breathing when I reached her, and she knew who I was. Her last words to me were, 'Get Anton, get Anton!' I panicked! I did not know what to do. I had your address, but; I needed to know how to reach you immediately on the tele. This was an emergency, so; I called her aunt and she said she would take care of everything."

Alan was listening in shock. He immediately assumed there was really someone else. Then he had trouble asking, "Who...who...who is Anton?"

"She always called **you** Anton when you were not here. She never thought the name Alan suited you properly. She would always talk about her Anton and how he would soon be coming to marry her and take her to the United States with him. If you want to know more about 'Anton' I suggest you talk to her aunt."

He asked, "Does anyone have any idea who and why anybody would do this?"

"No one seems to know. Two groups of people are suspected; one, the people of Brussels who accused her of being a Rexist during the occupation and the other is, former unknown Gestapo agents who discovered she was with the Resistance and acting as a sincere German associate considered her a traitor. Our inspectors suspected they labeled her an Allied Spy. She had German descendants, from her mother. One was a Gestapo Captain in Italy who was used to win the Germans confidence in her when she was with the Resistance."

Government investigators, in addition to our inspectors have investigated the incident. Three suspects have been investigated and confirming anyone has been very difficult."

"Would you tell me where she is buried," he asked.

"In the Leuven cemetery next to her parents and near her cousin Mimi whose parents and the entire family, grandmothers, grandfathers, have adjacent grave sites."

"Would you permit me to visit Michelle's apartment and reminisce a little while."

"Yes, you may, but; everything in there has been removed except the sitting room couch."

"Oh, that alone would be wonderful!" He received the key and went up to the apartment. On entering the kitchen, he couldn't restrain the tears from entering his eyes. He closed his eyes and saw Michelle standing radiant in her nightgown. A moment later he opened them, and she was gone. Maybe she went into the sitting room. There he closed his eyes again and she was standing more radiant than before, until he opened his eyes. He sat on the couch and reminisced of the many happy hours there nestling in each other's arms.

He felt his heart pounding and couldn't help crying and

repeating, "Oh LORD why...why...why? Then asked himself, "Are you punishing her because of me; is it my fault for not wanting to marry her when she desired to so much? Or was it because I made her pregnant? Didn't we suffer enough over losing our child? Why wasn't it me who had to die? I loved her so much!"

He blamed himself for the tragedy. He found himself unable to think or reason clearly before he finally got himself together and went to the British USO after dinner at Phillipe's Cafe and checked in. That evening he walked around Brussels to places; from The Grand Place to the Theatre de la Monnaie, to Colonne de Congres, to the Place de la Nation and to the Parc de Bruxelles. Alan could hardly contain himself when he walked in their steps to the park and sat on the benches where she and he spent some time; a place where they hugged and kissed and were so happy just to be alive together...!

Sitting there all he thought of saying was, "Now she's gone. Oh GOD.........help me? What am I going to do without her?"

Sunday, 14 April 1946

Alan walked back to the Red Cross club and to his second-floor room. He undressed, put his pajamas on; the new ones Michelle gave him, made in Sweden, and sat on the bed facing the window. The window seemed to be calling him to "come look where you and Michelle walked; take it all in now; for tomorrow it all shall begin to fade." He thought he was in some kind of spell and went into the lavatory, looked in the mirror and saw a face; tired and drawn. He asked himself, "Was that damn window talking to me? No; I'm talking to myself into a fervor to be with Michelle. I gotta get some sleep."

It was extremely difficult for him to sleep. He tossed, he rolled, he got up, walked around the room before closing the window's drapes. Then, walked to an armchair, in the corner, and sat down facing toward the door. He was tired, closed his eyes and was still wide-awake. He woke up at three thirty not knowing how long he slept and crawled in bed. His mind awake again wanted Michelle to be with him. He laid on his right side and fell asleep.

He woke at, 0815hrs shaved and showered. The water was cool. He began to dress and thought of Michelle with each thing he put on. First, clean underwear; clean shirt, clean socks; Michelle would be proud of him. Then, his pink trousers, tie, shoes, blouse, coat and last his crushed cap. Holding his B-4 Bag he checked out and walked to Phillipes.

Phillipe let him borrow his car and he rushed to Leuven and directly to Michelle's home. On seeing him Beatrix began crying. "I taught you'd never come again?" Then told him, "Aunt Marie is wondering and waiting for you".

He went upstairs looked in Michelle's bedroom; it was made up as if she was to sleep there that night and it was too much for him. He gave Beatrix a good-bye hug and kissed her cheek before leaving. When he reached Phillipe's auto he turned and saw Beatrix in the doorway crying. He choked a bit as he began to drive away and Beatrix waving to him until he was out of sight.

It was very close to noon when he arrived at Aunt Marie Louise's house. The butler answered the doorbell, let him in and took his coat and cap. Aunt Marie was surprised when the butler told her Alan was there. She hurried to the entrance hall, greeted, and hugged him, then; they both began to cry. "What brought you here," were her first words. "How long can you remain here? My home is your home."

"I came here wanting to ask Michelle to marry me if she still loved me and if you and Hubere would accept my proposal. I have four days, then; I..I... we would have had to return to my base. She could have gone home with me on a ship with staterooms for married couples. Aunt Marie I feel so bad. I break out and cry whenever I am near anyplace, we stood, walked, sat close to each other. I never knew my heart could ache so much."

Aunt Marie invited him to the sitting room and physically sat him on the armchair facing the love seat where she sat. Being settled she asked if he would like to have a cup of coffee with her?

"Oh...I would love to have one with you,"

She told the maid to have the cook make a large fresh pot and bring it in one of the better porcelain coffee containers that holds a few cups. Then, asked, "Do I have to ask you if you desire to visit Michelle's grave?"

"You know I do. But emotionally added, "But...but...I don't know if I can handle it?"

"Alan; I wrote you two letters telling you of Michelle's tragedy. Did you ever get either of them? I was concerned because I did not receive an answer from you. I feared something happened to you."

He asked when she began writing to him. "Initially I didn't know what to do. I was in shock for the most part of two weeks. When I began to accept her loss, I realized I had to write to you. I found your address among all your letters she saved." Carefully avoiding the use of murdered she added, "I wrote my first letter to you approximately two weeks, after Michelle died. It was the 24th or 25th of March then."

"That letter probably arrived, a few days after I was transferred from my base. I was transferred to Furstenfeldbruck, Germany and left my base on 25 March 1946. By your mailing dates the letters are probably trying to catch up to me. I may or may not see them before I leave for the United States and maybe never. I was so concerned when Michelle's letters stopped coming. I feared she found someone compatible with Hubere's social lifestyle thinking, and desired to remain in Belgium. I thought maybe; she found someone he liked and left me." He had to stop a moment. And it happened, but not the way I feared. I really didn't care who she would be with as long as she was happy."

She scolded him, "I remember Michelle once saying, ...sometime during this past January; I never met anyone like my Anton."

The maid interrupted them bringing in a silver serving plate carrying the pot of coffee, a silver sugar bowl and cream server with two rich looking porcelain cups. She set the plate on the coffee table and left. Aunt Marie poured the coffee, and each added what they wanted. Then, Aunt Marie asked, "Where was I when the maid brought the coffee? Oh; yes, I was saying she told me, there was no one like you and added you were her one in a million. And you were concerned if she was happy in your presence and were always concerned if you satisfied her in every way or with anything she desired. Her thoughts were always about you. "She enjoyed calling you Anton when ever your name entered our conversation."

"Aunt Marie...you know...I never felt secure in the presence of Michelle; she was so beautiful and so good to me I never knew what to say. I always feared I would disappoint her in some way. I didn't think our relationship could endure. I never felt I looked good enough to hold on to her. I loved her so much and was afraid some other handsome guy would come along and take her from me. That's why initially I did not want to marry her. I believed if someone won her after we were married it would destroy me! Alan finally got around to saying, "Phillipe told me she was shot a few doors from him coming to the café from the USO. Do the authorities have any idea of the type of weapon from the bullets in her, or didn't they keep them to identify and mark the weapon used."

"Did not Phillipe tell you all this?" Alan looked at her and nodded no. "Didn't he tell you the bullets were from a nine-millimeter pistol, probably a German Luger?" She was so close to Phillipe's when he heard the pistol's shots." Marie started sobbing, "Yes she was on...her...way...home...from...the USO...Club." Aunt Marie suddenly stopped and said nothing. Alan seeing her flood of tears handed her his GI handkerchief. She continued, "Phillipe was the last one to see her; she was barely alive. He told me she was, with her last words, calling for you."

That brought tears to his eyes, and he had to use his blouse sleeve, temporarily, for his tears. Marie looked at him and tried to smile a bit. "He told me some of that. Mostly that she called for me using the name Anton. I initially felt pretty bad because I know Anton is a man's name and thought there really was someone else." After several quiet minutes, he asked if she had any thoughts on who did this to Michelle?

"The suspects are German sympathizers knowing she was with the Resistance, unknown free Gestapo agents, and disgruntled Belgians who saw her being escorted all around Brussels with German Officers."

"Phillipe told me a similar thing about the suspects."

They talked for over an hour and Marie asked Alan if he

would like, go to her gravesite. He just asked, “Where is it and how do I get there.”

“I will take you there.”

Aunt Marie had the butler tell her Chauffeur to bring the Limousine around to the front of the house. A few minutes later he entered the sitting room and told her, “*The limousine was out front waiting.*” She escorted Alan out and on entering the limo told the chauffeur to take them to the cemetery.

The Leuven Cemetery – Sunday, 14 April 1946

He asked Marie to have the chauffeur stop at a florist before reaching the cemetery. She so informed him and a few minutes later he turned onto a main street. Then drove for several more blocks before turning onto a narrow street. He stopped at a florist shop in the middle of that block. Alan entered the florist alone. He was in there for fifteen minutes and came out with a dozen long stem dark red roses in a cemetery vase. As he entered the limo, he and asked, “Aunt Marie do you think these are appropriate?”

She answered, “Anton, oh...I am sorry; I am so used to Michelle and me, referring to you as Anton. I remember how Michelle thought that name fitted you perfectly. And the flowers; I am quite sure she would love them; especially from you” and said nothing else. Being quiet for a while, she broke the silence with, “I am so happy you finally came. I thought you were gone. I am not thinking clearly anymore. Would you tell me again what took you so long to get here?"

"You understand I never heard from her or anyone else after her March 8th letter."

"In the letters I wrote to you, after she died, she never mentioned anything about any social class of people. The only subject she repeated was you, her and your University."

They arrived at the cemetery and Marie, leading Alan, slowly walked to Michelle's gravesite. He carefully placed the cemetery vase with roses in a retainer close to her headstone and stood there silent for several minutes praying for her. He ultimately became overwhelmed and fell to his knees, hands folded in prayer and sobbing. His mind was full of guilt for not having her with him shortly after Chamonix. He prayed, "GOD please have Michelle forgive me for not marrying her in or right after Chamonix? We had so much to live for."

With tears flowing out of his eyes and running down his cheeks; he walked on his knees to her head stone and kissed her name from the "M" to the end 'e'. Marie stood next to him, a hand on his shoulder and could not withhold tears while looking at him. This all became too much for her and after a few minutes she leaned over to him and whispered, "I am returning to the limo. and will wait until you finish saying good-bye. She knows you are here."

He did not respond; she understood and slowly walked

to her limo and waited. He could not stop crying and kept praying to God and Michelle to forgive him and finally let it all out while crying, “I came to marry you regardless of what anyone may have said against it!”

His heart was broken because it took him so long to make, what was an obvious decision. He stood up ten minutes later; hesitated, then turned and walked to the limo. There with his arms on the open limo window ledge of the door; looked at Marie with tear filled eyes and said, “Aunt Marie do you think I will ever be forgiven by her or God?”

She asked him to get in and handed him her lace handkerchief as he entered the limo. Alan looked terribly distressed, and the knees of his trousers were full of mud. Marie brought it to his attention, and he responded, “Maybe I'll never take the mud off. It's from her grave.”

Marie said they should go home and decide what to do about the knees of his trousers there. He nodded yes, got in the limo, and looked out of the rear window, then; at her grave area until it was out of sight.

During dinner Marie asked Alan if he would stay overnight with her. After dinner, she led him to the sitting room carrying their wine glasses in one hand and the decanter in the other hand. They began a conversation about Michelle and Mimi. Marie told Alan how much they really looked alike, which lead to her bringing out an album.

As little tots they looked like twins. In some of the color photos they both had big blue eyes and their hair was very light blond. Their hair was in curls and they both were wearing similar dresses with different colored patterns of flowers. The photos reminded Alan of how beautiful Michelle looked in October when he was in Brussels on a liquor run. Their eyes were moist as they paged through the album and talked about how the girls looked during different ages of their lives.

Uncle Hubere's absence was obvious, and Alan asked where he was? She told him, "He was in France Friday and would be home tomorrow." They went to bed at 11:00 o'clock.

Hubere arrived near midnight and saw an auto parked near the house. When he crawled in bed next to Aunt Marie, he asked who's auto was parked outside in our parking area. Marie told him it was Phillipe's auto and Alan had gone to bed in the next bedroom. Hubere asked how he was and now, for some reason, seemed, concerned about him asking, "*When did he arrive? How did he react when he heard about Michelle's death?*"

"He is devastated! He cried almost the entire afternoon; during and after they went to Michelle's grave. He kneeled on her grave in front of her headstone and kissed each the letters of her name. His trousers are so muddy I wonder if they will ever be able to be cleaned. He seems to break up whenever he is near something or place where he and Michelle were together. His emotional distress peaked in our sitting room when he laid down in front of the fireplace where they laid together a year ago in January."

"I knew he loved her, but never suspected how much. It is all very sad. I feel for him."

The Petremont Residence – Monday, 15 April 1946, Leuven, France

Alan came down to the breakfast nook at 0815hrs. He was surprised to see Aunt Marie and Uncle Hubere in the nook having breakfast. Hubere stood up, extended his hand as Alan approached him and said, "Good morning, Alan. It is so good to have you with us."

He refused to shake hands and responded, 'Good morning Hubere."

Then, Hubere surprised him one more time saying, "You and Michelle talked about being married for so many months; you should have married her when she wanted you to."

He looked at him with anger in his eyes, "We had too many obstacles in our way."

Hubere understood the insinuation and said, "I loved her too. I know how you feel."

"You have no idea how 'I' feel. The anger in me wants to destroy you now; right here!"

Hubere attempted to apologize to him for any inconvenience he may have incurred.

Alan thought, "What a time to apologize," and responded, "Excuse me Aunt Marie! 'God Damn it...Hubere! Now that my Michelle is dead you want to apologize." Alan stood up, walked to Aunt Marie, kissed her on the forehead and said, "I gotta go."

Hubere stood up and pleaded, "Alan do not leave now; please hear me out."

"Isn't it a little too God Damn late for anything you have to say? How the hell are you going to account for getting me kicked off the continent when Michelle and I first fell in love? And the letter you wrote to me last fall; I hope you have to deal with GOD about that. I've said enough; I have to return to my base!"

Marie caught Alan's arm in the hall as he was leaving and asked, "Please will you give Hubere an opportunity to talk. He feels very depressed about everything that has happened. This has been very emotional for him. Give him a few minutes before you leave. Will you for me?" Michelle took Mimi's place in his heart. Please stay a bit and be a part of our family? You are the only one who was close to her that we can relate with Michelle."

Alan returned to the kitchen. Hubere sat expressionless. He now feared to say anything.

"Please sit down and have some tea with us," asked Aunt Mari?

He sat down across from Hubere and asked, "Are you aware of everything you did to us."

Friendly now, Hubere again asked Alan if he would accept a sincere apology. Then he pleaded, "Please hear me out. So many men wanted Michelle for her wealth."

"What do you mean, wealth? You controlled everything. I told her I didn't care. I would have taken care of her; oh, we may have had to struggle until I graduated in Engineering."

"Marie convinced me you definitely wanted to marry her and leave her inheritance here! It was difficult to filter out those who loved her for herself," responded Hubere.

"Yeah; like me but not your sweet nephew Claude. Tell me he didn't want her money?"

"I used him in an attempt to shield her from all predators. I misread your love for her."

"What makes you now believe I really loved her? I wanted her to be my life-long wife."

"Marie told me of your letter she received addressed to her Brussels apartment dated the 12th of March 1946. She read it to me and said she was sure you meant everything. You wrote, Michelle meant more to you than anything you ever wanted."

Aunt Marie said, "Michelle loved you so much she went to London purposely to have your child."

"Now that Michelle is gone, I am truly very sad she lost your child," admitted Hubere.

Alan asked Marie, "When did he know Michelle was with child? Did she tell him?"

"No; Michelle always confided in me. We were as close as a mother and daughter could have been. Hubere and I always wanted to have someone to represent Mimi and Michelle. We never had an opportunity to have that from Mimi or Michelle. Now we have nothing. Marie, now in tears added, "Alan can you realized what I have said."

He asked, "I'm now aware of how a grandchild could mean so much to grandparents."

Uncle Hubere surprised him with, "If she had not lost your child part of Michelle would still be with us. Believe me, that would mean so much to me now that Michelle is gone."

"Michelle always wondered why you always tended to resist having a child. Would you tell us why you resisted Michelle's desire to have your child," asked Aunt Marie?"

"First of all; I don't believe in having a child out of wedlock. Don't you believe in that? Second; pilots in my group were being shot down, sometimes a dozen, in December and January. How long do you think I may have survived if I wasn't transferred to the 8th Air Force? I didn't ever want to burden anyone, especially Michelle, with a child who'd never ever see or know its father. I was wrong! Life is so unfair; I didn't die; I've lived... and she died!"

Alan finally made up with Hubere before returning to Brussels, but; knew it was a little too late to forget anything between them. He slept at the same room he had at the Red Cross club and had breakfast at a Café on the way to Phillipe's. That morning he said good-bye to Phillipe and his family as he hugged each of them, then left for the railroad station and caught the next train to LeHarve via Paris. On the way to Paris, he thought of never seeing Brussels, Phillipe and his family, Aunt Marie, or Uncle Hubere again.

Tuesday, 16 April 1946, LeHarve, France

Alan had cut short his leave and returned to LeHarve two days early, on the leave he so desired. He rented a taxi to get to the LeHarve transition station. The gate guard called for a jeep to take him to his quarters. Claire Strait wasn't there when he arrived at their room. Putting away his clean clothes and the ones to be washed in a bag reminded him of Michelle always eager to make sure he had clean clothes. He couldn't hold back the tears that came.

It was ten to five when Strait walked into the room; seeing Alan laying on his cot asked, "What you doin here? You had six days. Did she have a new boyfriend, or she didn't want to see you because you put her off for so long. Is it all over?"

Alan shook his head no and for a moment looked at Claire and said nothing. "Finally; he only said, "She's gone, but; gone alone. "Claire sat down on his cot and waited for him to say more. Alan sat up and was very quiet as he put with his elbows on his knees and head in his hands looking at the floor. Claire didn't understand what he meant when he said, 'gone alone' and asked him, "How about us going to the mess hall for dinner," where he hoped Alan would begin to talk?

Saying nothing he just nodded with a yes motion, then; stood up and walked slowly and silently to the mess hall with Claire waiting for him to say something all the way there. Alan only took a small salad and a small barbecue pork sandwich off the mess line. They sat and ate silently. Alan hadn't said two sentences since returning from Brussels. Claire tried to start a conversation during dinner to no avail. Claire knew he was deeply depressed about something and thought best to leave him alone for the rest of that day.

They woke up early the next morning, washed, shaved, dressed, and went to breakfast. Alan was still silent all the way to the mess hall. They went through the mess line and Claire loaded his plate with eggs, bacon, sausage, toast, and SOS on the side. Alan only took a small package of corn flakes, one small carton of milk and a cup of coffee.

Claire had to get Alan to talk. He knew this silence thing he was doing was not healthy for his mind and he asked, "Did you get to meet your girlfriend?" He didn't respond and just shook his head no. "Wasn't she there; waiting for you?"

He broke his silence with, "I didn't mean to ignore you; she was there, but; couldn't wait for me. I have to 'shake' this trip. I'll tell you all about it when I'm ready. Is that OK with you?"

Alan had been sort of a bore and Claire, being an understanding friend, now knew well; something severe had happened to him and was really walking around in shock. He thought he should coax him into seeing a doctor, but then; on second though these medics weren't the shrinks that he needed for his problem. Alan was very quiet and rarely talked to anyone other than Claire for the entire two weeks before hearing of being shipped out, and only talked about routine things when it was absolutely necessary.

They were informed to be ready to board ship for the USA at 1000hrs, 22 April 1946. That morning they were awakened at 0630hrs for breakfast and told to pack for traveling. They went to and returned from breakfast, finished packing and all Alan said was, "O.K. let's go!"

They boarded at 0900hrs and were given a cabin where Alan laid quiet on his bunk. Claire left the cabin to watch the ship being guided out of the harbor. He thought he heard him praying as he was re-entering the cabin. Knowing he was depressed he asked, "What's the matter? You're holding something in; it's not good; it'll make you sick. We've been close friends for a while now. I 'm your buddy; you gotta get it out, can't we talk?"

"I don't care if I get sick. Maybe I want to get sick so I can die too!" After saying that he let out what happened and surprisingly said, "She died? "Yeah; it happened!"

"I knew you experienced some sort of catastrophe. Won't you talk about it?"

"I took an oath and asked God to help me out of this terrible experience; I have been hurt so much; I've suffered the loss of someone close to me since I was five years old. First it was my wonderful Grandfather at five; then Katherine, a girlfriend at thirteen and Mary Lou, my sweetheart, at nineteen. I've had all these people in my subconscious mind all my life. I don't know how to forget them." After a long hesitation said, "And now Michelle! The three girls in my life were beautiful blue-eyed blondes." He stopped and banged on the sides of his temples saying, "Coincidence? No; it's an omen! So, I made an oath, to God and myself; not to ever court a blue eyed blond for the rest of my life,"

Claire approached him and said, "Hey; you can't live with that. Anytime you want to talk I'm more than ready to listen

"Are you willing to mostly listen and not say what I did wrong or point out my faults."

"OK, OK! Trust me. I feel like I'm your brother. All I want to do is to help you."He tried to smile and meekly said, "It's all so bad, I don't know how to begin?"

"Look I won't repeat anything. Why don't you just start wherever you want?"

"All right, but; you have to promise not to ever tell anyone about this."

"Alan, you know me better than that. It's only between us; I promise."

He slowly began, "It's about the girl I first saw in Brussels in November of 1944. She was the last of the three girls I was fond of. Hell no! That's not true! Eventually, I fell very deeply in love with this girl. It's so emotional, please be patient with me? This is so hard to talk about. It hurts just thinking about it. I don't want to believe it happened. He sighed, then; took a deep breath followed by a long swig of scotch and began; "My first girl was in high school. We were close friends for only fifteen months. She died of Scarlet Fever. I met the second girl at Cornell. With her too; at first only close friends, but; made a sincere promise to wait for each other until we both graduated. She died in an automobile accident. Then, Michelle, I loved her so much. I was going to marry her when I went to Brussels. Let me have time for my mind to settle down. Thinking about these girls has my mind spinning. When I slow down, I tell you the whole story."

"Take all the time you need as long as it's less than seven days before we dock in the US. Just tell me about this last one you are so depressed over. OK?"

"You have to promise not to repeat what I tell you to anyone, ever. Can you promise?"

"Trust me; no one will ever hear a word about it from me."

"OK...I first saw Michelle on a Sunday evening in a restaurant, in November, during the week I was at the Paris Replacement Center." He continued, meeting her through some paratroopers talking him into going to Brussels and on to his transfer from the 9th to the 8th Air Force. He related to the London incident as well as the Liquor runs, the Riviera Bowl period and Chamonix providing him with the best moments of his life. Then he sadly said, "I never saw her again after skiing together in Chamonix.." Then added, "What a way for the war to finally end for me. Now here I sit with you....... I'm not regretting being with you Claire, but; it's leaving LeHarve without her. After a few moments of silence, he boldly said, "Somebody killed her!God..., I'd love to stay and get those bastards."

EPILOUGE

Alan's voyage back home was very somber. He couldn't get Michelle and what happened to her off his mind. After he was home a while, he ran into Tom, a high school friend, on the street one day. Tom asked Alan if he was seeing anyone, and Alan said no. Tom said he knew of someone he wanted him to meet. Alan asked, "is she blond?" Tom told him no, so Alan agreed to meet her. Tom asked why it mattered if she was blond, he knew of the girl who died of scarlet fever, but not of the girl in college or of Michelle, so Alan explained what had happened to the other two girls. A couple days later Tom drove Alan out to a neighboring town and turned into the driveway of a farm. Tom was dating Maggie, one of the eight children, seven girls and one boy. They went into the house and introduced Alan to Amy, a twin, and the youngest of the eight.

In September Alan went back to college at the local State University and played football while continuing his engineering studies and dating Amy. Alan played first string guard every year until he graduated in December 1949. In June of 1949 Alan and Amy were married. Shortly after graduating, Alan was recalled to active duty with the Air Force for the Korean Conflict. Alan was a test pilot at the Air Base in Niagara Falls, NY. In July of 1950, their first child, a son, was born. In early June of 1952, while still on active duty in Niagara Falls, their second son was born. About three weeks later Alan was asked to take up a new plane that had recently arrived at the Base. As soon as he took off, the plane started having engine problems. Alan attempted to return to the Base and land but was having difficulty maintaining his altitude. One landing gear clipped a billboard which flipped the plane over. It landed in a field upside down, tore the canopy off, ripped him out of the cockpit, and continued to slide over him and finally stop about 100 yard past him. Crews rushed to the crash site. Initially they thought Alan was decapitated because his head was buried in the ground. They dug him out, and the Flight Surgeon performed a tracheotomy with a jack knife, then took his pen apart and stuck half of it in his trachea so he could breathe. Alan was rushed to the hospital and was examined thoroughly for several days. His face was all swollen, cut, brush burned, and bruised. Due to the fact that he was in such good shape from all the sports he played, these were the worst of his, injuries. The doctors were concerned with the possibility of brain damage due to the lack of oxygen when his head was buried. For several days they kept asking him questions about himself and his family. He always answered correctly, so they were confident he had no brain damage.

In 1956 the area where Amy grew up, was starting to get developed. Alan bought some land that once was the alfalfa field and build a three-bedroom ranch home. In October of 1957, their third and last child was born, a girl. Alan continued to serve in the Air National Guard, until 1966 when he retired as a Lt. Colonel. He never flew as a pilot after the crash in 1952.

Milton Keynes UK
Ingram Content Group UK Ltd.
UKHW020708310723
426074UK00017B/963